A RAGE OF REBELLION

Quivering, Evelyn watched her husband's handsome features harden and heard his voice turn stiff as well. "If you will conduct yourself in the manner of a demimondaine, you leave me no choice. I would be the fool you seem to think me if I sat idly by while you handed me my horns in public."

"You cannot prevent me from seeing my friends, David," Evelyn replied defiantly.

"We shall see," he said. "After breakfast, I shall send a message to Aunt Sophia in Northumberland advising her that you will be making her a protracted visit. You may have today to ready yourself for the journey. Tomorrow you will leave town."

"How dare you," she said, outraged. "I shall do no such thing!"

"The choice is not yours, Evelyn," he said, and turned and left Evelyn alone with her rage at this lord whom she could not help loving, but whom her pride would rather risk losing than meekly obey. . . .

(For a list of other Signet Regency Romances by Elizabeth Hewitt, please turn page. . . .)

AN INNOCENT DECEPTION

ELIZABETH HEWITT

A SIGNET BOOK

NEW AMERICAN LIBRARY

For Marcella:

*who gave me the joy of music
and so much more*

NAL BOOKS ARE AVAILABLE AT QUANTITY DISCOUNTS WHEN
USED TO PROMOTE PRODUCTS OR SERVICES. FOR INFORMATION
PLEASE WRITE TO PREMIUM MARKETING DIVISION, NEW AMERI-
CAN LIBRARY, 1633 BROADWAY, NEW YORK, NEW YORK 10019.

SIGNET, SIGNET CLASSIC, MENTOR, ONYX, PLUME,
MERIDIAN and NAL BOOKS are published by NAL
PENGUIN INC., 1633 Broadway, New York, New York 10019

First Printing, September, 1987

1 2 3 4 5 6 7 8 9

PRINTED IN THE UNITED STATES OF AMERICA

1

It had begun to drizzle slightly in the early hours of the morning when the town carriage of the Countess of Norwood drew up before the darkened portals of Norwood House. By the time the carriage had come to a complete halt, the sound of it had aroused the Norwoods' dozing porter and he opened the door to receive his mistress, revealing a faint light in the entrance hall. The groom, wishing to be helpful, held up the carriage lantern for Lady Norwood as he prepared to assist her from her carriage.

In spite of this noble effort to alleviate the gloom of the night, Evelyn, Lady Norwood, felt an unaccountable reluctance to leave the womblike security of her well appointed carriage. The large, dark house seemed to her to be unwelcoming, though she knew this was nonsense. Norwood House, which had been built by the sixth earl a scant ten years before her husband, the seventh earl, had succeeded him, was quite modern and not in the least forbidding. Chiding herself for her absurd fancy, Evelyn took the proffered hand of her groom and, gathering the skirt of her silk evening gown about her to protect it from wet, stepped out onto the street.

But when she was at last inside and the porter had closed the great front door, she felt a brief wave of panic that made her again want to escape the confines of the house. "What hour is it?" she said to the porter, who was waiting patiently for her to ascend the stairs so that he could at last extinguish the light in the hall and find his bed.

Deference and training made the porter forbear to tell his mistress that she might discover that for herself by looking over her shoulder; instead he read the time from the hall clock himself and said, "It is just past three of a Thursday morning, my lady."

Evelyn wanted to ask if her husband had yet come in, but she hesitated, decided against it, and nodded dismissal to the porter. Taking the bed candle on the table by the newel post, she ascended the stairs, admitting to herself that she did not really wish to know if Norwood were at home. If she were before him, that was to her good; if not, doubtless he would note the hour of her arrival and, come morning, he would make some caustic comment on the late hours she kept.

In fact, it seemed to her that more often than not her conversations with Norwood in the last month or so had a caustic edge to them and she dimly recognized that perhaps it was her worsening relationship with her husband that made her so reluctant to return to Norwood House after an evening of pleasure with friends. It had not been so when they had married over a year ago, and sometimes it was hard to understand how they had come to a state where hard words or cool civilities were more common between them than words of love. She wished it were otherwise, but she did not know how to make it so. In her dispirited moments she was inclined to think it was entirely her fault, but at other times she was equally certain that it was Norwood's unwillingness to understand her needs and humors and his unjust and disapproving attitude toward her friends and the pleasure she took in being fashionable.

Evelyn knew that the best way to avoid confrontation was to avoid her husband as much as possible. Norwood was generally out of the house before noon and she would take care not to leave her rooms before then. It was unlikely these days that he would seek her out in her bedchamber.

As she went up the next flight of stairs to the second floor she was relieved to see no light seeping from under the doors of her husband's dressing room or bedchamber. Her bedchamber was just beyond, adjoining his, and she passed his rooms as silently as possible. When she reached her bedchamber, she lit a lamp from the bed candle and decided against waking her maid Betsy to help her undress. She removed the pearl and emerald necklace and ear drops that she wore and slowly, almost wearily, removed the pins that held up her heavy reddish gold hair so that it cascaded about her shoulders.

Although her back was to the door that joined her husband's bedchamber to her own, she heard it open, and the heavy sensation of impending unpleasantness returned. Evelyn turned to see the dark, shadowed figure of her husband standing in the doorway.

Determined to shake the aura of melodrama, Evelyn said as lightly as she could, "Are you just come in, Norwood? I hope your evening was as pleasant as mine. I went to the theater with the Mulridges and then to a supper party given by Lord Malcome, to honor Mr. Kemble. All the theater people were there, of course, even Mrs. Siddons, which was quite exciting. I suppose you will say the company was not entirely proper, but I assure you, you are mistaken. It was quite elegant. Even Lord Sandingtome was there and you know what a high stickler he is."

"I fear my evening was not so happily spent," the earl said quietly as he came into the room.

Too quietly. When Evelyn spoke again her voice sounded a bit shrill to her ears. "I am sorry to hear that. You should have come with me tonight. I know you do not like Sarah Mulridge overmuch, but she is the kindest-hearted creature. She would have been very pleased to have had you as one of her party."

"Haymarket ware," Norwood said succinctly.

In spite of the fact that Evelyn was determined to keep their conversation light and to avoid any unpleasantness, she bristled. "That is unkind and unjust, Norwood. Sally is a very good sort of person even if she is not as well born as Mulridge. In fact, he is a sad rattle and everyone says that marrying Sally has quite settled him."

"Everyone also says that two of Mulridge's three brats call him father only out of courtesy."

"Stupid, vicious gossip," Evelyn said, turning away from him abruptly and beginning to struggle with the small buttons at the back of her dress. "I make a point never to listen to such talk," she added loftily.

Norwood came up behind her, pushing her hands aside to undo the buttons for her. "It is certainly ill-bred to further gossip," he averred, "but a wise woman—or man—may listen and decide for herself what kernel of truth lies within it."

"Seldom any, I should think," Evelyn replied shortly, not so much out of anger as unease. Where once she had longed for and courted his closeness, now she found discomfort in the intimacy. She regretted her decision not to call for Betsy.

"You attended Jonathan Dancer's supper afterward, I think you said?"

"Yes," she replied with a sigh, her hopes of avoiding an argument vanishing. She knew well what she might expect with this admission. The name of Mr. Dancer had figured before in several recent arguments. She had deliberately not mentioned him tonight, trusting that her husband would not know of his connection with the party she had attended. "But it was as much Lord Malcome's party as it was Mr. Dancer's," she added defensively. "And, actually, it was such a sad crush that I scarcely set eyes on either man. I spent nearly the whole of the night with the Mulridges and in conditions of such propriety that even *you* could not disapprove." Evelyn spoke with apparent ease, but in fact she was tensed for his reply.

"You also attended the theater in Dancer's company." It was less question than statement.

"He was in Lord Mulridge's party. He has been a particular friend of Lord Mulridge for years," she replied evasively.

"What was your number for the theater?"

Evelyn wished she might lie, but she feared her husband's acuity. "Four, but I was not aware that Mr. Dancer would be one of the party when Sally asked me to join them tonight," she said, and was at once angry with herself for behaving as if she had cause to defend herself.

"I suppose you sat with him in the Mulridges' box."

He had finished with the buttons and now Evelyn turned to face him. "Yes," she said, raising her chin a little, "and Sally Mulridge sat to my other side. What is there in that?"

"I think I have mentioned that I do not care for the way you encourage Dancer's attentions toward you."

There was no apparent anger in his voice, but Evelyn braced herself for the storm she knew was coming. She could see that his amber brown eyes were shielded, carefully keeping from her any depth of feeling. She knew that steely expression well. "And I think I informed you," she said, assuming a coolness in her tone, "that you concern yourself unnecessarily. Jonathan Dancer is a friend and I like him very well, but it is no more than that. What does it matter if he chooses to flatter me with a bit of attention? He never goes beyond what is proper. It is all just a game; all fashionable ladies have cicisbei, though I am certain most of them have husbands who are sensible enough not to make insulting insinuations."

In the circumstances she felt uncomfortable about undressing before her husband, but she would not allow herself to feel intimidated. She stepped out of her ivory silk gown, but she could not quite like to remove her petticoats before him and instead took a rose silk dressing gown from her wardrobe and put it on over these.

There was no hint of desire in his eyes; he watched her disrobe dispassionately. "The insinuations I make are more against Dancer's character than yours. Dancer hasn't the reputation of a libertine, but he is a cold fish, and if he makes up to you it is not without purpose."

'You would not suppose that he might simply like me?" Evelyn said sweetly.

"No." His voice was hard and blunt. "He means to bed you or ruin you or both. He is well on the road to accomplishing the last with your full cooperation, it would appear, so I am not at all sanguine that he has not also achieved the first."

Evelyn could scarcely believe her ears. His words cut her to the quick and furious tears stung at her eyes. She could think of no words stinging enough to pay him for the insult and she did the first thing that came to her, which was to pick up an object from the dressing table behind her and cast it at him. It was a small crystal bottle containing scent and it missed him and exploded against the wall behind him, casting a cloud of aroma throughout the room.

Norwood did not even flinch and gave no notice to her display of temper. "You constantly accuse me, Eve, of mistrusting you and attempting to order your life, but the exact reverse is true: I have not checked you in any way. I blame my tolerance for bringing us to this pass." His voice was level, all but devoid of expression. "You wished to come to town to cut a dash and I wanted you to be happy. I trusted your good sense and gave you your head, but it is obvious that I was mistaken in my faith. You've fallen into every trap devised for the unseasoned. I'll grant you Dancer is received, but he isn't good *ton*. He has introduced you to a set that can most charitably be described as fast. If he were your friend, he would protect your name, not cast shadow upon on it."

"That is *your* judgment of my friends," she said accusingly. "How is it that Lord Malcome and Lord Sandingtome associate with these same people and their reputations remain unsullied?"

"You are not so ignorant of town ways that you cannot answer that yourself. A man is not judged by the company he keeps in the same light that a woman is. I'll wager neither Lady Malcome nor Lady Sandingtome was present."

It was true. Evelyn felt herself flush and turned away from him again. She wished she had not broken the bottle of scent—a gift from Dancer. The aroma was heavy, and while pleasant enough in small applications, its overwhelming sweetness now was cloying. She was tired and she wanted her bed. Her petticoats, which she had dampened so that her gown might cling suggestively to her legs, still felt a bit clammy and she wanted to exchange them for a comfortable nightdress. The one thing she did not wish to do was continue this fruitless discussion with her husband.

Evelyn did not especially wish for the attentions of Mr. Dancer nor for estrangement with her husband, but no more did she intend to allow Norwood to dictate to her who her friends would be or how she would spend her evenings. But argument was pointless and served no greater purpose than to distance them even further. Quite deliberately she crossed the room and pulled the bell for Betsy after all to bring their tête-à-tête to an end. But even as she tugged at the rope, Norwood moved swiftly and caught her arm in a firm grip. "We have matters to discuss, and I have no wish for interruption," he said coldly.

"I have nothing at all to discuss with you," Evelyn

said with a fair attempt at matching his tone. "I am going to bed." She pulled her arm free and walked to her dressing table. To her astonishment he caught her roughly by the shoulders and spun her to face him.

"You think me complaisant, do you not, Madam Wife?" he said, and she could see now that the icy light in his eyes was sheer anger. She tried to pull away from him but he held her fast. "It is not complaisance that has kept my hand light on the bit, but affection and the foolish belief that it was returned. Did you suppose my regard so boundless that you could settle your affections elsewhere and I should not heed it?"

"You insult me, my lord," she said, torn between anger and alarm.

"You insult *me*, my dear," he said, and the endearment was an epithet. "Shall I tell you of my evening?" he added in a silky tone. "I had dinner at Boodle's with Hempstead. We parted for a time, and not wishing to join the play in the card room, I contented myself with strolling about, catching, quite unintentionally, snatches of conversation as I passed the various tables. It was what I heard at the faro table that particularly interested me: the latest bit of Crim. Con. The *on-dit* is that Dancer has made the conquest of the Season. A young matron, comely of face and round of heel. One of the Tulips at the table, a man fortunately unknown to me, made a play of words upon her name. He called her Lady Notorious and he and his fellows thought it quite clever."

Evelyn could not pretend to misunderstand him. "It isn't true," she said in a fierce whisper.

"Isn't it?"

At this moment, the connecting door to Evelyn's dressing room opened and Betsy entered, expecting to find her mistress alone and waiting to be assisted out of her gown. She came to an abrupt halt at the scene before her. Evelyn felt his grip slacken as he looked up in surprise at the interruption, but her attempt to escape him was foiled. He caught her by the wrist as she moved away from him. "Get out," he said, addressing the maid over his shoulder, and it was at this point that Evelyn felt genuine fear of his anger. She knew that her husband was not a man given to displaying his temper before the servants.

The young maid hesitated, uncertain whether to obey her master or champion her mistress. But Evelyn had too much pride to hide behind the skirts of a serving girl. "Please leave us, Betsy," she said with what dignity her situation would allow. "I shan't be needing you tonight after all."

When the maid left them, Evelyn rounded on her husband. "How dare you use me so in front of my servant. If I didn't know you better, I would swear you were castaway. I cannot help what people will say of me, nor that you choose to listen to them, but I will not be bullyed and humiliated at your hands for crimes of which I am innocent." With this she jerked her wrist out of his grasp.

He said nothing for such a long time, staring at her in an unblinking, unnerving manner, that she almost wished for his wrath again. "I wish I might believe you, Eve," he said at last with intensity, "but your own conduct condemns you. I have warned you repeatedly that the circles in which you have become involved would not add to your credit, and, finally, I told you outright that I found Dancer's constant attendance on you offensive. Yet neither entreaties of affection nor duty to your position have weighed with you. It is obvious that your concern for your pleasure is more to you than your concern for our marriage or your reputation. If you will not have a care to your name, I must see to my own."

Evelyn rubbed her wrist as if he had hurt her, though he had not. "That's it, isn't it? You are afraid that Perceval will believe this stupid gossip. It isn't my reputation that you fear for, but your own in the House." She wasn't sure she believed her own words, but she knew his political aspirations were important to him and he would be vulnerable to her accusation. "I won't be intimidated, David, or forced to comply with your straitlaced ideas of propriety, particularly as I have done nothing to deserve such Turkish treatment."

For the first time Lord Norwood smiled, but it wasn't a pleasant expression and his wife was not encouraged to believe that her brave front had been effective. "Don't underestimate me, Eve. I have told you my leniency toward you has been choice, not weakness. I do care for the opinion of Perceval and my friends in the government, but I care more for my opinion of myself. If you will conduct yourself in the manner of a demimondaine, you leave me no choice. I would be the fool you seem to think me if I sat idly by while you handed me my horns in public."

He turned as if to leave, but he stopped and stooped to pick up the biggest shards of crystal that lay on the sodden carpet. "This was a gift, I think?" he said, giving the pieces to her and leaving any further meaning in his words unspoken.

Evelyn was both annoyed and alarmed that he seemed to discern her secrets and evasions so easily. "You cannot prevent me from seeing my friends, David," she said defiantly.

"We shall see," he said, his voice quiet again. "After breakfast I shall send a message to Aunt Sophia in Rothbury advising her that you will be making her a protracted visit. You may have today to ready yourself for the journey, but on Friday you will leave town to discover if a little rustication cannot improve your conduct."

If he had slapped her, Evelyn could not have been more shocked. Though she had met Lady Sophia Cheviot only once before when she had come to

Blakenhill for their wedding, Evelyn remembered the older woman as a prunish spinster who lived a retired life by choice in the "wilds" of Northumberland. Norwood meant to bury her in the country, to punish her like a recalcitrant schoolgirl. "How dare you," she said, outraged. "I shall do no such thing."

"The choice is not yours, Evelyn," he said, and left her.

Evelyn stood for several minutes in the center of the room, her hand still stretched out and holding the shattered pieces of crystal. Her sense of outrage and frustration held her quite immobile while she raged inwardly at her own powerlessness. While she had no intention of meekly accepting his dictum, she felt impotent to combat it.

She was realistic enough to know, even in her anger, that further open defiance of her husband would only result in additional humiliating scenes and the result would likely be the same in any case: she had no protectors to come to her defense and no means at all to be independent of him. But she would not leave town in disgrace and at his bidding.

Evelyn was quite alone in the world. She had no living family that she knew of with the exception of an elderly connection, Mrs. Walker, whom she called aunt out of courtesy. It was while living at Hardwood Hall with Mrs. Walker that Evelyn had met and married the Earl of Norwood, whose principal seat, Blakenhill, marched with Hardwood.

Evelyn's first thought was to seek refuge with "Aunt Lottie," but Mrs. Walker had left Essex to spend the spring and summer months with her widowed sister who lived in Knaresborough, and these two redoubtable ladies were already embarked on a walking tour of Ireland and Scotland. Evelyn hadn't any but the most general idea of their present direction.

Her friends in town were few, consisting mostly of those people Jonathan Dancer had introduced to her. At first she had allowed herself to be taken up by this set to please Jonathan and because their eagerness to make her part of their circle had flattered her. But, though she might not admit it, her opinion of Sally Mulridge was not so very different from his, and there were others among her particular friends, such as Lady Henrietta Kennet, whom she was coming to regard as insipid, venal, or encroaching. But as Norwood had voiced his opposition to her choices of companions, she had pursued these friendships, willfully blinded to their faults by her anger at her husband's attempts to control her. There was not one among them to whom she felt she might turn for comfort or support.

Perversely, the thought occurred to Evelyn that she might seek refuge with Jonathan Dancer. Mr. Dancer was clever and witty and quick to sympathize with any complaint against her husband, but though Jonathan amused her, she felt nothing for him beyond friendship. In spite of what she had said to Norwood, she was coming to realize that Jonathan read something more in her *jeune* confidences and artless encouragement. Though she was affronted by her husband's insinuations and efforts to control her, she was uncomfortably aware that Dancer's attentions were becoming increasingly particular. It was mostly due to her evasions that there had been no impropriety between them.

She would not admit it and concede the point to her husband, but in truth when she had learned from her friend Sally Mulridge that Dancer would be escorting her to the theater, she would have backed out of the engagement at the last moment had she known how to do so gracefully. Now that Norwood had infuriated her so, it was very tempting to toy with the idea of running to Dancer to spite him. But though Evelyn was naive at times, she was not a fool, and she understood well enough what such an action would mean. She was shocked enough at the prospect of open adultery to abandon the thought at once.

The only other person who might possibly give sympathy to her plight was Norwood's younger sister Lady Jane Halloway, who had returned to live at Blakenhill since being widowed two years previously. Lady Jane was only a few years older than Evelyn and possessed a sunny personality. She had welcomed Evelyn to Blakenhill with such genuine warmth that they had quickly formed a binding friendship.

They exchanged letters on a weekly basis, and Evelyn had already hinted that she was finding the earl's notions of propriety confining. Jane did not come to her brother's defense, as Evelyn half supposed that she would, but had completely commiserated with her sister-in-law and complained that she had found her brother rather too high in the instep herself.

Evelyn was encouraged by this to think that Jane would feel, as she herself did, the injustice of Norwood's treatment of her. Impulsively, she came to a decision. She would not leave on Friday at her husband's bidding, but today, and she would not go to Lady Sophia in Rothbury, but to Jane at Blakenhill.

"Please, my lady, let me come with you," Betsy pleaded as she folded a sprigged muslin dress into the open portmanteau. "It isn't right that you should be goin' off by yourself like this. His lordship will be ever so upset."

"I don't care a fig for that," Evelyn replied. "I need you here so that you may keep Lord Norwood from knowing that I have gone until it is time for you to give him my letter. You must spend as much of the day as possible here in my rooms so that if he inquires for me you can tell him that I have the headache and cannot be disturbed. I have explained in the letter that you were acting at my command and are not to blame for the deception, so you need have no fear on that head." She selected another gown from her wardrobe, a pea-green morning dress,

and cast it on the bed to be packed in the portmanteau, which was the only baggage she meant to take
with her on her journey. She did not mean to make
a protracted visit at Blakenhill. She fully expected to
return to town a few days after she had won her
point with Norwood.

The abigail stifled a yawn, for it was not long after
dawn and only a few hours of sleep had been granted
her. She was not as sanguine as her mistress that his
lordship would give her no blame for deliberately
deceiving him. Worse, she thought her mistress's
scheme foolhardy and likely to bring her grief rather
than satisfaction. Evelyn had not confided the whole
of the estrangement between her and Norwood to
the abigail, of course, but Betsy was quick-witted
enough to guess much of the detail herself, and the
scene she had witnessed last night had only served to
confirm her suppositions. If the earl, who she knew
to be an even-tempered man, was as enraged as he
had appeared to be, then it was likely that things had
come to a pretty pass and the sensible thing for any
wife to do at this stage was to placate her husband,
not defy him and invoke further wrath.

Evelyn had not slept at all. In the intervening
hours since David had left her she had convinced
herself that she would not only find sympathy with
her sister-in-law, but practical assistance as well. Norwood's mother had died while he was at Eton and
Jane still in the schoolroom, and the sixth earl had
followed his wife to an untimely grave not many
years afterward. Closing ranks against well-inten-
tioned but tepid guardians, brother and sister had
developed an extremely close bond. If Jane were
willing to side with her, Evelyn believed that her
husband would listen to his sister in a way that he
would not regard her own protests.

The earl was generally an early riser, but Evelyn
was confident that given the late hour that he had
sought his bed, she could be away before he was

awake and aware that she had gone. A judicious bribe to one of the grooms, whom she had had Betsy awaken to send for her carriage, would be sufficient to see to it that Norwood was not immediately apprised of her leaving, for it was unlikely that he would ask after her carriage or horses without cause. It only remained for her to quietly let herself out of the house before the porter or other servants were up and about and to walk to the end of the street where she had arranged to meet the carriage in a half hour's time. She decided against a sky blue muslin trimmed in ivory lace as being too frivolous for the serious business of taming her husband, and she chose another, simpler gown of rich brown crepe, which she thought more suited to evoking sympathy. She closed her wardrobe and pronounced herself satisfied with her choices.

Betsy finished the packing while Evelyn brushed out her own hair to save time. For a while neither woman said anything, but finally Betsy, though she knew her mistress would dislike it, felt compelled to speak. "I wish you would speak to his lordship, my lady, and tell him the truth about you. I know you think he wouldn't understand, but I'd wager it's the root of your troubles and it'd be better, surely, than all this fuss and bother that's been goin' on between you."

Evelyn stopped in the act of placing a pin in her hair and turned to face the maid. "Betsy, you know I have forbidden you to ever speak of that matter in this house. You presume too much. In the first place you are mistaken. It has nothing at all to do with any differences that Lord Norwood and I may have, and second, I think I know my husband better than you and I can assure you he would *not* understand. He is a proud man," she added bitterly, "and I can see more plainly than ever that he cares more for his precious name than he does for me or my feelings. I had hoped one day that I might trust him enough, but . . . Well, it is not to be."

"It's not as if it's your fault, my lady," Betsy persisted. "You're as gently born as him, if I'm a judge of the matter and—"

"Betsy, that is enough," Evelyn snapped. "I won't discuss this with you or anyone. Mrs. Walker has acknowledged me as her niece and that is sufficient. If Norwood knew that there was any question of my parentage, it would cause far more trouble than it would erase. In any case, I have told you it is nothing at all to do with the present situation. It would only give Norwood one more cause to wish me banished as if I were a disobedient serf."

"But he be a generous man, all of his servants say the same of him, my lady. If he knew, he wouldn't—"

"Do you wish to continue as my dresser, Betsy," Evelyn said, raising her voice a bit to interrupt the maid. When Betsy nodded unhappily, she continued, "Then kindly obey me in this matter. Mrs. Walker and I have placed our confidence in you and expect it to be respected. I want your solemn oath that you will never ever speak one word of it to anyone, particularly not to Lord Norwood, no matter what may happen. Is that clear?"

Betsy nodded again and returned to her chore, but she had a sense of foreboding not unlike the one her mistress had felt a few hours earlier. She tightened the straps of the portmanteau at the same time that Lady Norwood pronounced herself ready to go down to meet the carriage. Over the brown crepe Evelyn wore a drab-colored driving coat designed to ape the gentlemen's caped coats that were all the rage. She was turned out as elegantly as if she were embarking on nothing more important than a drive though Hyde Park during the hour fashionable for promenading rather than on a flight to evade the design of her husband. Betsy tried one final time to convince Evelyn to at least allow her to accompany her to the carriage, but Evelyn, insisting that the maid's return to the house might be noted, refused.

Knowing that she had done all she could to prevent her mistress from taking a headlong course, Betsy watched Evelyn go down the stairs and out the front door. Sighing, she turned back to the bedchamber to straighten the effects of packing and dressing and to wait out what she felt in her heart would be a long day.

Though Blakenhill was not more than a few hours' comfortable drive from London, Evelyn insisted that the coachman spring the horses, and they traveled at such a spanking pace that they reached their destination before luncheon. The only stops they made were to change horses, and Evelyn did not leave the carriage to refresh herself with even so little as a glass of lemonade. She felt weary, parched, and dusty by the time the carriage rolled to a stop before the Palladian facade of Blakenhill.

The door was opened for her by the under butler left in charge when the earl was not in residence and he seemed mildly disconcerted to see his mistress, alternately protesting and apologizing that he had received no instructions to expect their return.

"None were sent, Hiller," she said lightly as he assisted her out of her driving coat. "I am quite alone; Lord Norwood remains in town. Is Lady Jane at home?"

"I believe Lady Jane is in the still room, my lady."

"Thank you, Hiller, I shall find her myself. Please have my portmanteau taken to my room," she added, and started down the hall to the east wing where the still room was located.

Jane was sitting at the wooden table in the center of the still room frowning in concentration at a cookery book that lay open on the table. She was dressed in one of the simple cotton round gowns that she preferred in the country, and her golden-brown hair, exactly the shade of her brother's, was done up in a careless knot. She looked comfortable and homey, and Evelyn felt a pang of nostalgia for the simple life she and her husband had led here before they had gone to town for the Season. Evelyn did not understand why it was so, but now everything was changed and she knew it could never be the same again even if they were to return to live at Blakenhill permanently.

Jane glanced up at the sound of Evelyn's entrance and her surprise was evident. "Eve, dearest, what a delightful surprise." She rose at once and put her arms around her sister-in-law. "Never say you have had your fill of balls and routs already?" she added with a quizzing uplift of her brows. "You so took to town life that I didn't think to look for you until Christmas. Where is David?"

"I am alone," Evelyn said, after a little hesitation. "Norwood is still in town." During the drive she had rehearsed all that she would say to Jane when she arrived and had remained convinced that Jane would agree in every particular, but now Evelyn's confidence waned a bit.

"Is something the matter, Eve? Have you and David been arguing again?"

Sudden tears welled into Evelyn's eyes and the cool dignity with which she had meant to recite her wrongs abandoned her. Jane, whose own short marriage had had its stormy moments, was all sympathy. "Oh dear, what has my wretched brother done to upset you so?" Evelyn was rummaging through her reticule for her handkerchief to stem her tears, and Jane drew a clean one from the pocket of her dress and gave it to her sister-in-law. "You must tell me everything, Eve, but first I think that we should go up to my sitting room where we can be more comfortable. Hiller may bring us some of Mrs. Allen's delicious Restorative Sherry to settle you." She rose and held out her hand and Evelyn, still trying to restrain her emotions, followed like an obedient child.

Evelyn was greatly encouraged by Jane's obvious

sympathy. She recited the events of the previous evening in detail and, except to ask one or two clarifying questions, Jane said little. But Evelyn knew by the end of her recital that she would not find in Jane the champion she had hoped for.

"I can see how you would find David's high-handed manner upsetting," Jane began cautiously, after a short but uncomfortable silence had fallen between them, "but in fairness, Eve, you must allow that his anger was not without cause. No man could like hearing his wife's name used in such a way by another man."

As Evelyn's tears dried up so did her hopes of Jane taking her side against her brother. "Then you believe as Norwood does that I have played him false and am deserving of banishment," she said coolly, her sense of ill-usage returning.

"No, of course not," Jane said hastily. "I am sure you would never do such a thing, but perhaps you have been a little indiscreet in your friendship with Mr. Dancer if it is causing talk."

"I have encouraged him no more than half a dozen other men who amuse themselves with light flirtation. Every one does so."

"But every flirtation is not discussed by strangers over the faro table at Boodle's."

Disappointment spurred Evelyn's resentment at these words. "I cannot think why I thought I might find a friend in you," she said, rising. "You think exactly as Norwood does. I am to be held accountable because some puppy in his cups chose me for the butt of his wit. Mr. Dancer is no more to me than a friend; but male friends appear to be a luxury that *I* am not allowed. Mrs. Fielding and Lord Renidick are seen everywhere together and Lady Bessborough and Lord Granville Leveson-Gower are obviously the greatest of friends, but I have never heard so much as a hint that anyone suspects them of being more than they ought to each other."

"It is old scandal," Jane said quietly. "Everyone *knows* that Maria Fielding and Renidick and Lady Bessborough and Lord Granville are lovers, they have been so for so long that the world does not find them interesting any longer."

It was not said in an unkindly way, but Evelyn felt an implied criticism for her ignorance and naiveté, and she was chagrined that her illustration had proven against her rather than for her. Faint color stole into her cheeks. "I think it would be best," she said, "if I had the horses put to my carriage again. I shall not trouble you for a bed tonight, but shall push on to Knaresborough to see if I cannot discover my aunt's direction."

Jane reached up and took her hand. "Don't be a peagoose, Eve. You would not get farther than Watford tonight, and you are so obviously distraught that I should worry myself to a flinder over you. You have no cause to rail at me, you know. I'm not suggesting that you have had any illicit connection with Mr. Dancer, only that your sweet nature and friendly manner have been misinterpreted and left your behavior open to criticism. I know it is not fair, but a slur against one's reputation is a dangerous thing whether it is deserved or not, and it must be countered. No Countess of Norwood has ever brought disgrace to the Cheviots and I am sure you would not wish to do so either, particularly since it is unjust. Please sit down again, dearest, and we will discuss what we may do to counter this vicious gossip and perhaps soften David's reaction to it."

Evelyn winced inwardly at this speech, for there were other areas where the Cheviots might well accuse her of betraying their trust. Knowing this made her draw in her horns and she did as her sister-in-law bid her, sitting again next to Jane on the spindle-legged sofa. Evelyn had once nearly confided in Jane as a preliminary to admitting to Norwood that her parentage was not what they supposed it to be, but if

he and Jane could be so upset and make so much of
the talk caused by her friendship with Dancer, she
shuddered to think what they would say if ever they
discovered that Charlotte Walker was not really her
aunt or that she could not even give a name to her
father. "What do you think I should do?" she said
with resignation.

"Perhaps, for now at least, you should do as David
has suggested. Go to Rothbury." Jane knew that this
was not likely to meet with a happy response, and this
proved to be the case.

In spite of her good intentions, a martial spark
flashed in the young countess' eyes. "Allow myself to
be punished when I have done nothing to deserve
it?"

"You need not think of it as punishment," Jane
said quickly to make her point before Evelyn could
again object. "If you are away from town for a bit,
any gossip which has been stirred up will settle. It
needn't be for a great length of time, just enough for
the *ton* to indulge in other gossip and forget you and
Mr. Dancer. Then when you return to town, you
and David need only show the world how well you
agree and there will be nothing for them to talk
about."

Evelyn's chin came up and her expression was
mulish. "But there is not the least need for me to be
buried in Northumberland. I could remain here and
bear you company. It would answer equally well."

"Actually, I don't think it would," Jane said, her
tone placating. "You see, Mr. Dancer is a neighbor
of sorts. His estate, Spedwell Manor, is near Faversham, not more than twenty miles from here; I
thought you knew that. I am sure that David has
thought the matter through and that is why he thinks
it best for you to go to Rothbury."

"He wishes me to go to Rothbury because Lady
Sophia is a tartar who will have me sewing altar
cloths and reading improving tracts all of the time,"

Evelyn said bitterly. "I assure you *he* means it as punishment." She sighed. "I hadn't the least notion that Mr. Dancer was nearly a neighbor. He may have mentioned that he had an estate in Kent, but he never told me that it was near to Blakenhill."

"Well, we are not precisely neighbors in the sense that we call on each other," Jane conceded. "There is too much distance for that. We have only met infrequently for as long as I can recall, generally at assemblies at Sittingbourne or Maidstone."

"Then if we are never to meet him, what matters it that Blakenhill is twenty miles from Spedwell?"

"People would suggest that it is close enough."

Evelyn, no longer able to contain herself rose again. "*On-dit*! I am so tired of concerning myself with what people say. Who are 'they'? May I not even visit my own home to bear my sister company without courting the tongues of vipers?"

"If you wish to avoid scandal—"

"Scandal seems intent on finding me. I doubt it matters what *I* do."

Jane opened her mouth to reply but was distracted by the clear sound of an arriving carriage which floated up to them from the drive below. "Oh bother," she said, getting up to look out of the window facing the carriage drive. "I hope it is not Mrs. Ardly come to call as she said she might. I should have thought to have Hiller deny me."

Evelyn followed her to the window, but what the women saw was not a country gig drawn up before the house, but a smart racing curricle pulled by four steaming grays. "It is Norwood," Evelyn said in a stricken tone.

Jane's countenance expressed confusion. "I thought you left him a letter which was not to be given to him until tonight so that he couldn't follow you until tomorrow."

Evelyn was more annoyed than alarmed. "He must have it already, but I can't believe that Betsy would betray me. Doubtless he bullyed the truth out of her." She picked up her reticule from the table by the door where she had left it. "I have no wish to meet him. You may tell him that I am in my bedchamber lying down with the headache. I shall lock the door."

"You must meet him sometime," Jane said reasonably.

"I won't have him venting his temper on me. If he has ridden *ventre à terre* to seek me, it is not likely to be to beg my pardon. It is doubtful his humor is improved since last night."

And, indeed, it was not. Before Evelyn could quit the room, far sooner than either woman would have expected, the earl came into the sitting room, entering without ceremony and closing the door behind him with a small but significant snap. "I see you have broken your journey to Spedwell" he said, addressing his wife in a hard voice. "I must say I admire your sangfroid. It is not every woman who would have the courage necessary to stop for her belongings at her husband's house on her way to elope with her lover."

"David, it isn't like that," Jane said before Evelyn could reply to him.

He seemed to notice the presence of his sister for the first time, and when he spoke his voice softened a bit, but his intent did not. "It would be best if you left us, Jane. I apologize for embroiling you in my affairs; I did not intend it so. I only stopped to warn you that I would be returning with Eve later in the day, but Hiller informed me that my dear wife was already before me."

Jane certainly did not relish involving herself in her brother's affairs, but she felt an obligation to be peacemaker between him and Evelyn if she could. "There is no elopement, David. Eve came here to me because she was upset by your argument last night," she said in a voice of deliberate calm. "It is not like

you to go into such a pother over a bit of unfortunate gossip."

"I see my wife has been *well* before me," he said
with a glance that flicked over Evelyn in a way that
was insulting. "I don't know what faradiddle she has
been feeding you, Jane, but I know what her real
intentions are, whatever excuses she may give to you.
If Dancer is not already at Spedwell awaiting her,
then he is well on his way. I have the knowledge that
he left town this morning for Spedwell from his own
man. I deeply regret not passing him on the road,
for I meant for him to taste my whip; he is not
worthy of my iron."

Jane had never heard her brother speak so intem-
perately before, nor had she ever seen him in such
an icy rage, and she began to feel some alarm that
there was more to their quarrel than Evelyn had
confided in her. "You are both distraught just now,
David," she said. "I think you should wait to discuss
this when you are calmer."

But her brother paid her not the least heed. His
attention was again focused on his wife. "Did you
suppose I would allow you to disgrace me with
impunity?"

'What I suppose," Evelyn said, speaking at last and
with heat, "is that you are raving."

"I could divorce you for this," he said icily, "but I'll
see you damned before I'll let you ruin me and
everything I've worked for. Destroy yourself, if you
must, but you won't destroy me. You'll go to Aunt
Sophia until I can decide what is best done for the
future, though I despair of her teaching you conduct. I am afraid your career as the dashing Lady
Notorious is at an end, my dear."

"You are determined to believe in my guilt, aren't
you? Then think what you like, damn you, but I'll go
nowhere at your bidding." Her voice caught on the
last words; furious tears formed in her eyes. Blindly,
she swept past him. He caught at her arm, but she

evaded him and, flinging open the door, ran into the hall.

She had nearly reached the door to her dressing room, which was at the head of the stairs, when he caught her up. "We will discuss this now, Eve," he said in a much more controlled voice, but she was not deceived by the tone assumed for the benefit of any nearby servant, nor did she much care that her own behavior might occasion even further gossip.

"We will not," she said emphatically, and swung away from him in the direction of the stairs.

At that moment Jane came out into the hall. "You are acting like children," she said, exasperated at the unwillingness of either to behave reasonably. She had more to say in this vein but she noticed how close Evelyn was to the top stair, which was at her heels. She called out a warning to her, but it was not in time. Just as Evelyn was wrenching her arm free of her husband's grasp, her heel caught in the hem of her dress. Off balance from the force of her action, she pitched backward toward the stairs. Jane caught her breath and ran toward her and David tried desperately to grasp her arm again, but it was to no avail. Evelyn had the sickening sensation of uncontrolled motion and then a sharp pain as her head struck the banister. I shall be killed, she thought, and then blackness overtook her.

2

Evelyn, in a state somewhere between waking and sleeping, felt a sensation of absolute weariness. Everything about her felt leaden, so much so that even opening her eyes was more effort than she cared to make. The sound around her was indistinct—several voices speaking in hushed, low tones. Once or twice she thought she heard her name spoken and she caught another word or two that puzzled her and at last aroused her curiosity.

She forced herself to open her eyes and saw that she was lying in a dimly lit room in a large, curtained bed. The curtains on one side were closed; on the other side, near the foot of the bed, stood a man and two women who were unknown to her. Nor was the room instantly familiar; her memory was hazy and elusive.

She knew the only sensible thing to do was to ask these people who they were and why she was here. She tried to sit up but the images before her blurred and danced and a wave of dizzying nausea swept over her. She lay back against the pillows, her heart beating rapidly, and willed herself not to be sick.

But her motion had not gone unnoticed. "Eve?" One of the women came over to her and stood looking down on her with obvious concern. "Are you awake, dear? You have given us such a fright. I'll fetch David. He has been beside himself since your accident yesterday."

The man leaned over Evelyn in a portentous way

that made her try to withdraw into her pillows, and possessed himself of her hand to check her pulse. He advised her (unnecessarily) against any sudden movement. The same woman spoke a few whispered words to the other, who appeared to be a serving woman, and the latter left the room. Almost immediately, the door reopened and closed and another man came into the room. He was elegantly dressed in appropriate style for the country, in buckskins, top boots, and a dark-brown swallow-tailed coat. His cravat was expertly tied and in a fashion no town buck would have been ashamed to sport, which proclaimed him polished as well. He was a handsome man, Eve decided as she observed his approach. His golden brown hair was cut in a short but deliberately careless windswept style and his light brown eyes were of the shade often described as amber. His features were regular with a slight patrician cast and a bit of height to his cheekbones. He did not smile, but gravity seemed to suit him.

The men spoke to each other and Evelyn, still feeling weak and disoriented, closed her eyes again, letting their low tones wash over her without heeding the meaning of their words. She wavered in and out of consciousness, without coherent thought. Images that were not quite dreams formed and dissolved before they were entirely grasped, until the face of yet another man, this one smiling and very well known to her, took shape. She opened her eyes quickly to rid herself of the image but the distaste and fear it evoked were not so easily banished. She struggled upright again, heedless of the giddiness and nausea. "Jonathan," she said aloud, but as if to herself, and then addressing the two men: "Where is Jonathan?"

The doctor looked puzzled and a bit embarrassed, and the younger man's features went as rigid as if they had been carved in stone. "I have no idea," he said in a clipped way. "I presume he is at Spedwell or returned to London."

His words were comforting to Evelyn, though she was not sure why it should be so, for there was hostility in his tone. The doctor placed gentle hands on her shoulders and advised her to lie back against the pillows, which she was not loath to do, as the dizziness threatened to completely overwhelm her. Though she lay quite still, she felt as if she were reeling. The figures before her seemed to fade in and out and the room became even dimmer. The doctor spoke to her, but his voice sounded so distant she could not divine his words. "But Jonathan will come, won't he?" she said with a flat finality, not really understanding what she said or why she said it. And then unconsciousness claimed her again.

When Evelyn next opened her eyes, her vision was clear and her mind alert. The room was familiar to her, but only from her previous awakening. She did not find its strangeness alarming this time for she quite understood now that she had been sick or had had some sort of accident that had temporarily disordered her mind.

It was brighter in the room than it had been before; the curtains were drawn back from the bed and the draperies at the windows at the far end of the room were opened to reveal rain-pelted windowpanes. There was still artificial light in the room and Evelyn turned her head to its source, a lamp on a table near to the bed. Beside the table, sitting in a straight-backed chair and reading from a slim volume propped in his lap, was the man who had been called into the room earlier. He appeared to be alone with her, and absorbed in his reading.

Evelyn regarded him for several minutes without him being aware of it, but despite her scrutiny, he remained a stranger to her. It upset her that she could not recall who he was or what her relationship might be to him that he should be sitting at her bedside on obvious terms of intimacy. She looked away from him toward the window and forced herself to concentrate, and gradually her memory began to clear, but haltingly, as if it were a story being read to her one line at a time with a pause between each sentence. Finally, she was able to put a name to her vague fears, but it instead of helping her, it confused her more than ever, for she still did not know this place or the man beside her. It made her a little afraid, for she was very conscious of her weakness and vulnerability.

She turned her head again to look at the man in the chair and discovered that he had put down his book and was silently watching her. His countenance was no longer as forbidding as she remembered from the first time she had seen him, but he offered her no reassuring smile. His expression was shuttered and she could not guess what he was thinking. Silence stretched between them until he finally broke it. "Are you feeling better, Eve?"

"I don't know," she answered truthfully.

"Dr. Carlyon has already been here this morning and is gone, but I can have him fetched back if you wish."

She shook her head against the pillows and was pleased to discover that the motion had no uncomfortable side effects. "Is Jonathan Dancer here?" she said tentatively, assuming that there must be some connection between the two men. At once his expression changed as it had before when she has spoken that name.

He closed the book with a little snap. "Did you suppose I would send for him to attend your bedside?"

"Did Jonathan bring me here?"

He caught at his breath as if her words had shocked him, but his voice betrayed no emotion at all. "I fear your wits are scrambled, my dear. It is the concussion caused by your accident, no doubt. As far as I am aware, you came here unattended."

The dizziness and the nausea were now explained

to her, and even the frightening lapses in her memory, for she knew these were symptoms of a head injury. Evelyn closed her eyes in an effort to remember the accident he spoke of. "The stream at the edge of the meadow," she said after a few moments, speaking slowly as the memory returned. "The banks were so high and rocky," she continued, her voice growing in firmness along with her certainty, "and I decided to take my horse over it. I was riding a hack, not a hunter, and I thought he meant to refuse. I remember wondering if we would make it. I gather we did not."

The man was silent for a long minute and then he said in a measured way, "You fell down the stairs here at Blankenhill yesterday afternoon. To my knowledge you do not ride or hunt. You do not even sit a hack with ease."

What he said was absurd, for she had been riding almost since she could walk, but there were too many other things in his words to disturb her for her to take him to task on this point. It was very obvious that they were speaking at cross purposes. She had a wild idea that some bizarre mistake had been made and she had wandered into the wrong house. Certainly she had never heard of anyplace called Blakenhill, and yet this man knew her name. "Who are you?" she asked, deciding at last to get to the heart of the matter before trying to sort out the detail.

He looked utterly blank for a moment as if unable to answer, and his voice, when he recovered himself, hardened. "What game is this, Eve?"

Evelyn sat up against the pillows, this time without any giddiness. "It is not of my making. I don't know who you are or why you are here."

After a moment he put his book on the table and stood. "Cut line, Eve. If you are trying to persuade me that your accident has deprived you of your reason, you should have better sense than to ask for

Dancer. We both know he was the reason that you came here."

"I don't even know where 'here' is," Evelyn said, a note of panic in her voice.

"You are condemned by your own words in the letter you left for me," he went on, as if she hadn't spoken. "I fear your lover has not come up to scratch, though. I don't know what he thought when you never arrived at your rendezvous, but he hadn't the courage to seek you out here." He reached inside his coat and drew out a sheet of folded paper. "It is in your own hand, Eve," he added, and handed it to her.

She took the paper and unfolded it. There was no salutation.

Since you have a high-handed disregard for my sensibilities, I have no compunction about what I am about to do. You shall certainly dislike it, Norwood, for no man likes to lose control of what he regards as his property. If you are honest, you will give yourself the blame that you have driven me to this desperate course.

I am going to one who truly understands and cares for my well-being. It is obvious to me that *you* care only to control me and that I cannot live under such tyranny. It is pointless for you to come after me, for I will not meekly follow your bidding and I cannot be turned from my purpose.

There was no signature, but it was unnecessary; Evelyn recognized the hand as her own at once. For the first time confusion began to escalate into real fear. She had no recollection of writing the letter and it made no sense to her at all. "It looks like my hand," she admitted reluctantly, "but I cannot recall writing it. What does it mean?"

His eyes rested on her for a long moment before he spoke again. "It *is* your hand. This is the note you

left for me when you fled Norwood House. I said I
would not divorce you, Eve," he said, speaking with
a curious intensity, "for there is my own name and
career to consider. Addleby is talking of resigning
his ministry when he removes from town and Perceval
has spoken of it to me. It is everything I have worked
for, and I want it very much, but it may be too high
a price to pay for the complete destruction of my
peace." He took the letter from her, folded it and
put it back in his pocket. "As soon as you are well
enough to travel, we shall go to Rothbury. You have
no choice at all in the matter, Eve, so you had best
resign yourself to it. If you attempt to defy me or
make any effort to contact Dancer again, I shall set
you aside, whatever the consequences to us both."

Evelyn felt as if she were reeling again, but this
time it had nothing to do with her physical injury.
Either this man was mad or she was; she could think
of nothing else to explain the astonishing things that
he said. He spoke to her as if she were his wife, but
he was a stranger to her. He spoke of an elopement,
but she had been fleeing *from* Jonathan, not to him.
She regarded him, speechless. She could not order
her thoughts sufficiently to know where she might
begin.

When she did not respond after a minute or so he
said, "If we are not to have a full-fledged scandal
about our ears, there are matters that must be seen
to. I did not bring your maid with me and I have
dismissed the nurse who sat with you yesterday; we
have enough difficulty to face without allowing you
to rave before strangers. Jane will sit with you until I
return, but you needn't think you can cozen her
again with a pretense of confusion. She was here as
well when you first awoke and asked for your lover."
He picked up his book and extinguished the lamp.

The increased gloom of the room exactly mir-
rored Evelyn's spirits. "I am not your wife," she said
in a small voice. "I don't know who you are, or

where I am, but I won't believe I have lost my mind." Silent tears fell from her eyes. "I don't know why you are doing this. *Why* are you doing this to me?"

"Oh, dear God," he said, and it was a moan. The book dropped from his hands as if he had forgotten it. "Don't be a damned fool, Evelyn. You can't trade on my love or sympathy anymore. It's over. Accept it." He spoke harshly, his voice raised, almost as if in anger. Then he turned on his heel and left her.

Evelyn had felt remarkably well when she awakened, but now her head ached abominably. She had no notion what it meant to be insane, but she was sure she could not have lost her wits. Yet if she was certain of her own rationality, then she must question his reason, and though he was obviously angry and upset, he did not appear to her to be out of his senses.

The first thing she made up her mind to do was to get out of bed, for lying about in this invalidish way made her feel uncomfortably vulnerable. She pulled back the sheets and noticed for the first time that she was clothed in a nightdress of pale blue silk that was unlike anything she could ever recall wearing. It clung to her sensuously and revealed her slender but well formed figure, particularly her full breasts, which were so exposed they nearly spilled free of the thin material. A belated blush rose to her cheeks to think that he had observed her robed so indecently. Unless, of course, he were her husband. But that was impossible, absurd; she would not even allow herself to dwell on the possibility that she could be married to a man who she had never set eyes on before yesterday.

She got out of bed very carefully, for whatever else was a lie, she could not doubt that she had been injured in some way, and she was still feeling the lingering effects. When she stood her legs felt rubbery and she clung helplessly to the bed curtains for a few moments while the room spun about her.

When this passed, she took a few tentative steps away from the bed.

It was at this moment that the door opened again and the woman she remembered from the first time she had awakened, came into the room, saying with obvious concern, "Eve, you must not. Dr. Carlyon said you were not to be out of bed for any reason." She rushed to Evelyn's side and took her arm.

Quite suddenly Evelyn felt overcome. Her confusion, her weakness, her insecurity and fears, combined with a helplessness which she could not deny, overwhelmed her and she dissolved into tears. The woman put her arms about Evelyn and led her back to the bed. She gave Evelyn a fine lace-edged handkerchief to weep into and murmured soothingly until Evelyn at last regained control of her sensibilities.

"You must not cry so, dearest," the young woman said as Evelyn's sobs began to diminish. "I know David has been a bit harsh with you, but it is only because he cares so much. He may say that he does not love you any longer, but I don't believe it. He was nearly sick with worry over you. It is just his pride that makes him so unyielding, but you must not refine too much upon it. I suppose it seems hopeless to you just now, but I am sure it need not be so."

Evelyn had no notion what to do except to throw herself on the mercy of this woman who at least seemed inclined to be sympathetic toward her. "Will you please help me?" she asked through her tears. "I don't know what is happening, and I am frightened half out of my wits." She laughed at her ironic choice of words. "At least, I hope I am not out of my wits. I know it will seem to you as if I am, but truly, even though you seem to know me, I have no idea who you are, and nor do I know the man you call my husband. Please help me," she repeated in a final pathetic plea.

The young woman was clearly upset by her speech. "Evelyn, you must not talk like this. If you are playacting to gain David's sympathy, you ought to know him well enough to realize that it is the wrong way to go about it. He has lost his trust in you, I fear, and this makes matters worse rather than better. It would serve you much better to admit to everything and throw yourself on his forgiveness. He can be very generous when he chooses."

Evelyn was regaining her control and she pushed down her fears and self-doubt, determined to make herself believed. "I swear to you I am not playacting," she said, making her voice as calm and sensible sounding as she could manage.

Indecision was writ on Jane's face. David had warned her that Evelyn was pretending confusion to excuse her inexcusable behavior and that she was not to regard it, but something in Evelyn's plea touched her. She said clearly, "I am Lady Jane Halloway, and David is my brother, he is the earl of Norwood, and you *are* his wife. This is your own bedchamber at Blakenhill, which has been your home since you married David last year."

These answers did nothing to reassure Evelyn. "I am Lady Norwood?" Evelyn asked, pronouncing the words as if by rote. She could not reasonably believe that both the earl and his sister suffered from the same mad delusions. A sudden chilling thought came to her and she said urgently, "What is the day?"

Jane blinked. "The day? Why it is Friday. You arrived on Thursday, but I fear you have lost a day to unconsciousness."

Evelyn waved an impatient hand. "Not the day, the date."

Jane's looked completely puzzled, but complied. "It is April twelfth." Anticipating the next question, she added, "The year is 1810."

"My dear God," Evelyn said on a breath. "It cannot be. Surely it is August 1808. It must be so; I can't believe even Jonathan would be this cruel. He could not gain my inheritance by coercion or subterfuge;

does he hope to convince me that I have lost my wits
so that he may control me in that manner?"

"Oh, Eve, please stop this. You will have me wondering what is become of *my* wits," Jane pleaded,
sounding as if she wished to cry herself. "The concussion must have been far greater than Dr. Carlyon
has led us to believe. You must lie down again and I
will find David and have him fetch the doctor at
once."

"It is not the concussion," Evelyn said placing a
hand on Jane's arm as she made to rise. "Or at least,
not the way that you mean. It is truly April 1810?"
Jane nodded and Evelyn went on, speaking carefully
so she could not be misunderstood, "The last day I
can remember was August fifteenth, 1808, and I
remember the date well, for it was a week exactly to
my twenty-first birthday. I don't understand it any
more than you do, but I swear to you it is the truth."

Jane stared hard at her sister-in-law for a full
minute before speaking. "Can this possibly be true?"
she said at last. "I have heard of such things . . .
people who lose their senses in an injury and cannot
recall who they are, but this is not the same. You
seem to think you are someone else."

"I am Evelyn Anne Catherine Fearne," Evelyn said
quietly. "I was raised in Berkshire at Limirend Hall.
Just before I turned sixteen my parents and only
brother were killed in a coaching accident, and I
was placed in the guardianship of my uncle, Mr.
Archibald Dancer of Spedwell Manor near Faversham
in Kent. He died about a year after my parents'
deaths and my cousin Jonathan Dancer was named
my guardian until I reached my twenty-first birthday. I lived with him and his mother, my aunt Lavinia,
at Spedwell until August fifteenth, 1808." She paused.
"And that is all that I remember."

Jane moved about the room restlessly, her distress
obvious as Evelyn spoke. "What am I to think of this,
Eve?" she said. She stopped, crossed her arms as if

she were hugging herself, and stood in front of
Evelyn, biting at her lip in consternation. "*I* know
you as Evelyn Walker. You are the niece of Mrs.
Charlotte Walker, of Hardwood Hall; you came to
live with her at just about the time that you say,
mid-August in 1808. She told us that you were the
daughter of her husband's widowed brother who we
knew had died not many months before; there was
no reason at all to question this. As soon as you met,
the attraction between you and David was obvious,
and within six months you were married." She broke
off her recital and reached across the bed to take
Evelyn's hands into her own. "Please, Eve, if this is
some scheme, give it up. It is frightening me and
David will never be cozened into believing it."

"It is the truth, Jane. I swear to it. I know nothing
of the things you have just told me."

There was no doubting the sincerity of her tone.
Jane sat down on the bed again and sighed unhap-
pily. "Did you know then that you were not Evelyn
Walker?"

"I don't know," Evelyn answered truthfully.

"Have you told David everything you've told me?"

"He didn't give me a chance."

"I think you should," Jane advised, "for he truly
believes that you are just pretending to be confused
to persuade him not to send you to Aunt Sophia."

"Whoever she may be," Evelyn said, with a faint
groan. "I doubt I can convince him, you know. He
doesn't want to believe me."

"I think he is afraid to believe you," Jane cor-
rected, but she did not elaborate. She stood up again.
"*I* believe you, Evelyn. It is too fantastic to be a
made-up story and I can see that you really are
afraid. If you tell David exactly as you've told me,
he'll come to believe you," she added confidently.
She then asked Evelyn if she felt well enough to be
left alone while she sought out her brother and,
receiving an affirmative reply, left to do so.

Evelyn was indeed well enough, at least physically. She could almost feel her strength returning to her minute by minute, but as her body strengthened, her mental state became increasingly troubled. Even less than Jane did she know what to make of her situation. It was as incredible for her to believe as it was for Jane and considerably more frightening to contemplate.

Pulling her mind away from what she could not comprehend, she concentrated on the memories of which she was certain: happy days she had known with her family at Limirend Hall; the dull misery after their carriage had overturned in a ditch on a journey that by rights she should have accompanied them on, remaining at Limirend only because she was recovering from a bad head cold.

When she had been informed by her father's solicitor Mr. Petersham that she was to leave her home in Berkshire to live with her uncle and aunt, she had accepted it without protest, actually looking forward to the change from the terrible silence that had fallen over Limirend. But within a few short months at Spedwell she would gladly have exchanged the life she led there for the loneliness of her former home. From the beginning she was treated with the disdain of a poor relation. Her uncle was virtually never in residence, preferring life in London, and her aunt, who only joined him in town on occasion, clearly resented having Evelyn foisted upon her care.

Evelyn's father's man of business, believing her too young to understand such things, had not discussed the settling of her father's estate with her, but Mrs. Dancer made it clear that Evelyn owed virtually her existence to her guardian's charity. When Evelyn had suggested that since she was a burden to her aunt, she might return to Limirend, Mrs. Dancer had informed her that the estate had been sold to cover debts. Most of the servants, taking their cue from abovestairs, treated her with less than the respect due her station, and when friends and neighbors visited, Evelyn was either dismissed or so relegated to the background that she went as unnoticed as an extra chair.

But Evelyn was not a poor spirited girl and she had determined to make the best of an unhappy situation if she could not change it. Her life might have been lonely, but she would not allow it to be so. Her aunt, a vague and petulant woman, used her as an unpaid companion and general maid, setting her to a constant number of stupid tasks or forcing her to do menial chores in the understaffed house. To offset the tedium of her life, Evelyn took what pleasure she could in long walks about the estate whenever she could escape the demands of her aunt, and she made constant use of the library, which stood virtually abandoned when Mr. Dancer was from home.

Evelyn was pleased that her elusive memory was returning, but memories of her life at Spedwell were disturbing; feeling restless, she again got out of the bed and this time made her way to the window without difficulty. The rain had stopped and a sluggish sun attempted to burn its way through the clouds. The sight before her was of parkland and shaved lawn which was a rich dark green and trimmed to the texture of thick velvet. She had had a similar view from her room at Spedwell, though the grounds had not been nearly so well kept.

She had never been able to make herself believe completely her aunt's claim that her parents had had debts and mortgages so great that she had been left virtually penniless. The Fearnes had not enjoyed grand wealth, but they had been very comfortable at Limirend, which was a moderately large estate, and Evelyn knew that her marriage portion had at least been respectable. She had determined that once she achieved her majority she would confront Mr. Petersham and insist that he tell her exactly how matters stood with her. Even if it were true that she was utterly impoverished, she would not stay at Spedwell. She intended to make her own way in the world by hiring herself out as a companion or governess, or even as a milliner's assistant in Canterbury or Tunbridge Wells, if no other course was open to her.

It was not only that her aunt used her as an unpaid servant. It had been bad enough that first year, before her uncle had died, but since her cousin Jonathan, with whom she shared a hearty mutual dislike, had become master of Spedwell, a difficult situation had become impossible. Like his father, he was seldom found in Kent, but he left his mark on the household, nevertheless. He had ambitions to set himself up as a man of fashion without the connections or fortune that generally went with such a life, and he did not scruple to bleed the estate for every penny it could afford him. What was far worse, he forced his own mother to skimp and sacrifice wherever she could, and seldom thanked her for her efforts. Since Lavinia Dancer doted on her son and would allow no criticism of him, it was generally Evelyn who bore the brunt of her unhappiness and resentment at the retired, tedious life she was forced to lead at Spedwell.

Less than a fortnight before her long awaited twenty-first birthday, the drudgery of her life came to an abrupt end and turned instead into a nightmare. Quite entirely by accident she discovered that she was not the pauper she had been led to believe she was and that the five years she had been virtually in service to her aunt were for naught.

On the rare occasions when her cousin was in residence, the library was lost to Evelyn as a refuge, for he used the large desk at one end of the room as a sort of makeshift office to go over estate accounts on the rare times his beleaguered bailiff could persuade him to his duties. But on that particular morning in mid-August, Jonathan had gone into Faversham and Evelyn slipped into the room to exchange the book she had finished the night before for another. Generally she would have ignored the desk and the untidy mess of papers that were perpetually spread across it, but a glance in that direction as she entered the room revealed a panel in the wainscoting near the desk that stood open to reveal a hollow in the wall she had not known existed. On the desk was a metal lock box that was roughly the size and shape of the cavity.

Curious, she went over to the desk to examine the box and what she found were deeds, certificates, stocks, and other documents that bore her father's name and were obviously a part of his estate. She had had no idea that these things existed and no notion why they should be in her cousin's possession. Risking the unexpected return of her cousin or intrusion by a servant, Evelyn sat at the desk and began to sort through the papers, hoping she would discover what had become of her father's estate. What she did find was a copy of her father's will, that even a hasty perusal of which showed that she was not the helpless dependent her aunt claimed she was, but a young woman who in only a few days would be quite wealthy in her own right.

In retrospect Evelyn could see that the prudent course would have been to have said nothing until she gained her majority and the right to handle her own affairs, but all the indignities she had suffered in silence at the hands of the Dancers had created in her a simmering anger, which now came to the boil when she learned how hardly they had used her.

Lavinia Dancer was cast into confusion by her niece's accusations, but Jonathan, not so easily ruffled, silenced her excuses and complaints and informed Evelyn that he controlled her fortune for her own good as he would continue to do when he became her husband on the day that she attained her majority. All Evelyn's anger vanished and was replaced by astonishment and horror. Neither reasoning nor outright refusal weighed with Jonathan. Her contemptuous evaluation of his character to his face resulted in her ears being boxed, which proved that his cruelty could be physical as well as verbal and filled her with a new resolve against the match. When she threatened to seek refuge with Mr. Petersham, she was locked in her room and she soon discovered that Jonathan had foreseen her objections and had taken steps to render her powerless to prevent being married against her will.

Dancer left that same day to return to town for a special license and an obliging cleric who would be well paid not to ask awkward questions. Locked in her room, for the first time since she had come to Spedwell she had no occupation beyond dwelling on the wretched state in store for her and inventing and discarding schemes to prevent it from happening. Mr. Petersham was doubtless negligent in his charge toward her, but she could not believe he was party to her cousin's perfidy. In the end, the only course she felt open to her was to escape through her bedroom window to seek the solicitor's protection.

In the gray darkness of early morning, she managed to get out of the window and down to the ground without breaking her neck, and she then made her way to the stables to steal a bridle, which she meant to fit to the first hack or hunter that she found in the enclosed pasture behind the stable and out buildings. Fearing Jonathan would follow her as soon as he returned and discovered her gone, and knowing that there was a market fair at Maidenstone and the roads would be well peopled with observers who might give Jonathan her direction, Evelyn felt her only choice was to ride crosscountry as much as possible until she reached Croyden, where she was reasonably certain she would be able to get a stage that would take her to Reading and Mr. Petersham.

Evelyn was an accomplished horsewoman, so her only concern as she rode across brown-gray fields as

dawn approached was whether or not the few coins
she had put away since her arrival at Spedwell would
be sufficient to see her from Croyden to Reading.
But she reckoned without the fact that her cousin's
stable did not boast the fine horseflesh that her father's had. She was game, but her mount was not. As
she had told David, the very last thing she could
remember was coming upon the high-banked stream
and then nothing at all until she had first awakened
the previous day.

With all her heart she wished she might fill in the
gap between then and now, but no effort of concentration proved successful and at last she gave it up
and left the window to more closely explore her
surroundings. The room was graceful and well appointed, decorated in shades of blue and white with
no thought to expense. There was a door directly
across from the window at which she had sat and she
opened this and discovered a much smaller room,
which held two enormous wardrobes, an armoire, a
high and elongated chest, and a dressing table on
which was arrayed a vast number of small bottles
and jars.

Evelyn walked over to one of the wardrobes and
opened it. It contained more dresses and gowns than
she had ever seen in one place before in her life.
The other wardrobe was less full, but the chest and
armoire contained more clothes, all of which appeared to be of a size that would suit her, and she
came to the conclusion that this must be her own
dressing room—Lady Norwood's dressing room. Evelyn was utterly astonished. Since she had left
Limirend, she had had no new dresses besides her
aunt's castoffs, which had to be remade to fit her.
She delighted in the possession of so many beautiful
things, but at the same time it dismayed her a little
because it emphasized her ignorance of the life she
had led as the Countess of Norwood.

Discovering what was surely the matching peignior

to her diaphanous nightdress in one of the drawers of the armoire, Evelyn unfolded it and put it on, and the act made her feel a bit less vulnerable in her strange surroundings. She heard a door open in the other room and she returned to the bedchamber to find her "husband" had come into the room.

"I must compliment you, my dear," he said dryly as he approached her. "You seem to have convinced my sister of your nonsense. I have no doubt of her sense, so your success must be attributed to your skill."

Jane came into the room behind him at that moment and said, "David, please listen to Eve. You did promise you would."

"To please you," he said to his sister, but looking at Evelyn as he spoke.

It was scarcely encouraging, and Evelyn felt a spark of rebellion which urged her to tell him that she didn't care a fig for his opinion. But her common sense made her realize that she needed to make him believe her. She was caught in an impossible coil and, alone and friendless, she would need his assistance to unravel it, however much that might rankle. So she told him her history as she had told Jane, with many additions fresh in her mind from her recent reverie.

What he thought as she spoke, she could not guess, for his features gave away nothing of his thoughts. He didn't speak until prompted by his sister, who, finally goaded by his silence, asked him bluntly what he thought. "It is interesting," he replied noncommittally. "If it is fiction, it is quite well thought out."

Jane, determined to help Evelyn, seized upon this. "Do you believe that Eve could have made it up in the little time she has been conscious since her fall?" she asked.

David walked over to the window where Evelyn had stood and looked down onto the parkland for a few moments before turning and answering. Whether this was caution or simply a gathering of his thoughts, his slow response set Evelyn's nerves on edge. "He will probably say that I was feigning unconsciousness," she said caustically, "and using the time to invent a story."

The corners of his mouth turned up a bit, relieving the gravity of his expression. "Careful, my love. That sounds very like the Eve I know. It won't do if you mean to convince me otherwise."

"You need not take my word alone," Evelyn replied as she sat on the bed again. Some of her weakness was returning and she had no wish to display it before him. "Jane told me that you came to know me through a Mrs. Walker, who claimed to be my aunt. I have no notion why she would do so, though I must be grateful to her. Surely she will confirm at the least that I am not her niece and tell us how I came to be with her."

Brother and sister exchanged meaningful glances. 'Mrs. Walker is visiting her sister in Knaresborough," Jane said. "They are planning a walking tour of Ireland and Scotland. I am sure she may be reached but it will probably take a bit of doing." She glanced again at her brother with a quelling frown and he responded with a small sardonic smile.

Evelyn correctly interpreted this exchange to mean that he believed she had known only too well that Mrs. Walker would not be able to corroborate her story. But it was only a setback, not defeat, and she happily recalled another who could confirm at least some part of what she had said. "There is my father's man of business, Mr. Petersham, in Berkshire. He can tell you that I was sent to Spedwell to live and he doubtless knows of my father's will and my inheritance."

"If you are speaking of Mr. Elias Petersham, the solicitor who resided in Reading," David said, regarding her blandly, "I do not think he will be able to help you. I knew him slightly through some business dealings I had in that area. He died of a putrid fever about four months ago."

Evelyn let out her breath in a little groan of consternation. "But this is absurd," she said. "Surely there is someone who can confirm that I am who I say I am." A sudden thought occurred to her. "What of my cousin Jonathan? You say that I have known him since coming here, I can't believe he wouldn't know me; I couldn't have changed so very much in a year."

After another of his long pauses, David said, "He has never acknowledged you as a connection as far as I am aware."

Evelyn looked from him to Jane, searching their faces as if for an answer to her puzzlement. "He *has* to know me," she insisted. "He . . ." She came to an abrupt halt as enlightenment lit her features. "Of course, I should have realized . . . he does not choose to know me," she said grimly. "I don't know what he may gain by pretending not to know me, but it is doubtless to his purpose. I don't think he inherits if I die, but he may still have the means of controlling my fortune if there is nothing to prevent him."

"Or it may be that there is no one to confirm your fantastical story because it is just that—fantastical," David returned. "If what you say is true, then your luck is quite out, I fear. If the only people who could identify you and confirm your story are dead, unreachable, or determined for their own purposes to maintain the lie, then its only your word against what we know of you ourselves."

Evelyn opened her mouth to protest but closed it again. What he said was unarguable. It was seven years since anyone at Limirend had set eyes on her. She had been little more than a child when she left Berkshire for Kent, and living retired as she had at Spedwell, her Kentish neighbors were as unlikely to know her by sight as were their Berkshire counterparts. She had no friends among the servants at

Spedwell; none of these were likely to go against their master to help her. There was really no one at all she could think of who would be certain to know her or willing to come forward and say so.

It raised the fear in her breast that she might never be able to prove what she said, but she pushed the dispiriting thought out of her mind. "Why would I make up such a story," she asked reasonably. "It is, as you say, fantastical."

"Perhaps your injury gave you time to reconsider the consequences of the course you were set upon," he responded. "You are in a very difficult position, Eve. You face either banishment from my household or divorce. As ruinous as the latter would be for me, I think you might fare worse and you have come at last to realize it. Dancer exists on the fringes of the *ton* but he aspires to higher circles; I cannot see him allying himself legally or permanently with a ruined woman who would bring him nothing but discredit."

"So you think I am hedging my bets," Evelyn suggested.

"It is not an illogical conclusion," he said, smiling humorlessly.

"I must believe her," Jane said, going over to the bed and taking Evelyn's hand in hers. "It is so . . . intricate. It sounds like a story Mrs. Radcliffe might have invented."

"Yes, it does sound like a book," David agreed. "Or a play," he added after a significant pause. As he said this he held Jane's eyes, and noting her reluctant comprehension, he said with a slow smile, "Exactly."

Evelyn observed this exchange but did not understand it, and her expression showed her puzzlement.

"Mr. Dancer was one of a number of gentlemen who assisted Mr. Kemble in obtaining the funds to rebuild Covent Garden last year," Jane explained. "It is fashionable in some circles to be a patron of the theater."

"But what does that say to anything?" Evelyn protested.

David turned his back on the window and sat against the wide sill. "You have been introduced to these circles through him. It might in some way have given you the idea for your, ah, scenario."

Evelyn felt near to tears with frustration. This wretched man was determined not to believe her and had a means to twist her every word against her. "That is absurd. All that I have said is the truth and I *will* prove it to you."

"I hope you may," David said as he stood, but his tone was not expressive of hope. "If it is a lie, Eve, you would do best to rethink it. I won't be your fool again, you know." After regarding her unblinkingly for several moments, he turned and left.

Jane remained a bit longer to assure Evelyn that whatever David might say, he would not dismiss the matter without making some effort to learn the truth.

This was exactly the case. David went directly to a small room opening off the library that he used as his study. A young man, near his own age, was seated at the large desk that held center place in the room. Roger Ventry ran fingers through his already disordered light brown hair and closed the account book before him with a sigh. "I have tried a hundred ways to think the thing through, but I fear there is nothing for it. If we do not dredge the stream at the north of Guidrey's Vale we risk worse flooding next spring, but if we use the home farm's repair allotment for that we shall have to put off replacing the storage barn this season."

But Lord Norwood did not take his usual interest in the management of his estate. "Speak to Aldman about it and do what you think best, Roger," he advised in a dismissive way as he sat in a somewhat battered, but comfortable wing chair near the tall windows leading out to the garden. "Do both if you think it necessary."

"It will cut into the income of the estate if we do that."

"But will scarcely impoverish me, I think."

"Hardly that, my lord," said the young man, scandalized at the thought. Mr. Ventry knew the intimate details of Lord Norwood's income very likely better than the earl did himself. As his personal secretary he was privy to most of the details of his employer's life and knew to some extent even the fact that there were difficulties between the earl and his countess. "I hope Lady Norwood is recovering well from her fall," he said, selecting the most discreet of several inquiries he might have made.

"Remarkably well," the earl replied in the same offhanded way and lapsed into a pensive silence. His secretary, recognizing this humor as a brown study, returned to his figures until such time as the earl should require his attention. A number of minutes passed before this was the case.

"I have an errand I wish you to accomplish for me, Roger," David said at last. "I know I can rely on your discretion."

Ventry closed the book in front of him. Instinct, even more than the earl's behavior, told him that this was a matter of importance, perhaps the very sort of service he had been longing to perform for his employer this past twelvemonth. It was not that he did not enjoy the regular duties of his office: taking charge of the earl's correspondence, overseeing the disbursement of his lordship's comfortable income, and supervising the bailiffs of Norwood's various estates and holdings, but he was an ambitious young man and it was the political, diplomatic, and special personal portions of his position that most interested him. It was in fulfilling these duties that he felt he was doing the best job not only to his employer's advantage, but to his own. In the first place, he genuinely liked Lord Norwood, in the second, he was in love with Norwood's sister.

Positions that paid well and were yet genteel in character were few and far between, and as the younger son of a baronet of moderate means, it was very necessary for Mr. Ventry to support himself in the best way he could manage. Mr. Ventry might, of course, have chosen the two fields traditionally populated by scions of the aristocracy: the church or the army, but he felt no calling for either. Or he might have chosen the course so many younger sons followed and married to advantage, but it was not in his nature to be a fortune hunter or even to be thought one, and this was more of an obstacle to his happiness than his own lack of fortune.

He and Jane had been cast into each other's company since she had returned to Blakenhill after the untimely death of her husband, and their friendship had gradually blossomed into love. Though he was her equal in breeding, he was constantly conscious of his lowly status compared to hers, for she was the daughter and sister of earls and possessed a handsome fortune in her own right.

Compounding his feelings of inadequacy was the fact that Jane's deceased husband, Mr. Henry Halloway, had been a penniless younger son and Ventry had himself heard the earl comment on the fact that it was good thing that Jane was in no need of a jointure, for what had been left her was the merest pittance. Mr. Ventry read into these words disapproval, and perhaps condemnation, and though he was determined to make Jane his wife, he was equally determined to prove to her brother that his motive had nothing to do with his own advancement. Norwood's political star was rising, and if the services he performed for the earl were extraordinary and gave him cause to be grateful, he was confident of Norwood's assistance in his own rise to greater position, which would make him a more eligible match for Lady Jane.

"Of course, my lord," he said eagerly. "It is no more than my job to treat your private affairs as if they were my own."

A characteristic faint smile touched David's lips. "That would not always be a recommendation for trust," he said, and seeing the protest forming on the other's lips added hastily, "I was jesting, Roger. If I didn't trust you, I wouldn't employ you. Your father's estate lies fairly close to Faversham, does it not?"

The younger man nodded. "About five miles to the north."

"Are you familiar with Spedwell Manor?"

The young man nodded. "It is Mr. Dancer's estate," he said cautiously, well aware of the whispers that were circulating in town. "We are acquainted, of course," he added, "but my family is not on informal terms with the Dancers."

"Are you also acquainted with Mrs. Dancer's niece, a Miss Evelyn Fearne?"

The secretary knit his brow and then shook his head. "I don't believe so, my lord."

David chewed thoughtfully on a forefinger, and Mr. Ventry thought he had again fallen into a study, but presently he said, "I wish to know more about Miss Fearne, but I wish to do so without arousing any interest. Can you do that, do you think?"

Ventry's curiosity was rampant, but his breeding prevented him from displaying it before his employer. "I am sure of it, my lord. It shouldn't be too difficult. I am well known in the village of Wellmere and people will talk to me readily enough."

David nodded as if satisfied. "In that case, I think it is time you paid your mother a much overdue visit. Two days should do it. You will leave tomorrow and I shall expect you again on Friday."

"Is there anything in particular that you wish to know about Miss Fearne?"

"Any and all information that you can discover. I would be most interested, however, in where she is

to be found now. She lived at Spedwell for a time,
but I have reason to suppose that she resides elsewhere now." He paused and then added, "I don't
want to belabor the point, Roger, but it is important
to me that you don't call attention to your curiosity.
It is a somewhat delicate matter."

Mr. Ventry could not guess what was in his employer's mind, but felt instinctively that it must in
some way be related to the unfortunate gossip which
concerned Lady Norwood and her friendship with
Mr. Dancer. If that were so, it was possible that his
success at this task could in some way ease what must
be a very painful time for his employer and cause
the earl to be very grateful indeed. "My lord, you
may place your trust absolutely in me," he said with
a sincerity that bordered on declamation.

David did not smile again, but there was a bright-
ness in his eyes that might have been amusement.
"Very good, Roger. Oh, one other thing. You might,
if you can, examine the parish register in Faversham.
It is not out of the realm of possibility that Miss
Fearne is beyond the reach of us all."

"If she is not," the secretary asked earnestly, "shall
I pursue her, my lord?"

"That," said the earl with a trace of irony, "will
depend."

3

The doctor returned later in the day and pronounced Evelyn remarkably recovered, but advised her continued rest for the next several days. Evelyn obeyed, but not from choice. David returned to her when the doctor had left to inform her that he was making discreet inquiries and that he thought it best that she remain quietly in her room until these had been completed. She bristled at his commanding tone, but was pleased enough that he accepted her story at least to the extent of being willing to make inquiries, and she agreed to do as he asked.

He did not visit her at all in the days that followed, and Evelyn found herself feeling curiously disappointed, though she hardly knew why. In spite of her ignorance about her immediate past, it was obvious enough that there was much anger and hurt between her and Lord Norwood, and even now their dealings together were more confrontation than conversation.

Evelyn felt perfectly sound with no effects from her accident beyond those to her memory, and the inactivity and anticipation might have driven her to distraction if Jane had not spent much of her time with Evelyn. Evelyn was very grateful for this and had no reason to doubt Jane's word that they had been good friends before the accident, for Evelyn was already extremely fond of her sister-in-law.

Jane was completely sympathetic toward her and was only too glad to answer any questions she could that Evelyn put to her. She told Evelyn all that she knew of Evelyn's courtship with David, making it clear that she had never doubted that it had been a love match, at least on her brother's side. Though Jane had too much breeding to even hint that the marriage had been a *mesalliance* because of Evelyn's lack of dowry, Evelyn gathered that it was so by reading between her words.

"It is very difficult to imagine Norwood in love with me," she admitted candidly. "He behaves as if he quite disliked me."

"You must not judge him by what you see now," Jane told her. "It was not always so with him."

They were seated in two comfortable chairs which they had drawn up near the window overlooking the park. They were ostensibly engaged in fancywork but neither lady had used her needle for some time. Evelyn leaned across the space that separated them and placed her hand on Jane's. "Will you tell me what has happened to estrange us?" she asked. "I know you do not wish to be disloyal to David, but it is dreadfully uncomfortable being ignorant of the particulars of one's own life. I know one of the reasons he is so distrustful of me now is that I in some way betrayed his trust, only I don't know what I am supposed to have done. I am only certain of one thing: whatever Norwood may say, I could never have taken Jonathan Dancer as my lover, in or out of my senses."

Sighing, Jane said, "I don't know that I can tell you very much. I haven't any idea what happened in private between you, for David would not discuss such things with me. That is, he showed me the letter you left for him and he said he believed you were planning to elope with Mr. Dancer, and that he feared that he would have to divorce you if matters came to such a pass, but he told me none of the particulars that led to such a wretched state of affairs."

"I gather there was gossip about me and Jonathan," Evelyn prompted. "Did you know that?"

"Only what little David has told me," Jane said apologetically. "I was only in town for a fortnight this Season. While I was there, I thought myself that Mr. Dancer paid you a great deal of attention and that you did not dislike it, but I never supposed you would take it to the length of becoming his mistress."

"I swear to you I could not have done so," Evelyn said with quiet vehemence. "What happened when I arrived on Thursday, Jane? I remember nothing, not even my fall down the stairs."

Jane abandoned the pretense of working and returned the silks in her lap to the workbasket. She told Evelyn what she knew of her argument with David and the events that had led to her present condition.

Evelyn was very thoughtful when she had finished. "I hope all of my memory returns to me," she said with a sigh. "It is very difficult to defend oneself when one is quite ignorant of what actually occurred. I just wish I knew what Jonathan's part was in this. Why should he refuse to acknowledge me as his cousin and then pursue me to the point of scandal?"

"Why indeed?" Both women started, for they had not heard David come into the room.

"I can understand not acknowledging you, Eve, but what could he have to gain by destroying your reputation? There had to be some purpose to it," Jane insisted, her eyes glancing toward her brother.

"I daresay," was his only reply as he crossed the room. He sat across from them on the wide sill. "You are looking very well, Eve," he said, and when she assured him of her health, he added, "I think, then, that it would be best for you to dine with us again. It will cause comment if you remain so much in your rooms."

"That has not been my choice, my lord," Evelyn reminded him.

"It also will not do for you to continue to address me by my title. Whether or not you recall being my wife, you are, and an intimate form of address is more appropriate."

Evelyn bristled, for there was a slight, but definite edge to his voice, but she had already decided not to come to cuffs with him. It would certainly serve no purpose to alienate him, whatever the provocation. So she submitted meekly to both his censure and his request, and Jane took up the subject of what Evelyn might wear for her first night downstairs to put an end to less comfortable topics.

"The cornflower-blue silk with the Venetian lace will do for tonight," he said, and it was definitely more than a suggestion.

Evelyn's resolve to keep her tongue suffered a severe setback. "Is it a husband's duty to instruct his wife on her wardrobe?" she said sweetly. "You must advise me of such things, for I am woefully ignorant."

"So you claim," he replied dryly, but not accusingly and, in fact, he smiled, the first time he had done so in a humor that was not grim, causing Evelyn to blink and reassess his physical attractions. "For the moment, then, the advantage is mine." He got up and stood before her chair. He looked down at her for a long moment and then reached out and gently ran one long, tapered finger down the side of her cheek. "Do it to please me, Eve," he said softly, his voice gentler than she would have supposed it could be. She almost wondered if she had imagined it, for in a moment he took on his more usual gravity and suggested that it might be a good idea for Jane to familiarize Evelyn with the layout of the house and the names of the various servants.

"Even if he does not quite admit it, I think David must believe you," Jane confided a bit later as they went into Evelyn's dressing room to find the cornflower-blue silk gown. "At least, he is no longer behaving as if he were convinced of your deception."

Jane knew which of the two wardrobes contained the gown and she quickly picked it out and draped it in front of her for Evelyn to examine.

It was undeniably a beautiful gown and Evelyn knew it would exactly suit her coloring. As if reading her thoughts, Jane said, "This always looked superbly on you, dearest, and it is one of David's favorites. I think it is a very good sign that he asked you to wear it."

Evelyn dimpled, thinking that Jane was rather reaching in her search for good omens. "Do you mean he would not have asked me to wear it if he didn't believe me?" she asked quizzingly.

Jane laughed good-naturedly. "Not that." She hesitated while Evelyn waited for her explanation and then said, "I meant it was a sign that he still cared for you. If he were indifferent to you, he would not care a fig what you wore."

Evelyn did not reply as she removed her dressing gown. Recalling another remark Jane had made earlier about matters not being hopeless between her and David, it occurred to Evelyn that Jane had hopes that their marriage might somehow be repaired and continue. Evelyn had not really given it thought yet, but she assumed that when she was finally able to prove her identity and straighten out all the difficulties of her life, her connection with the earl would be severed as well. She had no notion of what the legalities would be, but she supposed that it would be a matter of annulment rather than divorce.

When Evelyn put on the dress, she was astonished by her own reflection in the cheval glass. Jane had insisted on pinning up her hair in a makeshift fashion and the pretty young woman who stared back at Evelyn from the mirror was about as far removed from the unassuming girl that she still felt herself to be as possible.

Her figure had filled out wonderfully in the time since she had last viewed herself in full length, or perhaps it was that the silk was cut to reveal her form to the best possible advantage. She thought that the gown revealed far too much of her figure, but Jane laughed at her and assured her that she had other gowns at Norwood House that made this one seem prim. Whatever her doubts, Evelyn was enthralled with her image and she stepped out of the gown reluctantly to give it to Jane's dresser for pressing.

Jane described the house in as much detail as she could, and promised to accompany Evelyn wherever she wished to go for the next few days so that Evelyn would make no foolish blunders that would cause the servants to wonder. The staff, too, she went over in detail, giving both physical and character descriptions which gave Evelyn a sense of familiarity that very nearly teased her into believing that she was truly remembering the things Jane told her.

It was with some trepidation that Evelyn took her first steps out into the hall. She felt a sense of disappointment that no rush of remembrance came over her as they walked through the house to the saloon where they were to meet David, but when they came to the corridor where it was situated, Evelyn turned to her left without being directed and crossed unerringly to the correct room which delighted Jane nearly as much as it did her.

David was slouched negligently in a chair near the fire and rose as they entered. "I think Eve is remembering the house," Jane said by way of greeting as they entered the room.

His brows rose slightly. "Is she?"

Evelyn wished that Jane had held her tongue, for she read into his words suspicion. "It was a small thing," she said as lightly as she could.

"Not at all," Jane insisted to Evelyn's consternation. "Evelyn found this room without any assistance from me."

David made no comment and whether it was because he sensed Evelyn's discomfort, or for reasons of his own, he changed the subject, and in a few minutes they went in to dinner. Dinner conversation proved a bit difficult for Evelyn. Whether they discussed estate matters or friends and acquaintances, there was little of the discussion in which she could take part. To her surprise, David solicited comments from her several times and she was forced to answer, even if vaguely, for the benefit of the footmen who hovered nearby. The murderous look she cast him on the last of these occasions elicited a devilish smile from him which was as enigmatic to her as the whole of his character.

Evelyn was relieved to withdraw with Jane, but when David still had not joined them nearly an hour later, she found she was piqued that he should continue to evince so little desire for her company. Jane was clearly mistaken about his feelings toward her, which she told herself was certainly for the best. Jane was inclined to speak warmly of her brother and give him an exemplary character, but it was obvious she doted on him and so was not a fair judge. Evelyn had yet to see anything in him but a chilling reserve and an inclination toward a mordant humor.

"Would you mind very much if I returned to my room, Jane?" she asked. "I am more tired than I thought I would be."

Jane was instantly solicitous. "Of course not, dearest, you should have told me sooner that you were tiring. The tea tray will be here at any moment but there is no need for you to wait for it. I thought David would be with us by now, for it is not really his custom to drink alone, but perhaps he has other matters to see to. Would you like me to come with you so that you do not lose your way?"

"No, I am sure I recall the way." She rose, but as she did so, the door to the withdrawing room, which had been ajar, was opened and a young man who was completely unknown to her came into the room.

Evelyn felt a sense of panic. She had not the least notion who he could be. His attire and bearing proclaimed him a gentleman, but whether he was a neighbor, a friend, or a relative she hadn't the least idea. She felt that no matter what she said, it must be the wrong thing. At that moment David came into the room behind the other man and Evelyn's panic turned to relief.

She did not know it, but the appeal in her eyes was large; she looked to David as if she were a lost child and he her savior. He very nearly caught his breath in an audible gasp; she looked so very innocent and unspoiled, as she had when they had first met. It took him only a moment to get himself in hand. "This is Roger Ventry, Eve, my secretary," he said, perhaps a little more brusquely than he intended. "He has just returned from Faversham. I thought it best to take him into our confidence so that he might better serve our purpose."

Mr. Ventry made her a very proper bow, but he looked away quickly, as if she had some deformity and he was afraid he would be accused of staring. Evelyn sat down again with a little thump as a flicker of anxiety took hold in her stomach. She had a sudden premonition that she would not be pleased by Mr. Ventry's information.

"Roger is the son of Sir Anthony Ventry of Ventry Hall," David explained. There was an inflection in his voice that told Evelyn that he had expected a response from her at this, but she had no idea what it could be. The name of Ventry was as unknown to her as Norwood had been only a few days ago.

Jane came to her rescue. "Ventry Hall is fairly close to Spedwell, though living retired as you did at Spedwell, you may not be familiar with the name." Evelyn was grateful to her, for it was the truth, but the look that David cast his sister was a warning.

"Roger has just returned from Ventry," David continued, "and I think you will find the information he gleaned in Faversham and the village of Wellmere, which lies between Ventry Hall and Spedwell Manor, interesting." He nodded at his secretary for him to continue the narrative.

Mr. Ventry looked a little uncertain, but an encouraging smile sent his way from Jane caused him to visibly relax. He cleared his throat and began. "No one that I spoke with really knew Miss Fearne," he said, casting Evelyn an apologetic glance. "In fact, I could find no one who could even recall having met her. But there is no doubt she existed. It is known quite generally that she was a connection of the Dancers, a charity case who came to live with them and acted as a sort of companion to Mrs. Dancer.

"The Dancers take little part in neighborhood society," he continued. "Archibald Dancer was at Spedwell as little as he could manage, and his son followed his example when he inherited the estate about six years ago. In any case, what visiting Mrs. Dancer did at that time she did alone, leaving Miss Fearne at Spedwell, and neither did she bring Miss Fearne forward to meet visitors when they called at Spedwell. I even spoke with a farmer's wife who had been a parlormaid at Spedwell for two years during the time that Miss Fearne resided there, and though she said she might know her on sight, she would be a poor witness for she clearly disliked her employers and would be glad enough, I think, to do them an injury. Miss Fearne, I was told, kept to herself for the most part and had little association with the servants, who I gather did not treat her with the respect due her station."

"But that is no information at all," Jane protested.

Evelyn, though listening intently to Ventry, was very much aware of David. He had walked over to the fire to stand with his back to it. His eyes were on his wife as if he were awaiting some specific reaction from her to the secretary's narrative. He removed his gaze momentarily to reply to his sister. "You must be patient, Jane," he said. "There is more."

Ventry cleared his throat and went on. "This was all I could discover until I asked if Miss Fearne could still be found at Spedwell. It seemed that there was no one who could not answer *that* question. It is common knowledge, and quite a local scandal that the girl ran off with an undergroom about a year and a half ago."

Evelyn gasped with angry astonishment. "How dare he!" she said vehemently. "Jonathan has set that story about to account for my disappearance, and to ruin me in to the bargain should I ever return."

"You still have not heard the whole of it," David informed her.

"I had the story from several sources and essentially it was the same," Mr. Ventry continued. "Dancer found her a few months later in a sorry state, abandoned by her lover and more than half out of her wits, which, I was given to understand, he claimed had never been strong in the first place. Mr. Dancer took it upon himself to place her in a private asylum where it is generally supposed she is to this day. I tried to discover, if I could, the direction of the asylum, but no one had information that specific."

"Of course they did not," Evelyn said indignantly. "It is all fabrication." She stood and walked a little away from her chair, almost wringing her hands in agitation. "Damn him! We must do something to expose his lies."

"What do you wish us to do, Eve?" David asked quietly.

Evelyn turned toward him. She was not certain of his meaning or how to answer him. "I would like to confront him and dare him to prove his lies."

"And what would you do if he could?" David said in the same ambiguous tone.

Her eyes sparked with indignation. "You still think

that I am the one lying. Well, I am not, and I am not afraid to prove it either to you or to Jonathan Dancer."

David smiled a little at her belligerent response. "There is no need to fly into the boughs. I meant that Dancer, who certainly cannot count on your memory never returning, may have been careful to cover his tracks. The story he has put about is a very useful invention. With one explanation he has accounted for your disappearance and has shown cause why he should control your inheritance. It is even possible that there really may be some unfortunate young woman known by the name of Evelyn Fearne in an asylum."

"There could not be," Evelyn said, her expression mutinous.

"Of course there could be," David said with maddening assurance. "There are a number of possibilities. He might have taken over the care of some Bedlamite by visiting the hospital and claiming her as his relative—they are so hopelessly overcrowded and overworked that they would accept the word of anyone willing to take a charge off their hands. Or he might have taken some poor half-wit from the streets of London, which abounds in lost souls with wandering minds, and placed her in private care."

"But if he needed to produce his Bedlamite, wouldn't it have to be a woman who at least resembled Eve," Jane said, her expression thoughtful. "His luck would be wonderfully good if he could also accomplish that."

"It would," David agreed. "But I think similar height, weight, and coloring would be enough to answer when there appear to be so few people who would easily recognize Miss Fearne on sight."

"Do you think that's what happened?" Jane asked.

"I haven't the least idea, dear Jane. It is only a possibility."

"What other possibilities are there?" Evelyn asked, her tone daring him to doubt her.

"He may be trusting his luck and have taken no precautions at all." He paused and then did not disappoint her by adding, "Or the story Roger was told may be the truth."

"If I had my father's will to show you," Evelyn said bitterly, "you would claim that I wrote it myself under the bedsheets when you thought I was unconscious." The last word of her sentence was barely spoken when her expression changed rapidly and became animated. "But that is the answer," she said excitedly. "If I had my father's will, it would prove that I am not penniless as Jonathan claims and you would have to believe that I am telling the truth."

Jane quickly took her meaning and shared her ebullience. "It would be the very thing. If we had the will, there could be no doubt that you are . . . were Evelyn Fearne."

The earl and his secretary exchanged glances that expressed no noticeable enthusiasm. Mr. Ventry cleared his throat. "Finding the will would not really prove more than that such a will existed. In any case, that is unnecessary. Since the will has doubtless been probated and the estate sizable, there will surely be a copy of it on record in London."

Jane looked crestfallen, but Evelyn was not so easily dispirited. "But if the original of my father's will is at Spedwell," she said, directing her words at David, "if it is where I said it would be and shows that my father left me a considerable estate, then it should be obvious to the meanest intelligence that I have been telling the truth."

"No doubt the meanest intelligence would be convinced," David said in a dampening tone, "but I would still have some misgiving. You might have learned of the will, where it is kept and its provisions, from Dancer."

"Can't you at least give me the benefit of the doubt for now?" Evelyn said with a small exasperated sigh, sitting again in the chair by Jane. "This could at least be a beginning. Eventually, Mrs. Walker will return home to tell you that I am not her niece and I may hit upon some other means to prove that I am Evelyn Fearne."

David walked over to them, seating himself across from his wife so that he still observed her changing expressions. "How will you get it? Ring the bell at Spedwell and ask Dancer nicely to hand it over?"

Evelyn took his question seriously in spite of the fact that he was obviously quizzing her. "No. You may be right," she said, giving ground reluctantly. "Confrontation wouldn't answer. It is only my word against Jonathan's and if he has any proof of what he claims and I do not, I would probably fail."

"I wondered if you'd see that," David said mildly.

Evelyn gave him a darkling look. "But I do not mean to fail, and your sarcasm won't dissuade me, my lord. One way or another, I intend to prove what I claim."

"You could call on Mrs. Dancer." Mr. Ventry spoke and all heads swiveled toward him. "It would be a means of getting into the house," he argued.

"And once there we would find the opportunity to search the library," Jane said, eagerly entering into the plan.

"Sounding the paneling in a casual manner during general conversation, I suppose," David said.

"If you have nothing positive to contribute, I wish you will be quiet, David," his sister said, annoyed. "Mr. Ventry and I mean to assist Eve if we can, with or without your help."

Ventry looked a bit taken aback by this speech, which questioned his allegiance to his employer, but he did not contradict her. "While I was at Ventry I learned that Dancer is in residence but is expected to return to town today or tomorrow, so he needn't be a concern," he said, speaking directly to Jane and carefully avoiding the earl's eyes. "It might look out of the ordinary if you were to call at Spedwell, my lady, when you are not in the habit of doing so, but if you were in the company of someone who does call at least infrequently, such as my mother, it would not seem so odd."

His words were greeted with silence, but it was the silence of thought and not of disapproval. "I think it is an excellent scheme," Jane said to encourage him. "But we would have to think of some reason for Evelyn to go into the library unattended. Perhaps if we were to go outside and I pretended to feel faint, Eve could run to fetch my vinaigrette."

"Which you had left in the library?" said Ventry, his brow knit with the effort to comprehend Jane's plotting.

Jane laughed. "No. Of course not. Eve could have it already in her pocket. It is just a ruse."

David smiled with genuine amusement and Evelyn noted again that the effect of his smile could be quite blinding. "I see you mean to have your part in the adventure, Jane."

"I should not miss it for the world," his sister assured him. "But what shall we tell your mother?" she asked Ventry. "She would think it most odd if we were to call on her to ask her to call at Spedwell."

The secretary glanced at David. The earl's expression was unreadable, but there did not appear to be any hint of displeasure in it. "I think it would be best to tell her the truth as much as possible. I vouch for her discretion absolutely."

Evelyn happened to look up and looked directly into the eyes of the man who was her husband. She was swept by a sudden wave of familiarity. There was in their exchanged glance an intimacy that she knew well. For one tantalizing moment she knew him, and then the sensation was gone. She looked away from him quickly, her heart beating faster. She had the feeling that he had felt the intimacy, too, and perhaps had disliked it, for when she looked up at him again his expression had become almost as forbidding as it had been when she had first awakened.

"I assure you the success of such an absurd scheme would be unlikely in reality," David said, with the return of a faint edge to his voice.

His sister regarded him in astonishment. "David, you can't mean you don't wish to go to Spedwell to try to find the will."

"I mean exactly that," he said, rising. "If we are to sort out this mess, it needs to be done with common sense and not as if we were living between the pages of a melodrama. Tomorrow Roger will start out for Scotland to see if he can find Mrs. Walker and fetch her back to confirm that Evelyn is not her niece as she claimed."

"But it may take him some time to find her," Jane protested. "Are we to sit and wait until then?"

"Yes," David replied. "Exactly."

He started to leave the room despite the protests of his sister. It was Evelyn who rose and went after him. "May I have a private word with you, my lord."

He turned and said coolly, "If you think you can persuade me otherwise, Eve, you are mistaken."

"Please, may I speak with you," she said with calm persistence.

His expression was stony, and she thought he meant to refuse her, but after a few moments, he said, "Very well. We can go into the library. I bid you good night, Jane, Roger. I won't be returning to you."

Evelyn followed David down the stairs to the library in silence. When they went into the room, he shut the door behind them and turned to her at once. "Well, what is it?"

Evelyn refused to be intimidated. "I know you don't wish to believe me, my lord," she said. "If it is true that you had cause to think I had played you false, you are hardly to be blamed for your mistrust of me."

"Thank you," he said dryly.

"But even if you cannot trust me without question," she continued, "please allow me to do whatever I may to prove to you beyond doubt that I am Evelyn Fearne and that my story is not a fabrication."

"Beyond a doubt? I don't think you can."

"You could at least keep your mind open to the *possibility* that I am telling the truth," she retorted, her patience deserting her despite her intention of remaining calm and dignified in her appeal. "If you are always so pigheaded, I am not surprised that we did not get on." She saw something change in his face and reined her temper belatedly. "I beg your pardon," she said, her voice stilted. "I should not have said that."

"Not if you wish for my goodwill, at any rate."

"Is gaining it possible?"

"I wish you no *ill* will."

"Then help me," she implored. Unshed tears were in her eyes making them extraordinarily bright. "Please. I don't know how to go on. I'm afraid that I shan't be able to prove anything on my own. I feel so alone that it frightens me."

They stood near the center of the room, only a few feet separating them. He regarded her silently, his expression inscrutable, but his eyes on her were intent. Impulsively, Evelyn moved closer to him, placing her hand on his arm to emphasize her appeal. Something passed between them like a current. She heard him catch his breath and their eyes held. A sensation not unlike weakness came over her, but before she could analyze her feelings, she found herself swept into his embrace. His hands caressed her possessively and his tongue expertly explored her mouth. She did not resist him but shamelessly molded her body to his, returning his kiss with an equal passion, as if were an entirely natural thing for her to do.

As unexpectedly as he had embraced her, he released her. "Damn you, Eve," he said harshly. "You ought to know the tricks of your sex won't work on me any longer."

Evelyn felt her cheeks burning. "I don't know what happened. I . . ." A sob caught in her throat and she could not go on. She turned from him, blinking to keep back the tears and biting at her lip to keep it from quivering. She had no idea why she should wish to cry, but she did.

He put a hand under her elbow and turned her again to face him. "I thought I was quit of you," he said in a dull voice. She looked up at him, shedding silent tears. "I'll give you the benefit of the doubt, Eve," he continued, his manner changing abruptly, "though I may be a fool to do so. If I discover that you are lying, Eve, nothing . . . nothing will turn me from my purpose. I shall divorce you, whatever the cost to us both." He was silent for a moment, then he drew a handkerchief from an inner pocket in his coat and handed it to her. "We shall go to Spedwell tomorrow and you will have your chance. I trust you to make the most of it."

The drive to Ventry Hall was accomplished mostly in silence, each of the occupants of the carriage preferring thought to speech. Evelyn spent much of the time scrutinizing the passing countryside, which she had found familiar from the moment she had stepped from the house. As they drove along the road she recognized passing landmarks and could even give a few of them names, which excited her so that it took all her self-control to say nothing to the others. Jane would doubtless be happy for her, but she feared that any admission of returning memory at this stage would only encourage the earl's doubts and disbelief, so she thought it best to keep her tongue. It was only as they turned off the main road to Canterbury toward Faversham that the scenery became alien to her and then changed again to familiar as they approached Wellmere, which she knew quite well from the time she had lived at Spedwell.

Mr. Ventry had ridden ahead of the carriage to apprise his parents of the impending visit and to explain to them as best he could the incredible circumstances of Evelyn having lost and regained her memory. As they turned in the drive to Ventry Hall, Evelyn began to have misgivings, fearing that the Ventrys would disbelieve her story or think her deranged.

Ventry Hall was a modernly appointed Georgian manor house set in well-kept grounds. Its owners were very like their home, elegant and comfortable. Sir Anthony and his lady welcomed their party with sincere pleasure, expressing shock and concern at Evelyn's plight, but keeping any doubts they may have had to themselves. "My goodness," said Lady Ventry innocently as she took Evelyn's hand. "How can such a thing have happened to you? It sounds like a story from the lending library in Canterbury."

Evelyn involuntarily looked toward David at these words and caught the mocking gleam in his eyes. "We do not understand how it can have occurred, either," she said to her hostess, "but it has, and now I am learning that identity is not a thing to be taken for granted. If I am to claim my inheritance, it isn't enough that I say I am Evelyn Fearne, I shall need to prove that I am. You are very kind to help me, Lady Ventry."

Lady Ventry looked long and hard at Evelyn, but at last she shook her head. "I wish I could help you in the most practical way, my dear," she said, addressing the young countess. "I am not a particular friend of Lavinia Dancer, though I have known her forever. I suppose I may have been at Spedwell a number of times during the years you lived there, but I simply cannot recall ever meeting you. I do seem to remember there being *someone* about, a companion of sorts, but the memory is quite vague."

She sounded so unhappy about this that Evelyn hastened to reassure her. "It is not too surprising, Lady Ventry. I was seldom asked to be present when there were guests and I hardly objected. It was humiliating enough to be treated like a servant without suffering my humiliation before others."

"Dancer ought to be horsewhipped for allowing it," Sir Anthony said gruffly. "I never liked him overmuch. Damned commoner. Too young to be in my set, of course, but wouldn't have had much use for him if he was. Raised on a fine piece of property like Spedwell and can't even sit a horse with distinction." It was obvious that the baronet thought that nothing greater could be said to Jonathan Dancer's discredit.

"Nor can I recall hearing gossip of an elopement from Spedwell, though I suppose the servants would know of it," Lady Ventry said musingly. "Oh dear, I am not being much help at all, am I? It is just that I do not pay much mind to servants' gossip, and if it was discussed amongst my friends, it must have been in a passing way."

"It doesn't matter, Mama," her son said soothingly. "You can be of great help now, if you will."

"But of course," Lady Ventry responded and gave her attention to Jane, who had taken upon herself the task of mapping out their course of action. "Visiting Lavinia will present no difficulty at all," she said when the plan had been outlined for her. "Today is an at home day for her and the only rub may be that we shall have to alter our plans if there are other callers. Certainly she will see nothing at all odd in a call from me, or that I should bring with me my own guests."

"Might wonder though at so many of you," Sir Anthony interpolated. "She must have cause to be wary of any visit from Lady Norwood, which would only be natural."

Lady Ventry bit thoughtfully at a thumb. "It might put her on her guard a bit," she agreed.

"Suppose only Eve and I were to go with you, Lady Ventry?" Jane suggested, already beginning to amend her campaign.

"I think it would be best if I accompanied you," David said.

"Surely you can trust Eve in this, David," Jane said, and at a warning glance from her brother added quickly, "Eve will manage to find the will by herself, and thinking on it, I am sure that Mrs. Dancer would consider it odd if you came to Spedwell considering . . ." She came to an abrupt stop, realizing that yet again her tongue was betraying her.

"Considering that Dancer is not in residence, and we are not, in any case, more than the merest acquaintances," David finished smoothly. "I am sure you are right. I shall remain here with Roger and Sir Anthony."

Sir Anthony promised the diversion of a visit to the stables to show the earl the fine hunter he had recently acquired, and the matter was quickly settled. Lady Ventry's carriage was sent for and in a very short time Evelyn found herself traveling the road to Spedwell.

She did so with very mixed feelings. She was exhilarated by the prospect of possessing her father's will, but she was also a little anxious that she would be discovered removing it from the house. But as they drew closer to the house she had not seen in more than a year, the unexpressed anger she felt toward her aunt and cousin who had used her so hardly, rose up in her, and finally this removed much of her doubt and made her almost impatient to get on with her task.

They were admitted to the house by the butler, Harper, who knew Evelyn well. If he was startled to see her, he did not give himself away, regarding her with the polite impassivity reserved for strangers. When he opened the door to them, she had the hope that he would involuntarily exclaim at the sight of her. She smiled to herself for her optimism as they were shown into a saloon opening off the center hall. Harper and his wife, who was the housekeeper at Spedwell, were cut from the same mold as their employers and it was now obvious to her, as perhaps it should have been before, that the Harpers were in her cousin's confidence. No doubt Harper was well paid for his poor memory.

It was also likely that in the eighteen months that had passed since she had left the house, the butler and housekeeper were the only servants remaining who would even know her. It was not a comfortable household and the underservants were given wages as small as they would take. Maids, footmen, and even the outdoor servants were inclined to stay only as long as was necessary for them to find a better position or some other means of escape.

Yet the house had a prosperous, well-cared for look to it that Evelyn did not remember. There was a new table and two rosewood chairs in the entrance hall and the saloon into which they were shown held furniture and draperies that were obviously new. The rug was the same, but it had been cleaned to bring out the pattern, and the mantel, which was wood over marble, had been repainted. Evelyn could not but wonder if these signs of affluence were visible throughout the house, and it gave her a cold, angry feeling in the pit of her stomach to think that it was probably her own money that had paid for them.

When Lavinia Dancer joined them, she too evinced no surprise to discover her niece in her well-appointed saloon. "My dear Elvira," Mrs. Dancer said, holding out her hand to Lady Ventry. "What a delightful surprise. I have not set eyes on you since before

Christmas, though I have called twice when you were from home. But I quite excuse you. Since you have brought Lady Jane and Lady Norwood to visit, it is an unlooked for pleasure." Turning to Jane, she said, "We do not meet often enough, Lady Jane, though we are near enough to Blakenhill that I quite think of us as neighbors. I feel I am almost better acquainted with your dear sister-in-law, whom I met in town last month when I went there to have a few gowns made. I wish I might have remained for the Season, but Jonathan does prefer his bachelor existence at Grove Street, and I fear I am *de trop*."

Evelyn was a little taken aback by this speech; she had not supposed that she had known her aunt in London since Jonathan had always discouraged visits from his mother to his house in Grove Street. She took the hand that was offered to her, but before she could speak, Mrs. Dancer continued. "Jonathan will be quite disappointed to learn that he has missed you, Lady Norwood, for you must know he is quite taken with you and speaks often of his dear friend Evelyn Norwood. He was here until yesterday, but now he is gone back to town. You know how he prefers it despite a mother's pleas that he spend more of his time in his ancestral home."

Evelyn blinked at her in surprise. There was a confidentiality in her tone that made her think that her aunt was toying with her, with more than one meaning to her words. But Evelyn dismissed this idea as the result of her own nerves, for though her aunt was not a stupid woman, Evelyn doubted she had the wit to engage in a game of cat and mouse. "I, too, am sorry to have missed him," she said with more equanimity than she felt. It was one thing to plot with the others at Blakenhill or Ventry, but it was quite another to face her aunt, acting out this odd charade and fearing to give the game away. A sudden panic welled up in her and she cravenly wished that she had listened to David and never come.

As if sensing her fears, Jane caught her eye and gave her a reassuring smile. She then addressed her hostess to draw that lady's attention away from Evelyn. The usual commonplaces were exchanged as is to be expected on a visit among people who are not well acquainted, and these were of a particularly insipid nature as Mrs. Dancer tended to vagueness and generalities in her speech and appeared to be willing to agree with just about any statement her guests chose to make.

The rules for a country visit were not so rigid as they were in town, but after a quarter hour had passed Evelyn began to fear that their purpose would never be achieved before it would look odd that they remained so long. Once again Jane seemed to share a similar thought for she remarked, "Lady Ventry has told me that your gardens are delightful and I had the hope of seeing them before we leave, if you would not mind."

Mrs. Dancer seemed a little surprised, as well she might, for Evelyn could recall nothing special about the gardens at Spedwell. But the older woman smiled and very nearly simpered, clearly flattered by the attention. "I would be most pleased to show the gardens to you, Lady Jane. Are you interested in horticulture?" Jane expressed herself delighted with that subject above all things. "Then you will probably wish to see the succession houses as well, though I think it may be early in the year for them to be at their best." She got up and pulled the bell near the mantel. "I shall have Harper send a note to the head gardener to expect us at the glass houses, and then we may go out to the formal gardens that open off the morning room."

The entire party expressed themselves well pleased with this plan, and if Mrs. Dancer was at all suspicious, she gave not the least sign of it. As she led them out of the saloon, Evelyn saw Jane deliberately push her reticule into the side of the cushion of the stuffed chair in which she had been sitting and the young women exchanged a conspiratorial glance. The stage was set and Evelyn's pulse quickened with the excitement of the challenge that awaited her.

The gardens were pleasant enough, if unremarkable, and Jane, playing her part to the hilt, exclaimed over each shrub and early blossom and cast out gardening terms at every opportunity. Evelyn marveled at her, wondering if her knowledge were genuine or gained by virtue of a bit of research.

By the time they reached the glass houses located on the other side of the house behind the kitchen garden, Jane had managed to remark several times on the unusual warmth of the day—which was fortunately true—and to mention, in passing, that the only time she had ever fainted had been on a day when she'd had too much sun. It was not very surprising, then, that after several minutes in the warmth and humidity of the glass house, her steps became uncertain and she declared herself to feel a bit queasy.

Mrs. Dancer's brow puckered with concern and she suggested they return to the house at once, but Jane would not hear of it. "I beg you to forgive me my stupid weakness," she implored, "but do not deny me the pleasure of a bit more conversation with your excellent gardener, Mr. Kearney. If only I had my vinaigrette, I am certain I would be quite the thing again and able to continue. But I fear I left my reticule in your saloon. Evelyn, dear, would you be so kind as to fetch it for me?"

"You must not put yourself out so, Lady Norwood," Mrs. Dancer interjected. "Kearney can go up to the house and tell Harper to bring it to Lady Jane."

"I would not dream of disturbing Mr. Kearney at his work," Jane said as if horrified by the thought. "Evelyn does not mind, do you, dearest?"

"Not in the least," Evelyn replied with alacrity. "I believe I know exactly where you left your reticule."

She did not wait for further objection but turned at once toward the house at a brisk pace, her heart pounding in her ears at every step.

As soon as she was out of sight, she gave a wide berth to the kitchen gardens for fear of encountering any of the servants. She knew there was a side door through which she could enter unobserved, but the fear that she would find it locked, coupled with the risk of having to cross the entrance hall to reach the bookroom decided her against it and she returned to the house by the French doors in the morning room. There was a narrow terrace before the doors and as she crossed this a man materialized from a grouping of yews beside the house, giving her a start that nearly made her panic and run back across the garden.

But it was not Harper or Jonathan, as she had supposed in her first fright. The man proved to be David, and speaking in a whisper, she rounded on him as soon as he was near enough to hear her. "Why are you here? Are you mad? You will ruin everything."

He was unperturbed. "You said yourself last night that you didn't blame me for not trusting you. I don't. If finding the will is to have the value you place upon it, I need to see it with my own eyes."

"I would have brought it to you."

"But you will have so much more credit if I see that it is found as you claim it will be," he pointed out.

"I shall probably not find it at all now," she said crossly. "With two of us we are far more likely to be caught out in the theft."

"We shall certainly fail if we waste time talking about it and make Lavinia Dancer suspicious," he said reasonably.

Evelyn knew he was right, and since it was unlikely in any case that she would be able to dissuade him from accompanying her, she contented herself with casting him a smoldering glare and then turned and went into the house, letting him folllow her as he chose.

She had not the least difficulty recalling the layout of the house and knew that the library was on the ground floor at the back of the house, unfortunately near to the service stairs. She looked out into the hall cautiously, prepared to explain her presence if necessary, but the hall was as empty as she could wish it to be. She did not turn to see if David were behind her, for she was very conscious that he stood close to her near the doorway. "We must be particularly careful until we are in the library," he said into her ear.

She turned and looked up at him, her expression making it clear that he was stating the obvious. His hooded eyes smiled down at her and she suddenly felt the pleasurable anticipation of an adventure shared, which lessened her hostility toward him and made her think of him as an ally rather than an adversary for the first time.

David asked her which was the door to the bookroom, and then stepped around her and went into the hall, holding his hand out behind him for her to follow. Taking a deep breath, she did so. If there were anyone about, the observer remained unobserved.

They moved quickly but stealthily, and as they neared the door to the bookroom, she let out her breath which she had not realized she had been holding. But her relief was short-lived. There was the sound of footfalls on the service stairs and her pulse began racing again. Drawing her close to him, David quickly covered the remaining few steps and opened the door into the room, pushing her in ahead of him and then quietly shutting the door behind them. They leaned against it, like children hiding from punishment, scarcely daring to breathe while they awaited their fate. After a moment or so, footsteps passed by the library without hesitation. They turned to each other and exchanged a laughing, conspiratorial glance that made Evelyn feel quite like the lighthearted schoolgirl she had been before her parent's tragic accident, and she began to perceive that her forbidding husband had qualities and a side to him that she had not hitherto suspected.

It was the first time she had been in the bookroom since the afternoon she had found her father's will and she was unprepared for the emotions that assailed her as she stood there facing Jonathan's desk exactly as she had that day. Once again all traces of her anxiety were erased as indignation took their place. Not only had everything she was entitled to been taken away from her, now she was forced into the role of thief in order to prove her very existence.

"Which is the secret panel?" David asked in a stage whisper.

Evelyn pointed to the corner behind Jonathan's desk and he walked over to the desk with Evelyn following behind him. With all the panels securely in place and looking quite unmovable, she was not entirely certain which of these contained the cavity, but she indicated two or three she thought likely and David suggested that they search for the catch in the raised scrollwork that adorned each panel.

"How did you follow us here?" she asked, giving in to her curiosity.

"When I evinced concern for the success of your venture, Sir Anthony kindly lent me one of his hunters," David replied as his fingers moved slowly over the carved wood. "He has rather a fine stable."

"And you rode *ventre à terre* to my rescue," she said caustically. "I thank you, my lord, but it was not necessary."

He gave her a condescending smile that she knew was meant to annoy her. "That remains to be seen. Ah! I think this may be it." Evelyn heard a tiny click and the section of paneling directly in front of David moved and stood ajar.

The metal box fit the cavity exactly as she had guessed it would. There was a small handle lying flat against the lid and he pulled it up and the box slid easily out of the wall. He took it over to the desk. It proved to be locked and he rummaged through the top drawer of Dancer's desk until he discovered a small thin knife used to mend pens. The lock was not of a serious nature and was forced with little difficulty.

Evelyn held her breath again while he pushed back the lid to reveal an untidy bundle of papers. She reached inside the box and removed them, shuffling through the papers, impatiently seeking the one that mattered. "It isn't here," she said with what was nearly a wail. "None of these are the papers I saw that day. These are just receipted bills and things which pertain to Spedwell. When I last saw this box everything in it concerned my father or pertained to his estate." He regarded her without comment and she said dully, "You don't believe me, do you?"

"I think you had better return to the others," he said, ignoring her question. "I'll see to matters here and return to Ventry." He began to gather the papers and return them to the box.

Evelyn pushed him aside and pulled open the nearest desk drawer, pulling out papers and whatever else came to hand. He put his hand on hers and restrained her. "You are only wasting precious time. You won't find the will in there, I promise you."

She looked up and met his eyes, biting at her underlip to prevent it trembling. "It must be somewhere," she said in a voice which shook with emotion.

"Quite," he returned, "but not here. What we have found in the box makes that obvious. Go back to the garden, Eve. Mrs. Dancer may be witless, but she is not a fool."

She was not so easily convinced and left to herself, she would have torn the room apart to find the will, so great was her frustration. But she knew he would not permit her to do so and she allowed her will to be bent to his.

Swallowing her chagrin, she nodded and closed the drawer. When she reached the door, she put her ear to it for a moment, but no sound at all came to her from the hall, and looking back at David for a brief moment, she let herself out of the library and returned to the corridor with more haste than quiet this time.

She went into the saloon where Jane had left her reticule and stopped short; Harper was removing the tray of Madeira and seed cakes they had been served on their arrival. He looked up at her unceremonious entry but his expression betrayed nothing, not even surprise.

Evelyn was certain that her appearance must be suspect; she had come into the room nearly at a run, and she could feel the color mounting in her cheeks, but somehow she managed to raise her chin and say calmly, "Lady Jane has need of her reticule, which I believe she has left in here."

"I have not seen it, my lady," Harper said, his voice as expressionless as his face.

Evelyn looked about the room. "I think Lady Jane sat in that wing chair by the fire."

Harper followed her gaze and walked over to the chair. He looked on it, beside it, and under it and finally put his hand along the edge of the cushion and found the reticule that Jane had earlier thrust there. "Would this be it, my lady?"

"Yes. Thank you," Evelyn said, a little too breathily. "I'll take it to her." She put out her hand and the butler gave her the purse. He took a step backward and then stood waiting in a way that disconcerted Evelyn. "Th-thank you," she said again, and resisted the desire to explain herself further which would certainly have made him suspicious if nothing else had already done so.

She returned to the garden the way she had come.

She resisted the temptation to look behind her to see if David would safely emerge from the house. She had no notion whether or not he had managed to leave the library undetected by Harper, and it served no purpose to dwell fatalistically on the outcome of their fruitless search, or possible repercussions if it were detected.

She walked briskly to the end of the formal garden and then broke into a run only slowing to a walk just before the succession houses came into sight. Her rapid breathing had calmed to a reasonable rate by the time she found her party seated on iron benches in the shade of an apple tree. "I beg your pardon for taking so long, Jane," she said as soon as she came up to them, "but your reticule was *not* where I thought it would be, and, in fact, had fallen behind the cushion of your chair. Your butler was kind enough to discover it for me," she added addressing her aunt, in case Harper should mention her encounter with him. But what Lavinia Dancer thought of Evelyn's long absence was unknown, for she did not comment on it, merely asking Jane a little wearily if she now wished to return to the glass house to inspect the plants.

Jane took a sniff of her vinaigrette to be convincing and was nearly overset by the strong odor which brought tears to her eyes. She managed to keep her composure to say, "No, I fear I must curb my enthusiasm for another visit, Mrs. Dancer. You have already been more than kind and I pray you will indulge me by saying that I may return again on a day more suited to my constitution."

Her hostess was nothing loath to make this promise, for she had had quite enough of horticulture for one day. They returned to the house, Jane still languishing a bit, and at once took their leave of Mrs. Dancer.

Jane and Lady Ventry had nobly refrained from any attempt to satisfy their curiosity as to their co-

conspirator's success until they were safely installed in their carriage and had started along the drive toward the main road. "Well," said Jane impatiently, "have you got it?"

Evelyn shook her head unhappily.

"Oh, dear," Jane said, cast immediately into a gloom. "Whatever will David say?"

"He already knows," Evelyn replied to the astonishment of both ladies. "He was waiting for me when I returned to the house and he helped me in the search."

"Why?" asked Jane.

"He still doesn't trust me, Jane, whatever you may think," Evelyn said, heedless of the presence of Lady Ventry. "Now it is made worse. I wish we had never come."

"But what did he say?" Jane persisted.

"Nothing," Evelyn said flatly. "He simply told me to return to the garden."

Jane appeared to take an equally dim view of this reaction.

"You could return to search more thoroughly," Lady Ventry suggested to be helpful.

"I suppose we might go back to view the glass house again," Jane said without enthusiasm.

"*I* doubt Lavinia would accompany you to the glass houses again," Lady Ventry said sagely. "When you engaged her gardener on the proper care and planting of bulbs, her eyes glazed over."

"David doesn't believe that there are any papers of my father's to be found in the library at Spedwell," Evelyn said, "and neither do I. The box was full of other papers that were pointless to keep in a locked box in a secret panel. Jonathan has destroyed my father's papers or has taken them to London and put them in safekeeping there."

"Then I suppose we shall simply have to wait to learn anything further until Roger has found Mrs. Walker," said Jane as the carriage turned into the road that led to Ventry Hall. "Unless you can think of some other means to support your story."

Evelyn shook her head but even as she did so a thought came to her. "There is something else that occurs to me, but I am not sure if it would signify."

Jane's flagging spirits brightened a bit. "What is it? Anything is bound to help when you have nothing at all."

"My mother had a miniature oak chest in which she kept all the little things that mattered to her. She called it her treasure chest." Evelyn spoke slowly. It was the first time she had thought of the little chest in many years and the sudden memory of her mother displaying treasures to fascinate her little girl brought her unexpected sadness. "There was nothing of value in it beyond the sentimental, things like a pressed rose from the first flowers my father gave her and locks of my hair and my brother's when we were infants."

"I suppose it would be something to have it in your possession," Jane said, sounding doubtful nevertheless.

"I was not thinking of that. It is an object that is in the chest that I wish I had. The year that they were married, my father commissioned a portrait of my mother."

"The portrait is in the chest?" Jane said uncertainly.

Evelyn laughed, the first time she had done so that day. "Of course not, goose. The portrait, I presume, is still at Limirend, or at least I hope it may be. My aunt told me that the house was bought as it stood, with nothing taken from it but those things which I brought with me to Spedwell and a number of other objects Jonathan had taken to his house in London."

"I am afraid I am not making the connection between this portrait and your mama's treasure chest, my dear," Lady Ventry interjected.

"In the portrait my mama was wearing a locket of wrought gold studded with amethysts and inscribed with her initials on the back of it," Evelyn replied. "It was unusual, but of no great value except that it was an early gift to her from my father. She always kept the locket in the chest. If I had it in my possession and if the portrait still exists, no one could deny that it is the same."

"Perhaps we should consider the portrait itself," Jane suggested thoughtfully. "Are you very like your mother?"

"A little, perhaps," Evelyn allowed. "But I was always held to favor the Fearnes. To have the locket would be much more telling. It is surely not something an imposter would know of, for I doubt that even my Aunt Lavinia or Jonathan is aware of its existence."

Jane considered this. "It might answer." She sighed. "I suppose that means we shall have to think of another means of searching Spedwell without arousing suspicion."

"It is not so easy as that," Evelyn said with a sigh. "The chest is in London. It was in a trunk with some other momentos I took with me from Limirend; the trunk was accidentally placed on the wrong cart with the things that Jonathan was taking to London. He said it was too much trouble to return it to Spedwell and it was placed in the lumber room in the Grove Street house."

"Is it still there?" asked Jane.

Evelyn shrugged. "It may be. But I am not sure it matters. I could hardly ask Jonathan for it outright and I don't see how else I am to find it."

The carriage rolled to a stop and Jane leaned forward and patted her sister-in-law's hand reassuringly. "We shall think of something. Depend upon it."

But Evelyn was not heartened by Jane's encouragement. Her spirits were quite cast down by her inability to find the will and the additional burden that David had witnessed her failure. She considered

it ominous that he had spoken no word of reassur-
ance or even of disappointment and supposed that
what little credit she may have gained with him was
destroyed.

David, who had been able to ride cross-country,
was before them. He sat at his ease in the saloon
exactly as he had been when the ladies had left
Ventry. He had not a hair out of place, no crease in
his coat, no soil on his well-fitting buckskin breeches
to show that he had ridden hard, and Evelyn could
almost imagine that he had never left the room. His
greeting to his wife was cordial and his manner expressed neither disappointment nor condemnation.

"Must have put it somewhere else for safekeeping," Sir Anthony suggested after commiserating with
Evelyn on her failure to find the will.

"Or destroyed it," said his son.

"A probated will is a matter of public record,"
David reminded them. "Our task has proved fruitless, but the end of it may still be achieved. I wish
you to go to Reading tomorrow, Roger, to discover
what you may about the dissolution of Mr. Petersham's practice and who might have inherited his
records. It would facilitate our quest greatly if we
knew more about when and how the transfer of
property took place."

Evelyn regarded him in some surprise. She had
half suspected that he would believe she had lied
about the will after all and would abandon all attempts to help her. "The accident which claimed my
family took place in July of '03," she said to be
helpful.

Mr. Ventry sat at a small writing desk near the
windows and wrote out this information and the
instructions of his employer. "I expect I shall have to
go to London, though, to confirm what information
I may find in Reading," he said over his shoulder.

"Perhaps we should go to London, too," Jane said.

"Why?" queried her brother.

"Then we would be on hand to learn what Mr. Ventry has discovered and perhaps even assist him with further suggestions should we think of anything else that might help Eve."

"Such as?" David said, raising his brows slightly.

Jane thought it prudent to retreat for the moment. She knew she had a better chance to persuade her brother in private, for he was not a man who would discuss more of his private affairs before strangers than was necessary, however sympathetic they might be. She shrugged one shapely shoulder with apparent unconcern. "I don't know. It was just a thought."

If David suspected that anything lay behind her suggestion, she could not tell. At that moment servants arrived with a tray laden with tea and biscuits, and for necessity's sake, the subject was turned.

4

When they returned to Blakenhill it was late afternoon, but David announced his intention to ride out to the home farm to inspect the site for the proposed storage barn. Evelyn, who had hoped that they would have an opportunity for private conversation before dinner, dreaded the idea of putting off the discussion that was necessary between them and boldly stated that she would join him. His surprise was patent, but he did not object, only remàrking again that he had thought she did not care for riding.

It was her turn to be surprised. "It used to be my favorite pastime," she informed him, "but I had little opportunity for it when I was at Spedwell."

Apparently David took her at her word, for the gelding that was brought out to her in the courtyard was a handsome raw-boned hunter which was obviously high-spirited. Evelyn was an excellent rider and had no qualms about mounting the sidling, restive horse, but she was very conscious of David watching her in that careful speculative way to which she was becoming accustomed. As she prepared to mount she saw one of the grooms regard her with obvious concern and then whisper something to his master. She saw David shake his head and guessed that both men were expecting her to be unequal to her mount. She was very happy to be able to prove them wrong.

She went into the saddle with the ease of a practiced rider and took command of the reins. It took her only a very few minutes to convince the raking chestnut that he had met his match, and by the time that David had mounted his own bay, her horse was standing docilely waiting for their ride to begin.

They went out of the courtyard at a smart trot, and as soon as they came out of the park at the edge of the wood they opened up their horses to a canter and then an easy gallop. As they came at last to the road and a more sedate pace, converstion was finally possible. "You sit Rufus well," David commented, as they slowed to a walk.

Evelyn leaned forward to pat Rufus' neck. "He is a fine fellow." She turned to look at David. "You didn't expect me to, did you?"

"You have never shown any particular liking for horses or riding."

Evelyn found this hard to credit and recalled that he had said so before. But she had no idea what "Lady Norwood" had liked or disliked. "I used to ride out every day with my father and brother at Limirend."

"I could never persuade you to do so with me," he said, but with no hint of reproach.

"It may have been because I came off my horse at the stream when I was leaving Spedwell," Evelyn suggested, "even if I did not consciously recall what had disordered my memory."

"Perhaps," he said noncommittally. "If that is what happened."

"You don't believe there was a will to find, do you?"

"I would be very surprised to discover that it did not exist."

She pulled up her horse to stare at him in amazement, and when he realized she had done so, he reined in his bay as well. "I cannot understand you, my lord. You question my veracity at every point and then you say you would be surprised to find I have lied. I wish you will tell me openly what you think of me, for I am beginning to doubt the order of my wits again."

He smiled at her. "I think that you should have the chance to prove your story."

"You mean you think I should have all the rope I need to hang myself," Evelyn said dryly, and made his smile spread to a grin. "But that is not what I meant, you know."

"I know."

"You do not mean to tell me?"

"It did you no harm in my opinion that there was a secret panel in the library at Spedwell and that it contained a metal box that exactly fit the cavity."

"Even though Jonathan might have told me of it himself?" she asked quizzically.

"As he might have told you of his mad cousin, Evelyn Fearne, and her father's will," he responded with a provocative smile. He pressed his heels into his horse's sides and started again down the road.

Evelyn followed. "Can you really believe this is part of some fantastic scheme set up between Jonathan and me?" she asked, incredulous. He met her eyes for a moment, but did not answer. She sighed with exasperation. "I think it is you who is possessed of an excess of imagination."

He pointed to a field on his left. "If we cross through there, it will be much quicker, though there are a number of fences and hedges to be gotten over."

Evelyn recognized his suggestion for the test that it was, and though she had not taken a barrier in seven years, with the exception of the stream which had led to such disastrous consequences, she knew that she had no choice but to agree. She nodded agreement and he set off at a spanking pace which she was determined to keep up with. At the first hurdle, which was a low, but wide hedge with a drainage ditch before it, she was very conscious of her own heartbeat, but Rufus was well-schooled and high-couraged, and he took it with ease. By the time they had cleared the third fence and the plowed fields of the home farm were in sight, she was exhilarated and happily anticipating the next challenge.

It came in an unexpected, but not unpredictable form, after they had spent a pleasant hour with Mr. Mathias, the bailiff of Blakenhill, and were returning to the house. The veneer of harmony between them was thin and easily cracked. It required effort and was something of an accomplishment when any discussion between them ended civilly, and this occasion proved no exception.

"What will happen after Mr. Ventry finds the record of my father's will?" she asked as they walked along the road, taking the longer route to cool their mounts.

"Then he will travel to Scotland to see if he can locate Mrs. Walker."

"Which may at last prove to you that I am telling the truth," she said, "but which I doubt will be sufficient to prove legally that I am Evelyn Fearne if Jonathan denies it and produces an impostor."

"If you do not wish Dancer to be aware that your memory has returned," he advised, "we would be wise to take it one step at a time and not tip our hand by rushing our fences."

Evelyn nearly groaned. "But how long may that take? I have no wish to live in this limbo indefinitely."

"Patience has never been your forte, Eve, has it?"

"Perhaps you should tell me what *is* my strong suit," she said tartly, "since you claim to know me so much better than I know myself."

"Perhaps you should let your epithet be your guide."

"My epithet?"

"Lady Notorious," he said, casting her a brief, sidelong glance.

She flushed as she took his meaning. "How dare you! Whatever your jealousy may have led you to believe, I don't deserve that."

"I don't dare," he said in an easy tone. "That is the title by which you are known amongst the gossips. How can you be certain it is undeserving?" he asked with a little more edge to his voice. "If, as you claim, you remember nothing of our life together?"

Evelyn looked stricken. "That is truly what I am called?" He favored her with a short nod and looked back to the road. "If that is true," she said with obvious concern, "I cannot think what I could have done to deserve it."

"Can't you?" he said in a clipped way.

"You mean that Jonathan was my lover," she said bluntly. "I will never believe that was true, in or out of my senses."

"You valued his friendship more than accord between us," he said coldly.

"If you were as volatile in our dealings then as you are now, I do not wonder at it." She had the dubious satisfaction of seeing anger kindle in his eyes. "But however well you thought you knew me then, you don't know me now. Not any better than I know you, and I find little in you to make me wish to improve the acquaintance." With this, she spurred her horse and rode back toward the house, knowing it was the only way to avoid a full-blown argument. He did not follow her, and though that was what she wished, she was annoyed and curiously dispirited that he did not.

Jane accosted David in the hall as soon as he returned and had obviously been waiting for him. "I must speak with you at once, David."

Her brother gave her a weary smile and held up his hand. "I know you mean well, Jane, but Evelyn and I shall do best to sort out our difficulties on our own."

Jane did not regard the setdown. "Well, of course you shall," she said. "But surely nothing may be resolved between you until all question of her identity is made certain. Evelyn has given me a notion how we may hasten that end."

It was in David's mind to refuse to listen to her. After Evelyn had left him he had ridden hard again through the fields to work off the spark of anger their words had kindled, using physical exertion to work off the emotional tension that was perpetually present between him and his wife. It had been a very long day, and he was tired physically and tired of the uncertainty and discord, which seemed to have become a part of his life. He had had enough of Evelyn, innocent or not, for one day. But Jane was eager, like a child, and he hadn't the heart to curb her spirits. "Come into my study," he said peremptorily and turned down the hall.

David sat in one of a pair of comfortable leather chairs, slouching into it to ease his tiredness. Jane closed the door, already beginning to speak as she did so. "Eve seemed rather upset when she returned before you. I think it is mostly because she fears that no one will believe in her."

"Fear did not seem to be her uppermost emotion when I was with her in the south wood," he said aridly.

"Yes, she told me you had words again." Jane sighed. "I wish you would not be so hard on her."

David let this comment pass. "What is your notion?" he said, hoping to bring her to the point so he could end the discussion as quickly as possible.

Jane was well aware that he was only humoring her, but she understood something of his feelings, for she too had loved and lost her love, though in a very different way. As succinctly as she could, Jane told him of the conversation in the carriage on their return to Ventry from Spedwell. "And if the portrait of Mrs. Fearne still exists—and why should it not?—it must prove, if nothing else, that Evelyn knew of the locket and where it was to be found."

"The same as she knew where her father's will was to be found?" he said blandly.

"David!" Jane said, exasperated. "If you are going to be a cynic, it will only make matters worse. You must give Eve the benefit of the doubt if you wish to straighten out this stupid coil."

David begged pardon. "I thought I was," was all he said in his defense.

"Don't you wish that all were settled?"

"Yes, but—"

"Then let us go to London to find the locket and take it to Limirend to prove that Evelyn is speaking the truth," Jane said, quick to make her point.

"Another goose hunt, Jane?" David said, skeptical.

"No. Eve knows the trunk is in the lumber room for she saw it there herself on the one occasion when she accompanied Lavinia Dancer to London to shop."

"And it may have been given to the ragman any time since in a turning out of the house."

"I wish you will not be so tiresome," Jane adjured. "Evelyn feels her failure this morning far more than you do, I promise you. It would be a kindness if nothing else, to let her have another opportunity to corroborate her story."

He rested his head against the back of the chair regarding her thoughtfully out of hooded eyes. "Suppose she fails again. Would it be a kindness then?"

"I don't believe she'll fail this time," Jane said staunchly.

His only response to this was to close his eyes, and Jane waited patiently, having sense enough not to push him. "It might be a good idea to return to town for a time," he said after a while. "The continued absence of us both is bound to give rise to talk and, in any case, there are matters which I should see to which have nothing to do with this."

"And while we are there we may find a way for Eve to procure the locket."

"No."

He spoke so sharply that Jane flinched a bit. "But why on earth not? It is ridiculous to do nothing when something positive can be accomplished."

His anger, so close to the surface these days, rose again and he vented it by slapping the end of his riding crop which he still carried against the arm of the chair making his sister jump again. "Do you suppose I would allow my wife to openly visit the home of the man who is rumored to have handed me my horns?"

"It is not so bad as that, David," Jane said, looking a little startled at the vehemence of his tone.

"It is near enough to it."

A silence fell between them and then Jane said quietly, "She hurt you very much, didn't she?" She got up from her chair and went over to sit on the arm of his.

David put down his crop and took his sister's hand. "I am being tiresome, aren't I?" he said with a faint smile. "I must seem unreasonable, but I cannot trust Eve as readily as you do."

"I do believe her, you know. Has it occured to you," she asked, her tone sobering, "that during the time when Eve was behaving so outrageously it may have been because she was troubled? Even if she didn't remember her earlier life, she had to know that the life she was living was a lie and that the truth might one day catch up with her as indeed it has. And think how awful to have no idea what that truth would be. She would scarce be the first person to try to forget her anxieties by plunging into gaiety."

"With the very man she claims caused all of her difficulties?" he asked, with an incredulous lift to his brows.

"If she did not realize who Dancer was, he would mean nothing to her." Jane paused and then said musingly, "It could not have been a comfortable time for him, wondering if she were going to de-

nounce him. Perhaps that is why he pursued her, to
watch for signs that her memory was returning."

"You will forgive me if I do not weep for the
troubles of Mr. Dancer."

"What I do not understand is why you do not wish
to see him paid out for his perfidy," Jane said, carefully. This was her trump card and she did not wish
to play it recklessly.

"Do you suggest I call him out? That would only
heighten the scandal, though putting a hole through
him might make *me* feel better."

"All you need to do is help Eve prove that she has
the rightful claim to her father's estate and you will
have a very fine revenge on him," Jane pointed out.
"You know he is an ambitious man; he wishes to
move in the first circles, and what hope of that the
possession of Eve's fortune may have given him will
be utterly dashed when he is denounced for the thief
and blackguard that he is."

He considered this for a long moment. "Once Evelyn is declared the rightful heiress to her father's
estate and Dancer is dishonored," Jane said, deliver-
ing the *coup de grâce*, "Lady Notorious will finally be
put to rest."

David raised his eyes slowly to hers. "Do you think
so?" he said with an inflection she could not interpret. He moved her a little aside and got up. "Very
well. We'll return to Norwood House at the beginning of the week," he said, looking down at her, "but
not to embark on another elusive search. Or at least,
not for a locket," he added enigmatically, and then
went up to his dressing room to change for dinner.

David was as good as his word, and by Tuesday
morning they were on the road to London. Jane
realized that her brother was adamant about not
wishing them to go to Dancer's house to look for the
locket, and had reluctantly abandoned the scheme,

but Evelyn, feeling the need to vindicate herself, was not as willing to let the matter drop. She and David had gotten through the remaining days before their journey began in relative harmony, for he had clearly exerted himself to be civil and even kind to her and she had prudently refrained from mentioning any burgeoning plans for getting into her cousin's house without further blighting her reputation.

Mr. Ventry's journey to Reading had proven inconclusive. Mr. Petersham's nephew who had taken over his practice had had little dealing with and not much recollection of the Fearne estate. A search through musty old files did not turn up a copy of Mr. Fearne's will, but it did unearth a sheaf of papers all predating the decease of Evelyn's parents, which at least proved that there ought to have been an estate of some considerable size. But since there was no documentation of debt, it was impossible to say if Mr. Fearne's fortune had survived probate. The only truly worthwhile information Mr. Ventry gained was that the will had actually been probated in London and the record of it would be found there. It was decided that he would accompany the Norwoods to town to complete his research before traveling on to Scotland to seek the elusive Mrs. Walker.

Again, much of the passing landscape was familiar to Evelyn, particularly as they neared London. When their chaise at last stopped before Norwood House in Portmouth Square, she could not prevent herself from catching her breath.

"Is something the matter?" David asked, his expression watchful.

Evelyn was not certain how to answer him for fear of what he would think, but she decided on the truth this time. "I know the house," she said quietly.

"Oh Eve, that is wonderful!" Jane exclaimed. "I know it is only a matter of time before your recall is quite complete."

Evelyn silently agreed with her, but was not certain that she would find it wonderful. David kept his counsel, as was his custom and, getting down from the carriage, waited to assist his wife and sister to the street. A tall, large-boned man stood at the door, the butler, who Jane had told her was called Tomkins, she supposed, but his face was not at all familiar to her.

The central hall was large, with a vaulted ceiling, marble floor, a number of doors leading to unknown rooms, and a gracefully curved staircase. Evelyn knew it as she saw it, but it appeared that her memory returned only on recognition, for she knew nothing of the house that she had not actually seen.

In spite of the fact that she remembered less at Blakenhill, she had at least felt comfortable there. Now she had to adjust herself to a new household and since she had no true idea of how she had conducted herself while she had lived at Norwood House, she feared she would give herself away and sooner rather than later. The servants, after all, were only the first hurdle; the entire *haute monde* awaited her and the pitfalls there would be innumerable. There would doubtless be a great number of people she would be expected to recognize, many of whom might be friends and know her quite intimately and countless others who were acquaintances and whom she might accidentally cut from sheer ignorance. With that cheerful thought, Evelyn almost wished she had elected to remain in Kent and waited passively for David and Mr. Ventry to do what they would to assist her. But such was not her nature.

Jane untied her bonnet and removed her gloves, giving them to her maid who had traveled with them. "I suppose you wish to have Cook prepare dinner for the usual time, do you not, Eve?" she said, addressing her sister-in-law and succeeding in nonplussing her.

Eve hadn't the least idea what the "usual time" was. "Y-yes," she said uncertainly, and then realizing that she needed to behave as the mistress of the house, added more assertively, "Yes, that will be fine. Does that please you, David," she asked, and realized it was the first time she had addressed him by his given name.

He was directing a footman who carried his portmanteau and said absently, "Whatever you wish." But then realizing what she had asked him, said, "No, I am forgetting. I have business to attend to in the city and shall probably dine with friends at Boodle's."

For some reason, Evelyn found herself piqued that he should not choose to spend his evening with her and Jane. "Then there will just be Lady Jane and myself for dinner tonight, Tomkins." Gathering up her skirts, she started up the stairs, without stopping to think that she hadn't the least idea where her bedchamber was. Yet she found it without error. Jane, who had followed her to guide her, came up behind her and she and Evelyn exchanged a significant glance as the latter turned the handle and entered her bedchamber.

"Do you remember all of the house?" Jane said, sotto voce as they entered the room.

Evelyn shook her head. "Not consciously, it just seems to happen as I see things."

"Maybe it is better if you don't *try* to remember. The time since you left Spedwell may just come back to you of its own accord, like a forgotten verse of a song, or a name that is on the tip of your tongue."

Evelyn gave her a wry smile. "I waver between hope and fear. I do so want to remember everything, but sometimes I am afraid I shan't like the person I was for the last eighteen months."

"You are not so very different," Jane assured her. "I don't really know what happened between you and David after I returned to Blakenhill at the beginning of last month, but we have always dealt very well together. I think you are a gentle, generous, and caring person. There were times," she admitted, "when you were given to brown studies and abstractions, but now that we know how the loss of your memory must have been troubling you, it is hardly to your blame that it was so."

As Jane spoke, a door at the opposite end of the room opened and a young serving woman entered. Evelyn only glanced at her as she was giving her attention to Jane, and the realization struck her belatedly that she knew the abigail by sight. She turned and said with a faint tremor in her voice, "Betsy?"

"Yes, my lady?"

"You know her, don't you?" Jane said, her eyes opening with surprise. "I told you how it would be."

The maid cast a puzzled look from Evelyn to Jane. "Is there anything the matter, my lady?" she said uncertainly. She had been in something of a state ever since the earl had bullied her into handing over her mistress's note barely an hour after Evelyn had left the house so surreptitiously. She had no idea how her mistress had fared since her departure for Blakenhill and had feared the worst when his lordship had gone in pursuit of his wife. She wondered now if Lady Norwood's troubles with her husband had disordered her wits, for Evelyn was regarding her in the oddest way and Lady Jane was saying things that made little sense.

"I knew it would be a good thing for us to come here," Jane said excitedly. "We should have remembered that Betsy came with you from Hardwood and she may tell us what we need to know without the help of Mrs. Walker. Betsy," she said, addressing the maid, "you must tell us how Evelyn came to live with Mrs. Walker at Hardwood."

The abigail cast a beseeching glance at her mistress. "Please tell us, Betsy," Evelyn said gently, leading her over to a chair near the dressing table and sitting herself on the stool in front of it.

"You be Mrs. Walker's niece," the young girl said, her tone wary. "When her brother was carried off by an inflammation of the lungs, you came to live with her."

"Is that what you really believe to be the truth," Evelyn asked her, "or what you have been schooled to say?"

Betsy fidgeted in her seat looking extremely confused. She was very conscious of having failed her mistress once already and dreaded doing so again. Evelyn had told her so many times that the truth was never to be spoken for fear of the consequences, that she did not understand why her mistress should press her now, and wondered if she was expected to tell the truth at last or to confirm the lie. "It—it is what I have always been told," she replied noncommittally.

"But is that what really happened?" Jane prompted.

The girl's face puckered as if she were about to cry. "You said we were never to speak of it," she said almost accusingly to her mistress.

"Then you *do* know what really happened," Evelyn said with a sigh of relief. "You must tell us the truth now, Betsy. It is of the greatest importance."

"No, wait, Betsy," Jane interposed hastily. "I think my brother should hear this and it will save telling it again, in any case." Evelyn had some misgiving about this, but she knew that truth had to be on her side, so she swallowed her qualms and made no objection.

David had just come upstairs to his own room to change out of his traveling clothes and it took scarcely a minute for Jane to fetch him. "I don't know why we did not think of Betsy at once," Jane was saying to him as they entered the room.

Evelyn glanced up at him as he came through the doorway and then averted her eyes. "When I first came to Hardwood, something had happened to me,

some sort of accident, had it not?" she asked the
maid.

"I think it would be best," David said in his cool
way, "if you did not lead the girl. Just let her tell
what she knows."

The look Betsy gave her mistress was positively
hunted, but Evelyn nodded and smiled reassuringly.
"Please do that, Betsy. It is what I wish you to do."

The maid looked uncertain and uncomfortable,
but she did as she was bid. "It was a year ago last
August, the time of the market fair at Wellmere.
Everyone was given leave to go to the fair and there
was only me and Mrs. Halper, Mrs. Walker's housekeeper in the house. Me because I had the toothache
and Mrs. Halper because she was the one left behind
to look after the house for the afternoon, Mrs. Walker
being gone to the fair herself in the gig."

Betsy saw that she had a rapt audience and some
of her diffidence slipped away; no one had ever
hung on her words before. "We never heard Mrs.
Walker come back to the house, but the bell in her
sittin' room rang so I went up and she says to me,
'You've always been a good girl, Betsy, and I'm goin'
to trust you now because I need help.' Then she
takes me into her bedchamber and there you were,
my lady, sittin' on the bed all bedraggled and lookin'
as if you'd been swimmin' in a mud hole in all your
clothes."

At these words, Evelyn cast David a significant
glance, for she was certain it confirmed her belief
that she had come off her horse at the stream she
had attempted to bridge. Noting the exchange, the
maid paused and Evelyn said, "Please go on, Betsy."

"Mrs. Walker says to me that you was her niece,
come unexpectedly to visit and met with a mishap,"
the maid went on. "It was easy to believe with you
sittin' there all dirty and ragged, with no baggage
and actin' like you were in a daze and scarcely knew
your name. But she made me promise to say nothin'

about you until she said to, and I knew there was somethin' havey cavey afoot."

Again Evelyn sought her husband's eyes and he acknowledged that her point was taken by the faintest of smiles.

"By that evening you were nearly ravin', my lady," the maid went on, her eyes growing large at the memory. "We had to send for Dr. Carlyon and he said it was brain fever, and you were in bed and sick with the ague for nearly a sennight. Mrs. Walker had me alter some of her plainer dresses to suit you so that no one would know you had come without a stitch 'cept what you had on your back, and by the time you was well again, no one remembered you had come to Hardwood in an odd way, and they accepted that you were Mrs. Walker's niece come to live with her. When you were confused, they put it down to the fever."

"But you knew the truth?" asked Evelyn hopefully.

The serving woman nodded. "Mrs. Walker was fretful that you were goin' to die of your sickness and she wanted someone else to know what really happened in case there were questions. She said she'd found you wanderin' by the side of the road near the north pasture on her way home from Wellmere. You were babbling and she thought you was half out of your wits with fright. The only clear thing you were able to tell was your given name."

"And she took me in, not knowing what manner of burden I might be," Evelyn said wonderingly. "She must be a very kind woman."

"Charlotte Walker is well known for her generosity and good works," Jane said. "Her husband, Henry Walker, died earlier that year and she may have been lonely and in need of something to interest her."

"But she knew nothing about me or what manner of person I was," Evelyn answered. "For all she knew by taking me in she was opening Pandora's box."

"Mrs. Walker always said that whoever you were and whatever your trouble might have been before you came to Hardwood, you was a lady born and had no cause to go fearin' that it mightn't be so," Betsy said helpfully.

Evelyn tried to imagine the horror of knowing nothing about herself, not even the whole of her name. It was disquieting enough to have lost eighteen months of her life. "And Mrs. Walker told no one the truth about me except you?" she asked her dresser?

Betsy nodded. "Wouldn't speak of it to anyone, not even his lordship," she said with a faint nod toward David.

"Why not, Betsy?" David asked her. "I can understand why she would not wish it published to the neighborhood, but it might be supposed that I would have a vested interest in the truth."

"Mrs. Walker was afraid you'd cry off if you knew the truth," Betsy replied readily. "She said the Cheviots were a proud family and you would never wed one as was baseborn."

David blinked at this estimation of his character. The truth was that in the eyes of the world his marriage to Evelyn was already a *mésalliance*. But he had married her for love and had never given her lack of fortune or connections thought. He had never had the slightest doubt that Evelyn was a woman of birth and breeding. He didn't believe it would have mattered to him in the way that Betsy meant if Charlotte Walker or Evelyn herself had confided in him, but it would have mattered greatly in quite another way. "As it happens," he said, "our ancestor, Arnaud Cheviot, who came here in the entourage of the Conqueror was baseborn, as was William himself."

Jane begged the abigail to tell them anything else that might be of help to Evelyn, but beyond describing something of Evelyn's life at Hardwood before she became the Countess of Norwood, there was little to tell. Evelyn had apparently developed an almost superstitious dislike of discussing her loss of memory, so whatever her feelings or fears may have been she kept to herself.

When it was obvious that there was nothing further to be learned, Jane and David left Evelyn to change and rest before dinner. "Now you must believe her," Jane said as soon as they were in the hall and the door to Evelyn's bedchamber closed behind them.

"I believe she is not Mrs. Walker's niece as we were told," he replied, causing his sister to describe him as odiously stubborn. He smiled. "Perhaps the person I mistrust the most is myself," he said, and ended the discussion by entering his dressing room.

By the time he had changed out of his traveling clothes into a coat of dark blue superfine and buff unmentionables suitable for the streets of the fashionable quarter of London, Mr. Ventry, who had gone immediately to discover the record of Mr. Fearne's will, had returned. David had just finished with the final touch of applying a pearl stickpin to his expertly arranged neckcloth when the secretary came into the room.

"Well?" Norwood asked, "did you find it?"

Ventry nodded. He handed David several folded sheets of foolscap. "I copied what I thought would interest you most, but I shall return tomorrow and make a more complete copy if you wish."

David sat against the edge of his dressing table and read the copy carefully. Most of his lingering doubts that Evelyn was Evelyn Fearne, as she claimed to be, were virtually banished, but his trust in her was not yet complete. The fact that she had been able to keep from him a secret of such magnitude in spite of the intimacies of marriage made him wary of her ability to deceive him again.

He handed the pages back to his secretary. "We had something of a revelation while you were gone," he said, and proceeded to tell him about Betsy and the manner in which she had confirmed that portion of Evelyn's story.

"Then you no longer wish me to go to Scotland to find Mrs. Walker?" Ventry said when he had finished, sounding a little disappointed.

David regarded him in that measuring manner that Evelyn so often found disconcerting. "Do you so wish to go, Roger?"

"If it is what you wish me to do," he replied promptly.

"Well, I think I do," the earl returned. "There will be no need to persuade Mrs. Walker to accompany you on your return, though. I think if you could obtain from her a written confirmation of the abigail's story, it will suffice. We need not infringe on her holiday." The secretary brightened so perceptibly that David added, "Ah, I see I was not mistaken. You are pleased that I am sending you to Scotland after all."

Ventry looked a little discomposed, but replied with alacrity, "I wish to be of service to you, my lord."

"Do you? Why?"

The secretary was taken aback. "It is my duty to do so."

"That isn't what I meant."

Mr. Ventry had the clear look of a man who is uncertain whether or not he should speak and is rapidly weighing the advantages of doing so against remaining silent.

"Come, Roger," David said, smiling. "You know I think well of you and value all that you do for me."

"As I, my lord, value my position," he replied sincerely. "But it is only natural that a man must wish to advance to—to secure his future. I have thought that if I could be of special service to you in such a delicate matter, you might be willing to mention my name to Perceval."

"The most natural thing in the world," David agreed. "Of course, I shall do so if you wish it. You need perform no extraordinary tasks to gain my goodwill, Roger."

"I would as lief earn it, my lord," the younger man said earnestly.

"You have. Is it simple ambition or some other motive that prompts you to wish to advance at this time? You have only been with me these two years, you know."

Mr. Ventry lowered his head. "I know my experience is slight, but . . . but I am nearly six and twenty and I have been thinking of marriage."

David gave him an arid smile. "I felicitate you. Do I know the lady?"

"It is Jane," the secretary blurted, and bit at his tongue as he saw his employer's expression change.

"Jane?"

"I should not have spoken," Ventry said hastily. "That is, I am not speaking, I mean in the sense of asking your permission to address her."

To his consternation David laughed. "My dear Roger, Jane is four and twenty and free to marry where she will."

"Then you would not object?"

"Why should I?"

"Lady Jane is possessed of a comfortable fortune and you know how matters stand with me," Ventry said simply.

"Lady Norwood came to me without dower," David said without inflection. "It is not who may have the fortune that makes for a comfortable marriage, but those things which pertain to the heart."

"There is none of that lacking for my part," Ventry assured him.

"And on Jane's?"

"I have not yet spoken to her of my feelings," the secretary admitted. "I wish to wait until I have some manner of future to offer her."

"In the circumstances, an unnecessary sentiment but one which does you credit," David said. "I'll speak with Perceval before the end of the week."

"I wish you will wait to do so, my lord, until your own difficulties have been cleared."

"With your assistance?" David asked, smiling and raising his brows.

"Exactly so, my lord."

They then returned to the topic of the secretary's proposed journey to track down Mrs. Walker and plans were made for him to leave on the following day.

5

For the next several days, Evelyn spent her waking hours learning all that Jane could impart about the people she would be expected to know to function amidst the *ton* without tippng her hand. She and Jane even went out in the closed town carriage the next afternoon, so that Jane could point out various personages to Evelyn, giving their names substance.

On Sunday morning the sisters-in-law went to services at St. George's, both veiled and sitting well to the back amongst the visitors, though the Norwood family had their own pew near the front of the church. It was a further opportunity for Jane to coach Evelyn. But by the following morning, Evelyn finally revolted.

"I don't want to hear another word about Lady Hertford, the Duke of Clarence, or Emily Cowper for the rest of my days," Evelyn declared as they sat in the morning room at the back of the house sipping lemonade. "And I am coming to hold Sir Henry Mildmay, Lord Ponsonby, and Lady Caroline Lamb in positive aversion. I only hope I shall be able to be civil to them all when we finally meet."

"Only hope that you put the right name to the right face," Jane suggested a little waspishly, for she was almost as weary of the lessons as Evelyn herself.

Their conversation was saved from descending into argument by the entrance of David. "I have news from Roger," he said at once. Both young women riveted their attention on him so earnestly that he laughed a little at their eagerness. "It isn't all that much, I fear. He has arrived in Edinburgh and has discovered that Mrs. Walker and her sister were there a fortnight ago and put up at the Royal James. He means to question the staff there to discover if she discussed her itinerary with anyone, even in passing. There is also this which arrived with the post," he said and held out a sealed letter for Evelyn. She took the letter from him, her expression questioning. "I believe it is from Mrs. Walker," he said.

Evelyn opened it and it proved to be exactly that. It was a long chatty letter, much crossed, detailing a great deal of information that meant absolutely nothing to Evelyn.

"Does she give you a direction where you may reach her?" David asked.

Evelyn quickly skimmed the letter and at the end of it her face fell sufficiently to tell its own story. "No. She only says that they expect to make the crossing to Ireland by the beginning of June after they leave Glasgow, but nothing about where she means to travel between now and then."

David took the letter from her and scanned it himself. "The letter comes from the Edinburgh Mail, but that means little; all mail from Scotland does so." He handed the letter back to Evelyn. "We shall have to rely on Roger to run her to earth."

"Does it really matter now that Betsy has confirmed what Evelyn had told us?" Jane asked.

"I wish to have it in writing from Mrs. Walker," David replied. "Stevens will be returning from his holiday in the lake country tomorrow and then we shall see what else he may advise us to do before we may safely make a formal claim on the Fearne estate."

Evelyn pinned a great deal of hope on the advice of Mr. Stevens, whose firm had been solicitors to the Cheviot family for three generations, but conversely, she also feared that he would dash these hopes by telling her that her claim was unprovable. The most telling thing against her, she knew without anyone needing to tell her, would be the refusal of Jonathan and his mother, her closest living connections, to acknowledge her. She would need more than proof that she was *not* Evelyn Walker to counter it.

She had once or twice hinted to Jane that she wished to find her mother's locket despite David's dislike of the plan, but this time Jane appeared to side with her brother. But with or without Jane's assistance, Evelyn felt that she ought to go on with it, for it made her feel less at the mercy of strangers and fate to be doing something for herself. Before she could even hope to go on with the plan, though, she would have to go into society again, resume her friendship with Jonathan, then discover a plausible reason for going to his house without arousing comment and, once there, find the means of searching the lumber room without being detected.

This, looked upon as a whole, did seem an impossible task, so Evelyn decided prudently to take it a single step at a time. Though it had surprised her a little that David, though he was against her going to Grove Street, had permitted her to return with him to London, it was the first hurdle cleared, so she did not question it. The next was surviving in that world without giving herself away, and with Jane's coaching that obstacle was well in hand. Her current anxiety was for the first time she would face Jonathan again, which she knew must be very soon. Though Evelyn would have delayed her "coming out" a bit longer, Jane thought it was best gotten over quickly, and had accepted for them an invitation to a rout party for the day following the next.

The selection of dresses that had so astonished Evelyn at Blakenhill was nothing to the collection of fashionable gowns which awaited her in her dressing room at Norwood House. With the help of Betsy, Evelyn tried on several gowns exactly right for dinner, a rout party, or a musicale, as distinguished

from those gowns suitable for a ball or the opera.
For the party, she decided on a forest green gown of
watered silk with a contrasting gauze overdress, which
was, as Jane had warned her, even more revealing of
her figure than the gown that had made her blush at
Blakenhill. But familiarity had made her fairly comfortable with the style, and she knew it became her
magnificently. Betsy and Jane assured her that she
would be dressed in the first stare of fashion, and
she was willing to trust their judgment as she was
quite ignorant of such things.

On the night of the rout party, Betsy dressed
Evelyn's hair in a style which she called *à la grecque*.
Fine emerald drops hung from her ears and a matching pendant gave unnecessary emphasis to her ample cleavage. When she and Jane descended to the
front hall the appraising glance that David swept
over her was openly admiring. Evelyn left Norwood
House filled with the confidence of a beautiful young
woman who knows she is looking her best.

The members of the *ton* whom she met at Mrs.
Linquist's helped to reinforce her self-esteem, for
many of the women plainly regarded her with envy
and the gentlemen with appreciation. After she had
surveyed the company, Evelyn came to the conclusion that David was one of the most attractive, well-
formed, and well-dressed men present, and not even
the displayed finery of the Dandies, Pinks, and Bloods
served to turn aside her opinion. Certainly he was
only one of a very few men whose shoulders and legs
showed to advantage in the tight-fitting silk coat and
knee breeches that were *de rigueur* for evening
entertainments.

Evelyn was understandably nervous as they entered the saloon where much of the company was
gathered. David gave her his arm to lean upon and
led her through the company, addressing as many
people as he could so that Evelyn would be able to
put names to faces. She wished she might spend the

night in the security of David's protection, but Jane had informed her that it was hopelessly *déclassé* for a husband and wife to be in one another's pocket and that she must not expect David's unlimited attention.

After they had progressed well into the room, David pointed out a young woman who was waving at Evelyn to attract her attention. "Lady Henrietta Kennet, known to her friends as Harry," David said into her ear, and Evelyn nodded. "It will look odd if you don't go to her; she is quite a friend of yours."

Evelyn could not miss the dry inflection in his voice and knew that he thought poorly of her choice of Lady Henrietta as a friend. She had received a similar impression from Jane, though Jane had not had anything particularly derogatory to say about Lady Henrietta. She scarcely knew what to expect, but it hardly filled her with confidence. "I think it is that which frightens me," she replied. "There are so many things I may say or do wrong."

"Fear no one, Eve. Most of the people here are so taken up with themselves that your behavior would have to be bizarre or scandalous to gain their notice. A little forgetfulness won't be remarked." He removed his arm from beneath her hand and stepped a little away from her. Evelyn knew he was sending her out on her own and that if she were to succeed in convincing David Norwood and outwitting Jonathan Dancer, it was time she made a beginning.

Lady Henrietta greeted her extravagantly, as if she had been away for considerably longer than a fortnight, and as soon as she had done so, pulled Evelyn a little aside and whispered in a voice throbbing with melodrama, "I feared for your safety, my dear Eve. I know what a tyrant Norwood is, and when you disappeared so immediately after Jonathan's party for Mr. Kemble, I was certain he must have incarcerated you in a jealous rage."

Evelyn scarcely knew how to answer this. Obviously this woman, who hovered about her in an

excessively familiar manner that she could not like,
knew the intimate details of her life. Evelyn wondered how, even out of her senses, she could have
made Lady Henrietta a confidante. Though she would
have liked to snub the woman, Evelyn knew it would
not be prudent to do so. In the first place it would be
thought odd, and might cause comment, and in the
second, if Lady Henrietta had intimate knowledge of
Evelyn's friendship with Jonathan, she might be able
to give Evelyn information about Jonathan that she
herself lacked. She decided the best thing to do was
to stick as closely to the truth as she safely could. "He
was furious, of course," she confided, "so I thought
it best to go to Blakenhill for a few days until he
regained his temper."

"But Norwood followed you there, did he not?"
Lady Henrietta asked with an avidity that Evelyn
found repellent. "Was he in a rage? Did he forbid
you to see Jonathan again?"

"He was annoyed," Evelyn replied dampeningly,
"but nothing so dramatic as that. He was right, I
suppose. It was improper for me to attend a party
such as that, particularly in the company of an unmarried gentleman."

Lady Henrietta looked a little taken aback at these
words, but her expression changed to a knowing
smile. "Of course, we cannot discuss anything freely
here, but I shall call on you tomorrow and we may
have a comfortable coze." With this promise, which
Evelyn found daunting, she squeezed Evelyn's hand
and left her.

Evelyn's attention was then claimed by Maria Sefton,
who hoped she had not been ill, and Evelyn passed
from her to Lord Harry Bentick and soon it seemed
to her that she had had at least a word or two with
every person in the room. It proved not nearly as
difficult as she had feared, and as the evening wore
on, she was beginning to relax and even to enjoy
herself. Eventually she felt confident enough to

risk living up to her reputation as a flirt, responding to the attentions of the gentlemen who formed her court with coquettish smiles and badinage that seemed to delight them.

This was heady brew for a young woman who had not been encouraged by her aunt or cousin to think of herself as pretty or desirable and she quite forgot her husband and the fact that it might not be in her best interests to behave in a way that might reawaken his suspicions of her.

Though David gave no appearance at all of a man who was keeping an eye on his wife, there was little she did that escaped him. He did not join his friends in the card rooms, preferring to mingle with the guests in the principal rooms, and this was where Jane found him.

"Evelyn seems to be doing very well," she said, putting a hand on his arm and drawing him a little aside.

"Quite well," he said dryly.

"I have seen nothing in her conduct to condemn,'" Jane said, coming to Evelyn's defense. "She is only behaving as we have told her the world would expect her to do."

"Or the way that is most natural to her."

Jane protested at his cynicism, but it was only a mechanical comment, for her attention was on the door that led to the hall and the gentleman who had just entered. She saw Jonathan Dancer pause to survey the company and her heart sank. She thought it would have been better for Evelyn if she could have had one or two successful nights in company before facing the test of meeting her cousin.

She was staring so intently that David turned a little and followed her gaze. "Ah," he said, "the cat is set among the pigeons."

"Perhaps you should go to her, David."

"Evelyn is doing very well without me. I never doubted she would do so."

Jane would have continued to persuade him if she thought it would serve but she recognized the finality in his tone. With her brother she watched Jonathan advance into the room, speaking to various people but stopping for no more than a few moments with each. Having reached the center of the room, Dancer raised his quizzing glass and again surveyed the room in an affectedly bored manner. Apparently his search was successful for he allowed the glass to drop back on its ribband and began to make his way across the room with obvious purpose.

A well-dressed, sandy-haired man of about David's age and height strolled casually over to where brother and sister stood. "You're looking well enough," he said to Jane with the mildly insulting familiarity of a lifetime's acquaintance. "I thought you must be wearing yourself into a decline rambling about that damned pile of David's. Must be bored to flinders with no one to talk to but cows."

Jane took not the least offense at his words. Martin Danbury was a cousin and a childhood playmate who with maturity had remained a good friend both to her and to David. "Not even a little bit," Jane countered. "Cows are excellent conversationalists, Marty, as you'd know if you weren't too high in the instep to become acquainted with one."

Martin ran a finger down the side of his nose in a thoughtful way. "Do you know, I rather thought it was the conversation of someone quite different that gave you a taste for rustication."

"I live very quietly at Blakenhill," Jane replied with sudden coolness. "The rector of St. Mary-of-the-Glen came to dinner every other Thursday but other than that I saw little of the neighborhood. There is Cynthia Ponsonby just come in. I should ask after her sister who is to be confined at the end of the month," she added, and with this excuse left the gentlemen.

"I said the wrong thing, I take it," Martin said to

his friend. He had, in fact, been alluding to Mr. Ventry, but as he had not the least notion that there was any interest between these two, he had meant it as harmless banter and was startled by Jane's reaction."

"I begin to think so."

"Do you mind?"

"Jane is old enough and sensible enough to make her own choices," David replied. "Ventry is a younger son, but Jane's jointure is handsome—enough to tempt most fortune hunters—but I don't think that Roger is of their number."

"Then why haven't the invitations been sent out?"

David smiled. "I believe he has some notion that his lack of fortune makes him unworthy of her."

"Sounds like a slowtop to me," Martin said with an air of pronouncement.

"No. He is definitely not that. Quite a clever fellow, in fact. That's why I employ him as my secretary."

There was a parting in the company and directly before them at the other end of the room, Jonathan Dancer was bowing over Evelyn's hand. "Eve's lookin' well," Martin said with a mildly speculative note in his voice. "I hadn't seen you in a few days, and when I called, they said you'd gone to Blakenhill. A bit sudden, wasn't it? We were engaged to Dudley Carenton on the tenth, you may recall?"

"Really?" David replied, with no particular emphasis. "I'd forgotten. I'll have to apologize to him." Several people moved and again blocked the view of the opposite end of the room and David looked away, making some light comment on the sartorial splendor of a well-known dandy who was near to them.

But Danbury was not so easily deflected. He was a man of the world and he had heard the whispers about Evelyn and Dancer, and for David's sake, he had more than once taken it upon himself to rout the fellow when Dancer's monopolization of Evelyn was about to cause comment.

"It's been a while since I've had the chance for

more than a word with Eve," he said casually now.
"You've such a damned pretty wife, David, one has
to fight off a whole court of admirers just to get near
her. Does you credit."

David said nothing, but the brief sardonic glance
he sent Martin's way said more than had he confided
in his friend.

Danbury would have gone at once to Evelyn, with
the purpose of deflecting Dancer, but David put a
restraining hand on his shoulder. "I know you mean
well, Martin," he said quietly but in a voice that
brooked no argument, "but trust me to see to my
own affairs. If you need occupation, find Jane and
amuse her. Ventry's gone to Scotland on an errand
for me." He then proceeded toward Evelyn, but in a
circuitous way that called no attention to the fact.

Evelyn did not notice Jonathan until he was quite
close to her, and when she did, she could almost
feel the blood draining from her face. It would not
do for him to see that he had had any unusual effect
on her, so she turned to a young captain of the
guard and gave him a dazzling smile which was more
encouragement than that gentleman had dared to
hope for. But Evelyn scarcely paid him heed; co-
vertly she watched her cousin's approach.

Jonathan looked exactly as she remembered him.
He was not a particularly tall man, but a lean, well-
formed figure gave him the appearance of height.
He wore his light brown hair in an elaborate cheru-
bim and his cravat was perfect in every snowy fold.
His coat was exquisitely cut, his black silk breeches
creaseless; he was the epitome of elegance, and one
glance at him was enough to tell Evelyn what she
had already guessed on her visit to Spedwell: Jonathan was in full enjoyment of her inheritance.

Swallowing the ire this engendered, Evelyn raised
her head and met his gray eyes levelly; she was in
control now and a welcoming smile was in place.
"You are well met, dear sir," she said, lowering her

eyes flirtatiously. "I have a message for you from your dear mama, whom I had the pleasure of visiting while in Essex."

He bowed over her hand, his ready smile in place. "Indeed? I have had a letter from Mama only this morning. You must tell me what Mama would say to you that she would not put in her letter." He took her arm in his and favoring the captain and a young lordling who had been following Evelyn about most of the evening like a puppy with a curt bow, he led her off to a small sofa in a corner of the room.

Evelyn felt acutely uncomfortable. She had only said what she had as an opening gambit and now had not the least idea what she would say to him. Of all things she did not wish for his attentions to be particular. When he sat beside her, it was very close, and she moved a little away on the pretext of smoothing her skirt. "It was no great thing," she said lightly. She opened her fan to have something to occupy her hands. "Mrs. Dancer wished me to tell you that she wished your visit had not been so short and that you would spend more time with her at Spedwell." This was a safe enough thing to say, for it was one of Mrs. Dancer's constant complaints that Jonathan spent so much of his time in London and so little at Spedwell.

Jonathan smiled pleasantly. "No doubt she trusted your influence to persuade me," he said with a clear insinuation that made Evelyn want to box his ears, "but I fear that the rural life bores me. I do what I must for the well-being of the estate, of course, which is why I make the journey at all, but I see no reason why my interest in that quarter should extend to the extreme of living there." He shuddered delicately. "I fear the smell of manure holds no enticement for me."

"And have you no wish to spend time with your mama?" she asked a bit archly, though she knew the answer well enough.

"Mrs. Dancer is perfectly welcome to stay as often and as long as she wishes with me in Grove Street,

but I fear *she* does not care for city life." His tone
suggested both boredom and impatience. "Is Norwood here?" he asked abruptly changing the subject.

Evelyn turned her gaze toward the room and quite
without intention, spied David's dark head some distance from her as he stood talking with friends. This
both pleased and dismayed her. It meant he had
observed her tête à tête with Jonathan, but it also
gave her a little bolstering to know that he was nearby.
"Yes," she said, but it was hardly necessary, for his
gaze had followed hers.

"When I returned from Spedwell last week, Lady
Harry told me about your sudden departure from
town after Kemble's party," he said, dropping his
voice to nearly a whisper. He was quiet for a moment and then, taking her hand in his, said in an
intense way, "I have been worried nearly to the point
of having my nerves overset. It was Norwood's doing,
was it not?"

Evelyn nodded. She was more concerned at this
moment with how to withdraw her hand from his
without giving him unnecessary offense and without
calling the attention of others to the intimacy. If she
had been in the habit of permitting him to take her
hand in public, it was not wonderful that she had
earned such a sobriquet as Lady Notorious.

"You must tell me all that occurred," Dancer said
earnestly. "I know what a hard man Norwood is and
I don't doubt he used you cruelly."

"I would as lief not speak of it," she said, her voice
sounding a little strangled, but not with the emotion
Dancer assumed. The desire to tell her cousin the
degree to which she held him in contempt nearly
overwhelmed her, but prudence prevailed. "We argued, but it is over and I find it only painful to
recall."

Dancer squeezed her hand, just as she was about
to attempt to slip it free of his grasp. Evelyn felt as if
every eye in the room must be upon them. "How I

wish I could remove you from his tyranny," he said in a voice vibrant with emotion. "He does not deserve that he should call you his wife."

With these words he would have raised her hand to his lips, but Evelyn pulled free of him not caring what he thought. "You forget yourself, sir," she said, more coldly than she intended.

He raised his brows in mild surprise, and she felt herself color. It made her dreadfully uncomfortable to think she might have encouraged such advances from him. "Forgive me, dear Eve," he said, his practiced smile still in place but with a shade less warmth in his voice. "It is the wretched thought of Norwood's mistreatment of you which quite carries me away."

In spite of her assurances to Jane, it was obvious to Evelyn that her friendship with her cousin had gone beyond what she would have thought possible. Though she could not like it, she was forced to admit that Jonathan had a superficial charm that was not unattractive, and doubtless, he had taken pains to conceal from her his true nature. She knew his character from the years she had lived at Spedwell, and now she was aware that his address was only assumed, but before, when she had not recognized him or remembered his coldness or cruelty, she might well have believed that he was sincere in his attentions and concern for her.

She still did not believe that she had taken him for a lover, but even the degree of intimacy that had been between them was, nevertheless, highly improper and she was ashamed in spite of the fact that she had not been herself at the time. She heard a sound beside her and looked up to discover that David was approaching them. There was appeal in her eyes, but there was nothing in his to acknowledge it.

A less experienced or self-assured man might have reacted guiltily at being caught out making love to another man's wife, but Dancer favored David with a lazy smile. "Ah, Norwood," he said with an audacity that shocked Evelyn, "we have just been speaking of you, have we not, dear lady?"

"Were you?" said David without apparent interest. He held out a hand to his wife. "Jane wishes you to meet a friend of hers who has just come up to town." Evelyn took his hand with alacrity, pleased to have escaped from her cousin before further conversation landed her in greater difficulties.

Jonathan rose and said, "Who is it that Lady Jane wishes Lady Norwood to meet? Anyone I might know?"

Evelyn froze, for she was certain that David had simply made an excuse to get her away from Jonathan. But David was not so easily perturbed. "Mrs. Hartley," he said, turning again to Jonathan. "She was Miss Beckstone who came out the same season as Jane."

"Ah, yes," Jonathan said. "I was not aware that Hartley and his wife had returned from their visit to his family in Ireland. I must pay my respects to them before the night is out as well."

Then he smiled, bowed, and left them, and Evelyn let out an audible breath. She glanced up and saw that David was regarding her with an expression that could not be considered approving. "I suppose you saw that he held my hand in his," she said to forestall the accusation she assumed was coming.

"I and a good third of the company."

"I am sorry for that, but I could not prevent it. I was afraid that he would suspect me if I pulled away from him too abruptly."

"You might have been concerned with what others would think if you did not," he said, but without anger.

"You would hardly wish me to make a scene."

He gave her a slight smile. "That is what it will be if we continue to stand here looking as if we are coming to cuffs."

Evelyn sighed. "I do not think I shall like society very much if I have to watch everything I say or do for fear of what people will think."

"It is only those who have lost their credit with the world who must do so assiduously," he said, and this time there was a slight edge to his tone.

"Will you never miss the opportunity to lecture me?" she said wearily.

His head came up and he looked down at her through slitted eyes. "I am not your tutor, madam, but I am your husband and I will school you if I deem it necessary."

"It is a pity *you* did not spend a bit more time in the schoolroom for lessons in address," she said sweetly.

He smiled. "We had better find Jane and Mrs. Hartley," he said, refusing the bait.

"Then Jane did send you to find me?" she said, surprised.

"No, but she is in conversation with Mrs. Hartley and the excuse served." He proffered his arm and she took it, smiling up at him as she had at the smitten young captain and though she had no idea of it, with much the same effect. Her only purpose was to confound the gossips, but he blinked at her radiant loveliness and was reminded again that he was not as immune to the charms of his young wife as he chose to believe.

On the whole, Evelyn was not displeased with her first foray into polite society. If her meeting with Jonathan had discomfited her, she was not entirely displeased with the result of it. At least she knew now what to expect of him and she did not think that she had done anything to arouse his suspicions. She wished that she might put him in his place the next time he chose to be too familiar, but she knew that her purpose would be best served by playing up to him, not warding him off. She also had no doubt that he had no real interest in her. She did not relish the prospect of being the object of his attentions, but until she could safely confront Jonathan, she knew she would have to accept his familiarity with the best grace that she could muster. It also made her excessively uncomfortable that David should witness Dancer's impudence, and her patent acceptance of it. She did not regard herself as David's wife in any true sense of the word, but she was at pains for him to believe that she had never been her cousin's mistress.

Though she was green in the ways of the world, she could see well enough what Dancer was about. A discreet man would have been at pains to protect her name. His purpose, she had no doubt at all, was to ruin her, and though she could only guess at why he should wish to do so, she knew his end purpose must be to gain full control of her inheritance.

That night, as she lay awake in bed, too stimulated by the events of the evening for sleep to come to her easily, she forced herself to think of her future. The most important thing, of course, was to prove beyond doubt that she was Evelyn Fearne, but she had thought of little else beyond this. Once she was in possession of her inheritance, her physical comfort would be assured, but that was the only thing of which she could be certain. She had little family, only cousins in the north who she did not know at all, and, of course, the Dancers.

Though in a sense, Jane and David were virtually strangers to her, in her vulnerable state she looked upon them as her family and the prospect of leaving them and being entirely on her own when all was resolved was a little daunting. One solution would be to remain as she was, Countess of Norwood. She had no doubt that David was a man of honor, and no matter that he had not married the bride he had supposed, he would give her the protection of his name as he promised. But remaining David's wife on a point of honor was distasteful to her. She supposed herself to be beyond the age of indulging in Lochinvar fantasies, yet she wanted to be wanted and loved in that complete way, loved by the man she would love, and loved entirely for herself.

During her unhappy days at Spedwell, she had often indulged in fantasies of handsome and dashing young men who would rescue her from her unhappy situation, and with whom she would spend the remainder of her life in undefined bliss. Men, in appearance at least, not unlike David Cheviot, Earl of Norwood. It was not difficult, lying in the dark with her eyes closed, to imagine him riding *ventre à terre* to save her from some grisly fate. She smiled to herself for her foolishness, yet she carried the fantasy a little further until it brought a warmth to her cheeks that was not due entirely to modesty.

It was excessively disconcerting to be a wife without really understanding what that meant, to have shared with this man the greatest of intimacies and yet have no recollection of it. She found it impossible to keep from wondering what that most intimate aspect of their lives had been like. It seemed to her that her body recalled what her mind could not, for she was always very aware of him as a man, and physical nearness to him had the power to increase her pulse. And she had surprised that look in his eyes which made her suspect that she could have a similar effect on him. But in her circumstances such thoughts were unprofitable, and she forced her mind to ideas more conducive to sleep and finally fell into that state.

On the following morning, Jane assured her over breakfast that she had done splendidly at the Linquist rout. "If I did not know better, I would swear there was no difference in you, Eve," she said. "You are a splendid actress."

Evelyn could not forbear glancing at David and the brief sardonic smile he sent her way made it clear that the unintended meaning in his sister's words had not escaped him.

"I think Mr. Dancer is a dreadful man, and certainly no gentleman," Jane went on as she poured a second cup of coffee for both herself and her brother. The servants had been dismissed from the breakfast room so that speech might be unfettered. "Did you notice that very shortly after he had spoken with you he left the party? Lady Anastasia Bullers, who is a nasty old cat, made a point of calling my attention to his departure. He had to know how particular his behavior would seem. It was probably the *on-dit* of the evening."

"You may depend upon it," David said, without glancing up from his perusal of the *Morning Post.* "You may see for yourself that his intent is to ruin Eve."

"Well, he won't succeed," Evelyn replied, determined. "When he first met me in town and realized that I had lost my memory, he could have helped me, and I might have forgiven him and my aunt for all that I suffered at their hands. Now I intend to pay him back in his own coin. You will have to be understanding if I appear to encourage his outrageous behavior."

"Shall I?"

"I won't disgrace you, I give you my word," she promised.

"If you do, I give you mine, Eve. I'll do nothing to save you from your ruin, not even for the sake of my own name."

Though her brother's tone was no more than conversational and Evelyn did not appear to take offense at his words, Jane, fearing the start of another domestic skirmish, quickly turned the discussion to their plans for the evening.

"Wherever we go, I only hope that Jonathan is present," was Evelyn's comment, which both surprised and dismayed her sister-in-law.

"I should think you would wish to avoid him as much as possible," Jane said.

"The better I know him, the easier it shall be for me to think of a means of getting into his house to find the locket," Evelyn replied and only then recalled David's presence and his stated objections to this plan. She looked up at him, half hoping that he had been involved in his reading and had not heeded her remark.

But the hope was as forlorn as she had known it would be. He put down his paper and gave her one of his long, enigmatic looks. "I have told you that I wish you to abandon all thought of going to Grove Street to look for the locket. It is likely to end as did the search for your father's will, with considerably more risk. It is one thing for you to flirt with Dancer in public; it is quite another to go to his house. The first is scandalous, the second, ruinous."

"I know that," Evelyn said impatiently. "And *you* must abandon the notion that my accident left me witless. I shall find a way to accomplish the thing with perfect propriety."

"It is both dangerous and unnecessary."

"Perhaps after David has spoken with Mr. Stevens, it will prove quite unnecessary, Eve," Jane suggested, again stepping in as peacemaker.

Evelyn sipped her coffee without comment, David returned to his paper and the difficult moment passed. But Jane was well aware that the awkwardness and delicacy of their situation would mean that there would likely be many more such moments and she could not always be present to deflect them.

Jane wished with all her heart that it wasn't so. She loved her brother and was extremely fond of Evelyn, and she wished them both to be happy. Though Evelyn had spoken to her of an annulment once her difficulties were resolved, Jane knew the world better than her sister-in-law did, and she doubted the efficacy of such a course or, for that matter, her brother's willingness to pursue it. Yet, if they were to remain man and wife and were forever coming to cuffs, it would be a wretched life for them both.

But during the next sennight, though David and
Evelyn were often in each other's company, harmony reigned. Evelyn did not again mention her
intention of finding her mother's locket, and though
she met Jonathan twice during that week, the en-
counters were brief and public. He did not call on
her at Norwood House, and she supposed that despite his boldness in his pursuit of her he would not
dare call if he knew that David had expressly forbidden it.

However, Lady Henrietta did call, and Evelyn did
not find that she improved upon acquaintance. As
David had predicted, Lady Henrietta was so self-
absorbed that she scarcely noticed any lapses in Evelyn's memory of their previous intimacy. Evelyn found
her vain, silly, mean-spirited, and foolishly romantic,
and was mortified that she could ever have chosen
her for her confidante. The most difficult aspect in
dealing with Lady Henrietta was discouraging her
constant disparagement of Norwood and her equally
constant extolling of the character of Mr. Dancer,
and Evelyn found that the only means—short of the
truth—of curbing her absurdities was to avoid her as
assiduously as possible, which proved no easy feat.

In addition to Lady Henrietta there were Sally
Mulridge—a woman whose vulgarity was patent and
only tolerated by the *ton* for the sake of her husband—
and one or two others who claimed to be on terms of
intimacy with Evelyn, though she could scarcely credit
that she had consistently chosen as her friends per-
sons signally lacking in breeding or principle. She
did not understand how she could have ignored the
influence of her husband and Jane who were both
impeccably bred and of sterling character. It made
Evelyn realize, as nothing else had done, that there
was some justification to David's hard reading of her
character.

On the Sunday morning of her second week in
London, David accompanied the ladies to St. George's

and this time they sat in the family pew. No entertainments were planned until evening, when they
were to attend a musicale at the home of an old
friend of Jane's. As soon as they returned to the
house from church, David went out again and Jane
went up to her room to write letters which she claimed
she had sadly neglected.

Evelyn had no one to whom she might write even
if she wished, and she was in a restless state of mind
that made concentrating on a book or even needle-
work difficult. Her life at Norwood House was very
different from what she had known at Spedwell.
There, she had seldom known an idle moment, for
there had always been some task awaiting her, but in
this, the house of which she was nominally mistress,
there was nothing at all for her to do beyond what
she chose for her own pleasure. Even at Blakenhill
she might have busied herself in the still room or
with some other domestic chore deemed suitable for
the mistress of the estate. The only thing she had
to occupy her were her own thoughts and these were
not always comfortable.

In desperation for something to divert her, she hit
upon the idea of walking through the garden at the
back of the house. The garden at Norwood House
was not wide, but it was deep. Compared to the
formal garden at Blakenhill, it was minute, but it
had been laid out by the finest landscapers and was
in every way a perfect gentleman's garden. Brick-
paved paths shaded by graceful trees led to miniature formal gardens and finally to a small but exquisite
rose arbor that already boasted the first blooms of
the season. There was a wrought-iron bench tucked
into the arbor, and when she had had sufficient
exercise strolling about the paths, Evelyn chose to sit
for a while in the cool and beautiful shade. The air
carried the scent of the blooms, which was delicate
and alluring.

She had not been sitting there long when she

heard footsteps and assumed it was Jane come to look for her, but it proved to be David who searched out her resting place. "Jane said I might find you here," he said and sat down beside her. "I wish you to know that Stevens is returned. I have had a note from him saying that he will call on us in the morning if it is convenient."

"How could it be otherwise?" Evelyn asked, her boredom putting a slight edge in her tone. "I wish it were over and done with," she added in a heartfelt way, "and as soon as may be."

"So do I," David agreed. "Perhaps by then the whole of your memory will have returned to you."

She favored him with a brief, rueful smile. "I only hope there may not be some things I do not wish to remember," she said earnestly. "I fear you may not have exaggerated my character as much as I wished to believe."

David looked a little startled by this admission. "No, I didn't exaggerate. What has made you realize that?"

She gave a little, self-deprecating laugh. "Lady Henrietta and Lady Mulridge principally."

He responded with an arid smile. "Both of whom were introduced to you by Dancer."

"I am not surprised. He no doubt wishes to see me in low company." She sighed deeply. "But there are things I do wish I could remember."

"In particular?"

The first response that came into her mind was not the sort of thing she would normally have said to him, but her humor was odd and it made her bold. "I feel as if I scarcely know you, and yet I am your wife. I have no memory of that," she added after a minute pause for emphasis.

"Perhaps we neither of us knew the other very well in any case."

"Why did we marry?" she asked baldly.

"I could only answer half of that question."

"Then you have the advantage of me."

He acknowledged this with a brief, self-mocking smile. "Within a sennight of meeting you, I knew . . ." He broke off for a moment and then went on, "I knew that you have affected me more deeply than any other woman I had known before."

"In what manner?"

"I wanted you very much."

"You wanted to sleep with me," she said, determined to have the bark off the tree.

A flash of annoyance crossed his features. "It was more than that," he said curtly.

"What then?" she persisted.

His eyes met hers, and though she could not read their expression, she knew there was strong emotion behind them. "I loved you."

Though she had half expected this reply, it made her catch her breath, for she felt a response inside of her that was something other than physical and which she had not expected at all. "Did I love you?" she asked, a little breathless, though she thought she already knew the answer.

"I thought so. At the time. Perhaps it was what I wanted to believe."

She wanted to speak, but her voice felt choked and she turned away from him so that he could not guess at her turbulent emotions. He put his hand under her chin and gently turned her head toward him again. He bent his head to hers and kissed her. She did not resist him because she had no real wish to do so. As soon as his lips met hers, she felt not only the delicious stirrings of desire, but also a sense of peace, and an elusive sense of belonging. Though the memory of their life together eluded her, it was as if she had always known his kiss, the feel of his strong arms encircling her, and the pressure of his hard body against her own.

His lips moved slowly down her throat to the hollow between her breasts, sending shivers of growing desire to every nerve. In her mind she remained virginal, but her body knew otherwise, and as his tongue and teeth found her taut nipples, she ached for a consummation she did not understand. She could scarcely believe how strong desire could be. When he touched her thighs, they parted involuntarily and she had no will at all to resist him.

She was a little frightened by what was happening, but anticipation was stronger than fear, and when he released her as abruptly as he had in the library at Blakenhill, she was both startled and chagrined.

"It won't do, Eve," he said after a long moment. "Not for either of us. I have never in my life wanted a woman as I want you at this moment, but we can't afford this entanglement to our affairs."

Evelyn felt as if he had slapped her. Not even the gentleness of his tone could deflect the sharp sting of rejection. She had offered him the gift of herself and he had cast it back at her. Yet she knew he was right. Renewing their physical intimacy would hopelessly complicate their already muddled and uncertain relations. But she wished that he had come to this conclusion before she had made it so clear to him that she was his for the taking. At the least she should have had the sense herself to resist giving in to her curiosity and vague longings. Gathering the shreds of her dignity about her she said, "Of course it would not do. You presume a great deal, my lord."

"Perhaps I do," he allowed. "But it is more difficult for me. I have perfect recollection of our marriage and of all that we once were to each other."

"We are nothing to each other now," she said stiffly, looking away from him out toward the garden.

"What has just happened between us gives that the lie."

"There is physical attraction," she granted, "but nothing more."

"I think I would call the fact that we are legally married something," he said a bit tartly.

"But only in name," she returned. "And as soon as my difficulties are resolved, there will be an end to that as well."

He did not respond to this. He rose and held out his hand. The corners of his mouth turned upward in a faint smile. "Then, since we are aware of our weakness, we should do what we can to guard against it. We had better return to the house."

Evelyn shook her head. "I think I would rather stay here for now."

"As you wish," he said, sounding indifferent. He turned and left her and she watched his retreating figure until a bend in the path took him from her sight.

Evelyn bowed her head and pressed her hands to her cheeks as if she were still flushed, but her skin was quite cool to the touch. Though she would not admit it to him, to herself she acknowledged that it was more than physical attraction that had caused her to behave so wantonly. She did not know him as her husband, but she knew beyond any doubt that there had to have been love between them, and far more disconcerting was the realization that she still did have feeling for him, though how it could be so when he was still nearly a stranger to her, she could not begin to understand.

She was frightened, for she was very aware of her vulnerability, and she could have no doubt from his behavior that however much he may have cared for her once, he did not do so now. He might desire her, but even that was not so overwhelming an emotion that he could not control it with the ease of indifference. He would be kind to her and would help her, but Evelyn knew she dared not mistake this for love. The woman he had once loved was not even her as she was today and she knew it would be fatal to her peace to allow the feeling she had for him to rekindle. By the end of her cogitations, she could only be glad that he had had more presence of mind than she to prevent an intimacy which she was convinced they could both only regret.

6

Evelyn and Jane attended the musicale alone, though Evelyn had no idea whether David did not join them by previous plan or because of what had occurred in the garden. Though the music of the evening was by Mozart and Evelyn was particularly fond of his work, she found little pleasure in either the music or the company. Her thoughts ran almost obsessively on David, the unexpected emotions he had aroused in her, and what this might mean to her already uncertain future.

On the following morning when she and David met across the breakfast table, his manner exhibited no change toward her and she was glad to take his lead. He invited her to ride in Green Park with him and she readily accepted, for she knew that for her peace of mind she needed to school herself to indifference in his company.

"Won't people wonder at my newfound skill if I suddenly display my horsemanship?" she asked as they walked their horses along Portsmouth Square heading toward Green Park. She was mounted on a sable-colored Spanish gelding named Cadiz, who was worthy of her mettle. It pleased her that David trusted her ability to the degree that he would mount her so well, and she was quite determined to be in charity with him.

"No. You always claimed you didn't care to ride. I don't recall you precisely saying you *could not* ride."

"I may have been afraid to put it to the test because I had no idea whether or not I could ride," she suggested and he agreed that it might have been so.

When they reached the park they broke into a trot, and as the park was virtually unpopulated except for an occasional nursemaid and her charges, they let their mounts have their heads to enjoy an invigorating gallop. Evelyn was exhilarated by the exercise, and it showed in the delicate, blossoming color in her cheeks and the sparkling brightness in her eyes. As they slowed again to an easy posting trot, David stayed just a little behind her that he might easily view her without his regard being remarked.

His feelings toward Evelyn were as unsettled as hers were toward him. He had really believed that the love he had once felt for her had been dissipated by their estrangement, but when she looked as she did now, there was a stirring in him that went beyond simple desire. The reserve and distance he had been determined to keep in her company was being constantly eroded and he was not at all certain whether he thought that for the good or for the bad. He had completely lost his heart to her once; he was not willing to do so again as readily.

Their pace dropped to a walk and Evelyn leaned forward to praise Cadiz and then turned to cast David a happy smile. "He is a beauty," she said. "As excellent a hack as Rufus is a hunter. You have superb taste in horseflesh, my lord."

"Thank you. But I thought we were agreed that you are not to address me by my title. You do so more often than not, you know."

Evelyn was readjusting the reins of the pelham bridle and did not look up at him. "I know. But I feel rather awkward addressing you so familiarly." She glanced at him then and caught the ironic gleam in his eyes. She knew he was thinking of yesterday and could not prevent the color that suffused her countenance.

"You seem to have no similar difficulty with Jane," he remarked. "Do you object to my addressing you by your given name?"

Evelyn felt foolish because she knew she was being missish and did not really know why it was so. "No. Of course not. I think it is just that I forget," she said, the excuse sounding false in her own ears.

There was the sound of other horses approaching them from a path to their left and Evelyn looked up expectantly, hoping for a diversion. A party of two women and four men approached them. The women were unknown to Evelyn but she needed only to observe their free manners with the gentlemen and the exaggerated fashionableness of their riding habits to guess that they were members of that set known as the Fashionable Impures.

David nodded in the direction of another path leading away from the approaching riders and Evelyn turned her horse to follow him, having no desire for an awkward encounter. As they rode away from the other group, Evelyn could not help wondering if David were acquainted with either of the lightskirts. She had ample proof of his virility and she doubted he was a man who would find celibacy to his taste. This possibility upset her more than she felt it should have and she realized she was not making much progress at learning to regard her husband with indifference.

Again there was the sound of approaching hoof-beats, though this time of a single horse. The canter reduced to a trot and Jonathan Dancer reined in beside Evelyn. "My dear Lady Norwood," he said as he possessed himself of her hand and brought it to his lips in a courtly fashion. "My eyes did not mislead me. I thought it must be you, though I had no notion you cared for the diversion of a morning ride."

"Riding is a pleasure I do not find as much time for as I could wish," Evelyn acknowledged, hoping he would not pursue the subject which might lead her to say something unguarded which would make him suspicious. "But my lord has provided me with such a splendid mount that I could not resist the pleasure." She turned and smiled a little uncertainly at David and discovered that he was watching her and Dancer in an unreadable manner. At these words, Dancer finally acknowledged the presence of her husband, favoring David with a sketch of a bow which was returned with equal coolness.

Evelyn wondered at her cousin's audacity. With the whole world linking their names in the worst sort of gossip she would have supposed he would avoid meeting David if he could. Jonathan gave her a faintly quizzing smile, which Evelyn had to admit was attractive. It would not do to underestimate him; he was clever and very personable when he chose to be. She still could not believe that she had taken his pretensions seriously, but she was beginning to understand why she might have found his company attractive. "Were you not with friends, Mr. Dancer?" she asked, hoping he would take the hint and return to his party.

"We would not wish to keep you from your, ah, diversions, Dancer," David said, with a quick, wry smile.

Dancer cast the briefest of glances in David's direction and then said, looking into Evelyn's eyes as if speaking only to her, "They are no more than diversion. My particular interests lie elsewhere."

There was no mistaking his meaning and Evelyn's wonder became astonishment; he was making love to her before David's eyes. She was acutely uncomfortable and wished she might think of something to rid them of his company without giving offense, for she still needed to be on good terms with her cousin at least until she had secured the locket. "Lady Harry tells me that you are at work on a play," she said, deliberately misunderstanding him. "That must be very interesting indeed."

"Yes. Mr. Kemble has encouraged my poor efforts," he replied. "It is a tragedy, the story of a beautiful woman who finds herself in a distasteful marriage and must choose between the longings of her heart and the good opinion of the world—which is ephemeral in any case."

This did not prove a happy topic so Evelyn ventured to a new one. "Do you attend the opera on Friday, Mr. Dancer? Madame Bartoli will be singing *Euridice* and all the world will be there."

He laughed a little. "Of course. I am sure you may meet me wherever the world is to be found."

"At least in large numbers," David said in a silky undervoice which was nevertheless loud enough to be heard by Dancer.

His words, implying as they did that Dancer would not be invited to partake in the more intimate entertainments of the *ton*, were clearly meant as an affront. Evelyn saw a spark of anger kindle in Dancer's eyes and his habitual smile became quite fixed. It did not at all suit Evelyn that the hostility between the two men should become an open thing, at least not at this time. She said quickly, "I hope I may see you at the intermission, Mr. Dancer."

"If I may share it with such a lovely companion, by all means."

She smiled at him. "Until Friday, then," she said, and it was a clear dismissal. He took it in good grace, again making her a brief bow, he turned his horse to return in the direction he had come.

Evelyn could not forbear a sigh of relief. She turned to make some light comment to David, but when she saw that he was regarding her with a seriousness that bordered on disapprobation, the words died on her lips. "You are not going to doubt me again just because Jonathan chose to make me the object of his attentions," she said disbelievingly. "I could scarcely prevent it."

"Could you also not prevent planning a rendezvous with him?" His voice had no edge to it, but she knew he was not simply quizzing her.

"It was only a means to get rid of him," she said.

"Then you do not plan to attend the opera on Friday?"

"I go with Jane and her friend Mrs. Carrington," she admitted. He said nothing, turning his head back in the direction of the road. "You are being unfair," she said, feeling a bit ill-used. "If I were to snub him suddenly, he would wonder at it and perhaps begin to suspect that my memory was returned. It was you who convinced me that my purpose would not be served by confrontation at this time."

"There is a deal of difference between confrontation and encouragement," he said levelly.

"Do you know you sound like a jealous husband?" she said, quizzing him.

From the look he flashed her she could see he did not care for her words. "We had better return to the house," was all he said in response. "Mr. Stevens will be waiting for us." He spurred his horse into an easy canter and Evelyn followed.

They did not arrive at the house before the solicitor, but Evelyn had barely finished changing out of her habit when a maid came to inform her that his lordship wished her to come to his study. Evelyn had half expected David to behave in an overbearing manner, insisting on handling her affairs as he saw fit, but he waited for her before explaining their odd situation to Mr. Stevens and she took full part in the discussion.

Mr. Stevens was cautious; he listened to the story without comment and little more expression. "It is most unusual" was his only comment before he began to reiterate the facts and discuss what could be done. He insisted on discovering for himself all matters of public record concerning Evelyn and her family, including her father's will and the settlement of the estate, the record of her birth and of her parents' deaths. Until such time as he had thoroughly acquainted himself with the case, he refused to commit himself to any definite course of action.

Mr. Stevens did not claim acquaintance with Mr. Dancer, but he pursed his lips at the mention of his name and admitted that he knew one or two matters of business that were not to that man's credit. He agreed with David that it was best not to tip their hand until they felt confident of success in spite of Dancer's failure to acknowledge Evelyn as his cousin and the rightful heiress to the Fearne estate. Nor could he like the idea of seeking out Evelyn's cousins in the north to identify her; they had not set eyes on her since she was a child, and in this case, he felt that a poor witness might be more harmful than none at all.

"Well then, what are we to do?" asked Evelyn, a little of her annoyance at Mr. Stevens' caution showing in her voice.

Mr. Stevens wore small reading glasses perched on the end of his nose. He removed these and addressed Evelyn in his grave manner. "First we shall gather all the necessary information. I fear you think that a tedious course, my lady, but I can assure you from my experience that it is not only prudent, it also often serves the purpose of suggesting the proper direction to take in a difficult and delicate matter such as this."

He removed a handkerchief from a pocket in his coat and began to polish the lens of his glasses in a careful way that made the chafing countess want to snatch them from his hand. "Then there is the search for Mrs. Walker that Mr. Ventry is undertaking. Her evidence, corroborated by that of your maid, will certainly be of assistance. Another suggestion I could make would be to find servants who were in service during the five years you spent at Spedwell but who have since left Mrs. Dancer's employ in happy circumstances so that there could be no accusations of wishing revenge on the Dancers. Any positive identification from a source such as that would be reasonably creditable. I have in my employ operatives who know that their jobs depend on their discretion so I think it could be accomplished without alerting the Dancers to what we are about. You may help us here, my lady, by supplying me with the full names of every servant you can recall at Spedwell, particularly any who left during the time you were there and the reasons for their departure."

Evelyn regarded him blankly for a moment and then said, "I think there were one or two maids who quit or were dismissed and a footman as well." She paused and then said, "But I am not certain I can give you their names or that they left Spedwell on good terms; it was not the most pleasant household in which to work. I might recall given names but I may never have known their family names. I never came to know any of the servants particularly well. Since I was neither servant nor regarded on an equal with my aunt and cousin, my relations with the staff at Spedwell were at best awkward. It is unlikely that anyone from the Grove Street household would remember me; I was only there once for a few days the first year I was with my aunt."

"Still, you must do your best, Lady Norwood," Mr. Stevens insisted. "It is an avenue of inquiry we can not afford to neglect. If you have a day or two to think on it, I am certain you will do quite well."

Evelyn had a question she wished to put to the solicitor, but she was uncertain whether it would be a good idea to ask it in front of David. As the solicitor rose to leave, she decided to risk it. "Mr. Stevens, would it help me at all in the way of proof if I had some article belonging to my family that I would be unlikely to have if I were not a Fearne as I claim?"

The lawyer's brow knit. "That would greatly depend. Such as?"

"An heirloom," Evelyn said, trying to sound as if the idea had just occurred to her. "Perhaps some object belonging to my mother which had belonged to hers."

"It would be a very subjective matter," the solicitor said after a few moments of thought. "You would have to prove beyond doubt that it had indeed belonged to your mother and it would need to be unique in some way so that it could not easily be copied. It certainly would not answer as proof in itself, but it might add to the weight of the evidence. Do you have such an object, my lady?"

Evelyn did not dare glance at her husband. "N-no. That is, not that I know of, but Mrs. Walker may be able to tell us of something I may have had with me when I came to Hardwood. It was only a thought," she finished lamely.

Mr. Stevens took leave of them then and David walked with him into the hall. Evelyn did not wish to wait for David to return, but the two men stood talking in the hall in full view of the stairs and she preferred to return to her room unobserved. Finally, Tomkins opened the wide door and while Mr. Stevens was being shown out, she quickly crossed the hall and started up the stairs. She was only a third of the way up when she heard David call her name. Resigning herself, she turned. He mounted the stairs behind her and they ascended the flight together.

At the top of the stairs he led her into a small saloon. He closed the door and turned to her. "I thought you had given up the idea of trying to find your mother's locket."

He did not sound annoyed, but there was certainly no approval in his words. "Mr. Stevens said it would add to the weight of the evidence," she said defensively.

"He said it might. It isn't worth the risk, Eve, for so little. What did your search of Spedwell gain you?"

"I am certain of this."

He smiled in a way that made her want to box his ears. "So am I," he replied. "You will abandon the notion of going to Dancer's house. You would be handing Dancer exactly what he needs to complete your ruin, and I cannot allow that."

Evelyn deliberately swallowed her anger, she should have known it was only a matter of time before he displayed his overbearing manner toward her again. "But we must do something. Mr. Stevens means well, but his ways are plodding. It could take weeks for him to gather the information he seeks and even longer to make the discreet inquiries he suggests."

"And if it does?" David asked, raising his brows.

"Jonathan is living on my inheritance," she said, outraged.

"As he doubtless has for the last eighteen months. What matters a few more weeks?"

She hardly knew how to answer that for it was true enough. She said the first thing that came into her head. "I am tired of playing a role for the benefit of society and living in constant quaking that I shall say or do something to make people stare. I wish it to be over so that I may be myself again."

"We could return to Blakenhill if you prefer."

Evelyn knew she did not prefer that. At Blakenhill they would be almost constantly in each other's company and much of the time alone. The rose garden at Blakenhill was extensive and it would be only one of many traps into which her vulnerable heart might fall. "No. I would rather remain here," she said.

"As you wish," he said perfunctorily. He turned to leave but at the door, he paused and said, "Permit those who are most capable of managing your affairs to do so, Eve. It is your only hope to succeed."

Evelyn's fingers itched for a breakable object to cast at him, but as it was, she simply flounced out the door past him and returned to her bedchamber, silently fuming and naming him in her thoughts by every unflattering epithet she could call to mind.

She might not have abandoned her desire to find her mother's locket, but neither had she greatly applied her mind to doing so. David's high-handed suggestions which amounted to commands decided her that she would use every moment she could spare to concoct a scheme for getting into her cousin's house without bringing ruin down upon herself. When this was accomplished and her inheritance secured, she would turn all of her energies to seeking an annulment to her absurd parody of a marriage to the odious Earl of Norwood.

The following morning brought another letter from Mr. Ventry, but no further news. He wrote that he felt he was very near to tracking down the elusive Mrs. Walker, but had no real progress to report. Evelyn chose to regard this as a sign that she was right to go ahead with her own plans.

She did not see Jonathan again that week, for there was truth in David's barb which suggested that Dancer existed only on the fringes of the first circles. Evelyn suspected that the more exclusive, less crowded entertainments Jane insisted they attend were deliberately selected to avoid meeting Dancer and further, she was sure it was at David's behest, which only served to strengthen her resolve to defy him. When Jane declared that she had seen *Orpheo ed Euridice* a dozen times and suggested that they cry off from their engagement with Mrs. Carrington, Evelyn was adamant that they attend, and on Friday evening Mrs. Carrington's carriage came to call for her and Jane. Evelyn feared that David would insist on making one of their party, but he left shortly before dinner to join friends at Mrs. Beamish's fashionable new gaming hell in Bond Street.

Mrs. Carrington was an ethereal blonde whose delicate appearance was belied by an energetic and outgoing personality. Evelyn had a difficult moment when Mrs. Carrington referred to a conversation they had had on a previous meeting of which Evelyn had no recollection, but fortunately Jane had also been present on that occasion and was able to respond in Evelyn's place. It was shortly after this that the opera began and Evelyn was able to relax and enjoy the unfolding story and music.

It was Evelyn's first time at the opera—at least the first time that she recalled—but like most well-bred and accomplished young women who had a taste for music she was familiar with most of the best-known operas from having heard portions of them performed in private homes as entertainment for guests. But the most elaborate private production had been nothing to what was displayed before her fascinated eyes and ears. The grotto that holds the tomb of Euridice at the start of the first act was lavishly adorned and she had never before heard voices so exquisite in quality and technique.

She was so enraptured by the performance that she quite forgot that her principle reason for coming was to meet with her cousin and to find the means of carrying out her plan to find her mother's locket. At the end of the first act, Mrs. Carrington, who had given far more of her attention to scanning the other boxes for acquaintances than to the stage, immediately suggested that they stroll the promenade behind the boxes. Jane agreed—reluctantly, since they were without male attendants—but Evelyn and Mrs. Carrington assured her that she was too nice in her notions and that it was not improper as long as they were amongst friends.

They met quite a number of their friends and acquaintances as they walked the length of the corridor, but Jonathan was not among them, and Evelyn began to think that she had refined too much on his promise to meet her at the intermission, or that he did not mean to put in an appearance until the interval between the second and third acts. But as soon as the ladies turned to retrace their steps to their box, Evelyn saw him coming toward her, with Lady Henrietta on his arm.

When the two parties met, Dancer bowed over the hand of each lady in turn, but lingered over Evelyn's a bit longer than was necessary. Lady Henrietta stepped forward at once, placing herself between Jane and Evelyn and saying, "My dear Lady Jane, you are the very person I most wished to speak with tonight. I shall be visiting in Canterbury next month and I know you are exactly the person to tell me what I may expect of the county."

As Mrs. Carrington was on the other side of Jane, Lady Harry's maneuver effectively set those two ladies apart from Evelyn, who was standing a little to one side next to her cousin. "We are blocking the way, Lady Norwood," Dancer said, loud enough for the others to hear. "Allow me to escort you back to your box."

Evelyn was very much aware, as Jane must be, that the behavior of both Lady Henrietta and Jonathan was prearranged, and she smiled a little to think that not even David, had he been present, could have managed to prevent her tête à tête with her cousin without causing awkwardness if not an outright scene.

Dancer misinterpreted her smile, and returned it with one of his own which was tinged with triumph. "We have outwitted your duennas."

"I don't know that I would call Jane that," Evelyn replied. "She is my friend."

"And Norwood's sister. It would be fatal to forget that."

Evelyn looked at him with mild surprise. "Fatal, Mr. Dancer? I think that is your flair for drama which speaks."

He laughed. "Perhaps. But I don't think I exaggerate too outrageously; she would prevent our friendship if she could, I believe. It goes against the grain, my dear, to force subterfuge into our friendship because of Norwood's jealousies and insecurities."

The urge to defend David was almost too overwhelming, but Evelyn overcame it. To serve her purpose, tonight it was necessary for her to play the role of an injured wife. "Norwood is being very difficult, nearly a tyrant," she confided in an urgent whisper. "Either he or Jane is forever with me and he plagues me constantly with questions about whom I have spoken with and what was said. If he had his way he would choose to bury me in Kent, I think, where there is nothing to do and no one who is amusing."

Jonathan gave her hand which rested on his arm an understanding squeeze. When he spoke there was an intensity in his voice that Evelyn knew was no more sincere than her petulant speech had been. "I sometimes fear the length to which his jealousy may take him." They reached the box and he stood aside for Evelyn to enter before him. It was improper in him to do so, but he closed the door, and before she could object, he took both her hands in his. "Perhaps the time has come for me to speak, my lovely one. It becomes insupportable to me to say nothing. That man does not value you as you deserve and I can no longer stand idly by and allow it to continue. Come away with me, Eve. The Continent is closed to us because of the cursed French menace, but I have some small holdings in Ireland and we may be away from the viciousness of gossip there."

Evelyn was startled by his declaration. She had always supposed that he was leading toward this, but it was happening much sooner than she expected. Her plan for the evening had been nothing more than to encourage his attentions and perhaps find an opening to suggest a way that she might safely go to his house. Her inclination was to box his ears for his impudence, but she was not yet ready to abandon her scheme to find the locket and so she said as if surprised, but not displeased, "Do you mean elope?

Oh, Jonathan, I could not. It is not as if we could be married, for I am already married. If I fled David's protection for yours, I should be consigned to the demimonde."

"It need not be so," Dancer assured her. "Norwood is too proud a man to keep a wife who has clearly shown her preference for another. He will divorce you and then we shall be free to wed. This damned war can't go on forever and then we shall be gay again in capitals that are more broad-minded than London."

His hold on her hands was so strong it was almost painful. Evelyn scarcely knew what to answer and wished that Jane and Mrs. Carrington would escape Lady Henrietta and rescue her by returning to their box. The absurdity of her situation struck her forcibly. She had fled Spedwell and fallen into her present predicament to avoid marriage to Jonathan and now she was forced to listen to his declaration so that she might solve her dilemma. The thought appealed to her rather wry sense of humor and she was forced to lower her head to hide a smile.

Dancer mistook this for confusion and said, "I've shocked you, haven't I? Blame my ardor if you will, but not my sense. My dear one, you must see you can't spend the rest of your life tied to one of Norwood's stamp."

"I don't know what to say," Evelyn responded, and it was true enough.

"Do you know your heart, Eve?" he asked, raising her face to him. Evelyn felt a tiny wave of panic, fearing that he meant to kiss her, but he made no move to do so. "You can't love Norwood," he said with conviction.

Evelyn found she could not quite bring herself to confirm this statement. Gently, she pulled her hands from his. "Please, Jonathan, don't press me. I don't know how I could agree to such a thing. It is such an irreversible step."

"There is no doubt at all in my mind or in my heart."

She looked up at him. "But in mine there is," she said quietly. "We are, as you say, friends. I hadn't thought beyond that. In many ways I barely know you."

"You must trust me, Eve. I would do nothing to harm you in any way."

No, Evelyn thought, you would only rob me of my inheritance and my good name. "What would Mrs. Dancer say?" she said as a thought finally occurred to her which might serve her own purpose.

"What has my mother to say to our happiness?"

Evelyn detected a hint of impatience in his voice. He must be very sure that she would ultimately accept his proposition. "Eventually, we would have to return to live at Spedwell, surely. What must she think of a daughter-in-law who has no reputation."

"She would love you for your dear, gentle self," he said promptly, and with mechanical suavity.

Evelyn had to bite back another smile as she thought of Lavinia Dancer and the pettish manner with which her aunt had always treated her. She knew now exactly where she was leading their conversation and now she prayed that Jane and Mrs. Carrington would *not* too soon escape the voluble, silly tongue of Lady Henrietta and upset her plan. "I wish I could be as certain. I am barely acquainted with Mrs. Dancer. If she should take me in dislike, it would be very uncomfortable for us all."

"It need not be," Dancer assured her, his impatience making his tone a bit testy. "We shall consign her to the dower house."

"Oh, I could not," Evelyn said, turning wide eyes toward him. "How horrid it would be for me to send her from her home. If only we could meet again, and I could see that she did not dislike me . . ." She let her voice trail away suggestively.

Evelyn had the feeling that he stifled an exasperated sigh, though he made no sound. "It would be impossible for you to visit Spedwell openly. Norwood would surely object."

"Mrs. Dancer does not come to town at all for the Season?"

"I have told you she dislikes town as much as I abhor being away from it."

Evelyn sat again in the chair she had occupied for the performance. The musicians were tuning again and it could only be a matter of moments before Jane and Mrs. Carrington returned to the box. Dancer sat beside her in Jane's chair and took one of her hands in his again. "Don't let your fears dissuade you, my love. You know I offer you a better life than you could hope to have with Norwood, who neither loves nor deserves you."

Evelyn ignored this conceit and said quickly, "I know you think me foolish, but knowing your mother did not disapprove of me would greatly help to ease my mind."

"Say you are mine, and I shall write to her in the morning," he replied, but his tone was a bit too short to be loverlike.

"That is not the sort of thing one writes in a letter," Evelyn protested. "And what if it should go astray?"

Before he coould reply and perhaps completely give away his growing exasperation with her, the door finally opened to admit the other ladies. Mrs. Carrington raised her brows a bit when she saw that Jonathan was still with Evelyn, but she said nothing. Jane looked uncomfortable and was also mute, but Lady Henrietta forged ahead. "I knew I should still find you here, Jonathan," she said, "but we had best return to our own seats. You and Eve should have things settled between you by now."

Dancer cast her a murderous look and Evelyn felt her cheeks grow hot, but Mrs. Carrington was too well bred to question Lady Henrietta's indiscretion.

Evelyn knew that Jane must surely understand only too well. All of Evelyn's pleasure in the opera was at an end, and she spent the remainder of the evening anticipating Jane's inevitable questions the moment they were alone. She would have to answer these without revealing either her cousin's declaration or her own plans for finding the locket. She was not at all certain that Jane would not go to David if she believed that Evelyn were about to fall into some scrape.

Evelyn's assumption that Jane would demand an explanation for her tête à tête with Jonathan was not mistaken. Though Evelyn declared that she was exhausted and wished only for her bed, as soon as they returned to the house Jane followed her to her bedchamber.

"It is not my place to question your conduct, Eve," she began, obviously disliking what she felt she must say, "but you must know how it looked for Caro and me to find you alone in such a way with Mr. Dancer."

"I know I should not have permitted him to shut the door," Evelyn acknowledged.

"You should not have gone into the box alone with him at all. I only hope that it was not as obvious to Caro as it was to me that Lady Henrietta was deliberately keeping us from joining you. Caroline Carrington is no fool, and though she is not a deliberate gossip, she may well mention to a friend or two that Mr. Dancer was quite particular in his attentions and that you did not spurn them."

"I am sorry, Jane," Evelyn said quietly. "I know it was unwise and I promise that I shall be more discreet in the future."

"Why should there be anything between you and Mr. Dancer requiring discretion?" Jane asked baldly. "You may not wish Mr. Dancer to know that you recognize him as your cousin, but that does not mean that you are obliged to encourage his pretensions."

This was so very nearly what David had said to her

on Monday that Evelyn bristled. "I could not avoid him tonight without giving offense. I wish you might trust my judgment a little; I've no more wish to court disgrace than you or David would wish me to."

"What did Dancer want?"

"Nothing that signified," Evelyn said, and hoped she sounded convincing. "He wished only for a bit of dalliance, but I promise you, he did not go beyond the line of what is pleasing or proper."

"It was improper for you to be with him so privately in the first place," Jane said, with just a hint of waspishness. But then she smiled. "I am sorry, dearest. I don't mean to ring a peal over you, but if David hears of this he might well fly up into the boughs and perhaps even insist that we return to Blakenhill— and I know you do not wish for that."

"No, not at all," Evelyn agreed. "I understand, Jane, and I shall try to prevent such a thing happening again."

Jane appeared satisfied with this, and bidding Evelyn good night, she went to her own bedchamber. Evelyn felt pangs of guilt. In some ways she disliked deceiving Jane about her plans more than she did David, for she regarded Jane more truly as an ally. But it could not be helped. Jane would doubtless object if she knew what Evelyn intended, and if she could not persuade Evelyn against it, she might even take it the length of telling her brother.

On the following night, Evelyn attended an assembly to which her cousin was also invited. She eluded his attempt to be private with her again, but a few minutes of conversation took place between them and she at least had the satisfaciton of discovering that the seed she had planted had taken root. Jonathan informed her that he had written to his mother to ask her to join him in town and that he had hopes that she would be arriving in the next day or so. Evelyn had scarcely dared to hope that he would act so quickly on her suggestion, but she had her wits about her sufficiently to take her plotting to the next step, suggesting that he give some sort of entertainment in his mother's honor when she arrived.

"It would be my pleasure," Dancer replied, though he did not sound particularly pleased, "but I doubt there will be time. My mother does not plan to make a long stay in town."

They were standing a little to one side of a larger group of people gathered around a long table where champagne and biscuits had been set out for the refreshment of the guests. Evelyn lowered her voice to avoid being overheard. "Yet it would be an excellent opportunity for us to spend a bit of time in each other's company without exciting comment. A simple rout party would do."

"Would it?" he asked, dropping his voice as well. "Yet I doubt Norwood would be complaisant about your accepting an invitation to my house."

"He'll know nothing about it," Evelyn replied promptly and quite truthfully. "You must invite Lady Henrietta and I shall come with her, but I'll tell Norwood that we are going somewhere else that will be quite unexceptionable."

Dancer made her no promise, but Evelyn was sure that he would do as she asked. She had no doubt he believed he was very close to success with her, and the fact that he had gone the length of summoning his mother proved that he was willing to do what was necessary to achieve his end.

On Tuesday, Lady Henrietta confided in her that Mrs. Dancer was due to arrive the following day and that a rout party was planned for Saturday, and Evelyn spent the next few days in growing but necessarily suppressed excitement. She declined Jane's suggestion that they attend the theater on Saturday by claiming a prior engagement with Lady Henrietta. David was present when she said this, and did not so much as look up from his perusal of the morning paper. Jane's brow creased a bit, and Evelyn knew that she was not pleased, but she said nothing and made no later objections.

Evelyn had no idea of the size of the gathering that was planned for Saturday, but it was not likely to be so small that her absence for no more than a quarter hour would be remarked upon. She did not think it would take more time than that to get to the lumber room, find the oak chest, and safely conceal the locket on her person. Her only fear was that she would face the same failure she had had trying to find her father's will. But she thought it unlikely that the chest would be gone, for Jonathan had no idea of its value to her.

7

Evelyn's complacency that everything was going smoothly and according to plan was rudely shattered late Saturday morning when Mr. Ventry suddenly returned from Scotland. She had no doubt that he had hurried to London to inform them of his success. It was, of course, both desirable and inevitable that Mr. Ventry should find Mrs. Walker, but the timing could not have been worse. Evelyn's one hope of appeasing David when he learned that she had gone to Grove Street against his wishes, would be to point out to him that neither his nor Mr. Stevens' methods had yet produced any success and that she had grown tired of waiting.

"The moment that she had finished reading your letter, Mrs. Walker corroborated your story in every particular that she could," Mr. Ventry informed Evelyn. As soon as the secretary had returned, David had summoned her and Jane to the library to hear of Ventry's success. "She was even willing to cut short her holiday to come in person to speak with Mr. Stevens, but I assured her that a sworn deposition would do until she returned to Kent in September." He pulled several sheets of paper from an inner pocket in his coat and handed them to David, who skimmed them and then passed them to Evelyn.

Evelyn was tolerably familiar with Mrs. Walker's handwriting, and as she read the missive, she finally learned most of what had occurred since her last full memory before she had awakened at Blakenhill.

Though, as of yet, Evelyn had no memory of the woman who had taken her in, it was obvious that she was something of a romantic, for there were references to Evelyn's obvious breeding and education and the older woman's conviction that she was fleeing a wicked stepmother or an unsavory suitor—neither of which was so very far from the truth—though Mrs. Walker confirmed that Evelyn had had no memory at all beyond her given name. Evelyn's history, she admitted, was put about to appease the curiosity of friends and neighbors, and was entirely her own invention.

Evelyn finished reading and returned the deposition to her husband. "I hope I may soon meet Mrs. Walker," she said quietly. "She is a very generous, goodhearted woman to have taken in a complete stranger knowing nothing of the possible consequences. Thank you, Mr. Ventry," she added, and meant it. It was hardly his fault that he had returned a day too early for Evelyn's purpose.

"It was mostly luck and sheer doggedness, I fear," Roger Ventry said with a self-deprecating smile.

"Nonsense, it was cleverness and hard work," David replied.

"I wish it might be more," Mr. Ventry responded, casting a quick glance toward Jane, who sat in a chair near her brother's desk. "With your permission, my lord, I shall call on Mr. Stevens on Monday and ask him if I might serve him in his inquiries."

"That is hardly necessary," David assured him. "Mr. Stevens employs competent agents. You have done far more for me that your position requires and, in any case, I need your assistance here now. I am speaking next week on the new bill that is before the House, you may remember."

It was clear from Mr. Venty's quick flush that he had forgotten. "Of course, my lord. But I am sure I may do whatever you require of me in addition to assisting Lady Norwood however I may."

"No doubt," David said a bit dryly, "but nevertheless it is unnecessary for you to do so." He stood straight and walked to Evelyn's chair. "Jane, if you and Mr. Ventry would excuse us, I wish to have a private word with Evelyn."

Evelyn felt her stomach knot a little. She knew her fear was irrational, but her first thought was that David had somehow learned of her plan to attend Mrs. Dancer's rout party. The library led into the smaller room which he used as a study and she followed him there.

"I believe that I owe you an apology, Eve," he said as he closed the door.

Evelyn turned. "Really? Whatever for?" she asked, surprised.

"For doubting you. Until today I still had at least a modicum of doubt about you," he admitted.

"I don't know that I blame you," she said handsomely, "but I am glad that Mrs. Walker's deposition has finally convinced you."

"It has not been the only thing to convince me. I admit that the principal reason I was willing for us to return to London was that I wished to observe you in Dancer's company again."

Evelyn knew this was dangerous ground and said warily, "And what did you see?"

"Nothing to signify. I know I have been unfair to you. As you have said, you could not change your manner toward him all at once without arousing his suspicions, but I have seen nothing in your manner to indicate that you have any real feeling for him."

Evelyn felt a twinge of guilt. She had at last earned his trust and she meant to betray it almost at once by doing what he had expressly asked her not to do. Self-reproach and the fear that she was endangering his newfound belief in her nearly made her decide to abandon her plans, but she recognized that there was more in her wish to find the locket than gaining possession of it to help prove that she was Evelyn Fearne. She wanted to steal it from Jonathan's house under his very nose. A small revenge, but it meant a great deal to her.

Evelyn smiled a little. "I only hope that the rest of the world is as willing to be convinced."

"I had a word with Stevens yesterday and he has seen your father's will and the parish records at Limirend where you were born and your family is buried. He is very optimistic that we shall succeed no matter what Dancer may do to counter us if we can but find anyone who knew you well enough, recently enough to identify you positively as Evelyn Fearne."

"How long does he mean to go on with his search?" she said, her tone clearly indicating that she did not expect an answer that would please her.

David shrugged. "As long as it takes. How pessimistic you are and how impatient," he said, smiling.

"I hate this uncertainty," she said. "What if there is no one to be found?"

"When we have exhausted all avenues, we shall take our chances and confront Dancer. That is always an option which we may exercise if all else fails." There was only a short distance between them and he closed it, coming so close to her that she was acutely aware of his nearness. "You may safely trust me, Eve. I have pledged my word to help you. I don't give a damn for your inheritance, but I know it means a great deal to you."

She had to raise her head to meet his eyes. "It is all that I have," she said simply.

"Do you forget that you are the Countess of Norwood?" he asked.

"But everything is yours."

"And yours, as my wife."

He leaned toward her, his lips lightly touching hers, sparking the now-familiar electricity between them. She pulled away from him abruptly. "I thought we were to guard against our weakness, my lord," she said with sarcasm. "I believe we are agreed that it would not do to give in to a mere physical attraction which might complicate our affairs."

"I deserve that," he said quietly after a moment of silence.

"You do," she concurred with a brief nod.

He smiled in a wry manner. "When this is finally settled we shall have a great deal to discuss. Perhaps we shall even gain the understanding of each other that has so long eluded us."

"You forget, David, that for me our history began scarcely a month ago."

"Jane has told me that you find your memory increases daily," he said.

"In a general way, of people and things, but not"—she hesitated, and then went on—"but not of any intimacy that we shared."

He smiled again and this time it ws clearly ironic. "I deserve that, too, I suppose."

Evelyn flushed a little because she had not been thinking of their lovemaking, which was how he chose to interpret her remark. "I meant that I believe it would be a mistake for us to attempt to regard each other at all in terms of our shared past. I am not that person now."

"You are and you are not," he said paradoxically.

"I am not," she insisted. "You had the misfortune to marry a woman who never really existed at all. It is as if we are only pretending to be wed and I think the sooner that is put to an end the better."

"I quite agree."

She thought his inflection ambiguous but she did not wish to examine it. She had enough to concern her for the moment. "I promised Jane I would go with her to the lending library this afternoon," she said a bit awkwardly, only wishing for an excuse to leave him.

He reached out and put a hand on her arm. "I pledge you my word, Eve, that you have nothing to fear. Dancer shall not only return to you all that is rightfully yours, he shall do so with interest. One way or another." His tone was so cool she nearly shivered, though she was not sure if it were that or the fact that he had touched her again. His touch, even in such a commonplace way, was erotic. Their eyes held for a long moment and she thought he might once again sweep her into his embrace, but he dropped his hand from her arm and she left unmolested.

Evelyn felt almost sorry that he had accepted her snub. In spite of his rejection of her in the garden, she knew in her heart that she was not averse to the renewal of his lovemaking. He was a controlled man, but perhaps his need for her *was* stronger than his insistence that there be no further intimacy between them, and though she castigated herself for a fool, she felt the first flicker of hope that his feelings for her might go beyond the physical. She could not help what she felt, but her sense told her she dared not refine too much on this or on his behavior. All that he said served to confirm her belief that his regard for her was growing, but she could not know if it was for her or for the woman he had known as Evelyn Walker. It was a fine point, perhaps, but the latter would not be acceptable to her.

Suddenly Evelyn felt like crying. With so many other difficulties facing her, how could she be so stupid as to fall in love with a man who might never be able to return her love as she wished. She reminded herself of her vulnerable state and the likelihood that it was more dependence she felt toward him than love. She would go on with her plans to have their marriage annulled, but considering the snail's pace at which her affairs were advancing, that would doubtless be many months from now, and in the meantime, who knew how either of them would feel toward the other. This bit of common sense helped a great deal to turn her mind to other things, such as the evening ahead of her, and the challenge it held to succeed at her task.

Neither David nor Jane showed the least suspicion when Lady Henrietta called for her. She had told them that she was joining Lady Henrietta for an evening of cards at the home of a mutual, and quite unexceptionable, friend. She had hit on this because Jane had no taste at all for games of chance and would not question why she had not been asked to join them, and David, of course, would not expect to be included with her friends in an evening spent playing for chicken stakes.

Evelyn could feel her heartbeat as the carriage pulled up before her cousin's house. It was nearly seven years since she had been in this house and she could not help but wonder if she would recall it sufficiently to reach the lumber room without hitch. But she banished the thought, knowing she would need all her self-confidence tonight to succeed.

When they entered the house, they were greeted by both Jonathan and his mother. Seeing them together gave Evelyn a little jolt. It was impossible to believe that she could stand talking commonplaces with them as if they were nothing to her. Her aunt was gracious to the point of being condescending, and Evelyn knew it must be at her son's instigation, for Jonathan had doubtless told his mother that she was to be the bait to convince Evelyn to elope with him. In the five years that she had lived at Spedwell, Evelyn could not recall her aunt even once speaking so kindly to her. Anger rose in her, and she used it, as she had before, to strengthen her purpose.

To Evelyn's relief the company, though not large, was sufficient for her brief disappearance to go unnoticed. Her only concern was Jonathan, who hovered over her as much as his duties as host would allow. As the evening wore on she saw her opportunities slipping away from her and her nerves were becoming strained. Once or twice she answered Jonathan rather sharply when he addressed a remark to her and finally he took her up on it.

"I think you are a bit vaporish tonight, my dear," he said as they sat on chairs at the side of the principal saloon sipping an indifferent champagne.

"A little, perhaps," Evelyn admitted, for it would be stupid to deny what was obvious.

"I had hopes it would be otherwise," he said, his smile becoming rueful. "Surely, you see now that you had nothing to fear from my mother. She finds you delightful."

"Will she find me delightful when there is scandal all about our ears?" Evelyn asked dryly.

"I must confess that I have confided in her a bit," he admitted, "though I know it is presumptuous of me when you have not given me your answer. Mama's one unhappiness is that the world will judge *you* unfairly, when it is Norwood who should reap their condemnation, for he has driven you to this step."

"She is all that is generous," Evelyn said, managing to keep the irony out of her voice, "but it frightens me a bit to think that I shall be so utterly in disgrace that I shall be quite at the mercy of both of you. Even my aunt, Mrs. Walker, shall probably disown me."

"My feelings for you matter more than what the world will say," he replied promptly. "And it is I who am at your mercy, beauty," he added. "Only you can decide whether my heart breaks or soars."

Evelyn looked away from him to her hands in her lap, to prevent him from reading in her expression what she thought of his syrupy style of lovemaking; she had not his trick of smiling perpetually to hide her thoughts. She found it difficult to believe that any woman would be responsive to such nonsense, and wondered that he would behave in such an absurd way that was so different from his usual cool and detached manner. He was obviously very determined to have her.

"For now, though, Jonathan, you must not be so particular toward me. I know lady Bessborough is a friend of your mother's but Lord Granville is a friend of David's. She has been staring at us these past several minutes."

"Lady Bessborough is hardly one to make scandal for you, my dear," he said with a dry smile, "but perhaps you are right. It won't do for me to neglect my guests and cause talk that is unnecessary. I shall leave you for a little, my sweeting, but I'll return as soon as I decently may."

Evelyn responded to these words with a smile as false as his own. Once she had accomplished her task she had every intention of pleading a headache and leaving as soon as she could. She did not give anyone else a chance to approach her and delay her further. She got up at once and made her way leisurely across the room to the doorway that led into the main hall.

The ladies' robing room was on the first floor, so it was in no way remarkable for her to ascend the stairs. Evelyn heard laughter coming from the robing room when she reached the upper hall, but the hall itself was empty and she continued on to the next floor.

At the top of the second flight of stairs Evelyn faced a long corridor with a number of closed doors leading off of it. She knew one of these was the lumber room, but for a moment her certainty as to which it was wavered. She hadn't the time to stand guessing, and to open each door and perhaps discover that one of the rooms was occupied was too risky. She decided to trust to her instincts again and went to the door that she *thought* was the correct one and opened it. Once again her intuition did not fail her and she looked into the dark and cluttered room filled with trunks, portmanteaus, and the odds and ends of a household.

The one thing she had not thought of in all her planning was that the room would be in complete darkness. Darkness had not been a factor in her

search of the library at Spedwell, and it had not
occurred to her that she would need to supply light
to find her mother's oak chest. It was too late to do
anything about it now, and she simply opened the
door to its fullest, hoping the light from the sconces
in the hall would illuminate the room at least in part.

She made the best of her situation and went to
work moving various objects as quietly as she could
to uncover the object she sought. It did not prove as
difficult as she feared. Behind two unused reading
lamps, a pie crust table, and a straight-backed chair
with a broken rung, she found the large trunk in
which the oak chest had inadvertently been placed.
Evelyn held her breath, hoping that the trunk would
not be locked, but it opened easily. Evelyn's suspense
was relieved at once; even in the very faint light
filtering in through the doorway, she saw the clear
outline of her mother's chest. She lifted it out of
the trunk and picked her way through the clutter to
gain more light by the open door.

The contents of the chest were in a jumble, no
doubt the result of traveling to London from Limirend.
At first Evelyn did not see the locket and she feared
that Jonathan had assumed it a valuable piece and
filched it from the chest, but she found it resting
beneath a pair of miniatures of her and her brother
when they were very young children. Evelyn felt her
throat constrict; it had been a very long time since
she had allowed herself to remember her brother
and parents and now the memories of a happy life
cut short flooded her thoughts, threatening to bring
her to tears and to jeopardize her mission.

She wished there was some way that she might
take the chest with her, for now that she had seen it
again, she could scarcely bear the thought of leaving
it in her cousin's possession, even if he was unaware
of its existence. But she allowed common sense and
the fact that it would be impossible for her to conceal
more than the locket on her person to prevail. She

closed the chest, put it back in the trunk, and then arranged the things she had moved to reach the trunk in a proximate order to which she had found them.

She stepped into the hall and carefully closed the lumber-room door. Standing in the light of a wall sconce, she opened the locket and revealed a thick curl of titian colored hair intertwined with one of a mahogany hue. She recognized the locks of hair as her parents', but the recognition, instead of deepening her melancholy, made her spirits soar. The redgold hair, which was her father's, was exactly the shade of her own, and she was certain that this must have some significance to her proof of her identity.

Evelyn's heart began to beat a little faster, both from excitement, and because she was very aware of the passage of time and feared that Jonathan must by now have noticed her absence. Her silk gown was designed to flatter and cling and allowed for no such practicalities as pockets, but the locket was not large, and she easily slipped it into her bodice. Feeling it against her breasts, she felt more secure of it than she would have it she had placed it in her reticule.

As she reached the first floor, two young women, vaguely known to Evelyn, came out of the ladies' robing room. Evelyn feared that they would think it strange to find her in the hall, but they returned her smile readily enough and appeared to find nothing strange in her behavior at all.

Evelyn started down the stairs in the wake of the other women, but Jonathan was at the foot of the stairs and came up them quickly until he met her. "Are you ill? I have been searching for you," he said, and Evelyn thought she detected something in his voice besides solicitousness.

"Surely I may spend a few minutes out of your sight?" she said in a voice that was meant to be amused, but which sounded sharp in her own ears.

"I wish you might never be out of my sight," he said, more mechanically than ardently.

His eyes seemed watchful and his smile more fixed than usual. She felt almost certain that he was suspicious. She was about to use a visit to the robing room as her excuse, but ebullient with the confidence of her success, it suddenly occurred to her that now that she had what she wished of him, she need no longer bear his attentions. "Actually, I wished for a few minutes alone to think. What I have realized is that I should never have allowed matters to come to this state. Whatever disagreement there has been between David and me, I could never subject us both to the disgrace of an elopement and divorce."

Jonathan looked startled, but his smile quickly became reassuring and a little condescending. "It is very natural for you to have doubts and fears for our future, but the bonds of our mutual love must see us through, my dearest. You have nothing to fear."

"I am afraid you are being presumptious," she said coolly, raising her chin. "I have never professed to return your feelings."

His smile faded at last and his brows went up. "Now what can have happened in the time since I left you in the saloon to cause this change," he said, almost as if to himself.

"Let us say I have come to my senses," Evelyn replied. "If you would be so kind as to send for Lady Henrietta's carriage, I shall find her and inform her that I have the headache and must leave."

"Do you have the headache?"

"No."

"I see."

"I hope you do, Jonathan," she said. "I have been very foolish to encourage your pretentions and risk losing the affection of my husband. In the future it would be best if we saw as little of each other as possible and conducted ourselves as mere acquaintances." What he thought of her sudden turnabout, she did not care in the least. She was so relieved that she would never again have to suffer his lovemaking that she recklessly decided that it didn't matter, now that she had the locket, if she gave him reason to suspect that her memory had returned. She moved past him and started down the stairs.

On the third stair from the bottom, she felt the locket slip between her breasts. It happened so quickly that she had descended to the next stair before she realized that it had fallen down her dress, and turning quickly, she saw the locket lying on the step behind her. Unfortunately, Jonathan saw it as well and was quicker than she; he scooped it up, but before handing it to her, he took a moment to examine it.

There were three intertwined initials on the back of the locket, "CLF" for Catherine Lydia Fearne. Jonathan traced them with a finger and then looked up at Evelyn, his expression unreadable. "A pretty piece," he said. "I don't recall that you were wearing this in the saloon."

"I wore it inside my gown."

"Would not the chain have shown?" he asked, with no apparent motive beyond curiosity.

Evelyn put out her hand. "May I please have my locket?"

"Are you quite sure it is yours, my dear? These are not your initials."

"It belonged to my mother," she said, seeing no reason to dissemble on that point.

Jonathan's brow knit. "I thought someone told me that your maiden name was Walker, but the last initial is an *F* not a *W*. Perhaps I was mistaken."

"The initial is for my mother's maiden name," Evelyn replied, knowing her voice was quite sharp but not caring. She only wanted him to return the locket to her and to leave him.

"And what might that be?" he asked her in a silky

voice, as he gently ran a thumb over the engraved letters.

"Fenwick," she said, and reached to snatch the locket from his grasp.

He pulled it away before she could take it. "Fenwick," he said musingly. "I am not familiar with the family, but I knew a Catherine Fearne once whose middle initial was L. She was wont to wear a locket very like this one during her lifetime. There is even a portrait of her wearing it, I believe. It is an odd coincidence, is it not? The locket might even be hers. Were it not your mother's, that is."

"Jonathan, give me the locket," she demanded.

"I think not, my dear Evelyn. Or at least not until we have had time to discuss this in more detail."

"You had best give it to her now, Dancer," David's voice said behind Evelyn, causing her to jump. Both she and Jonathan had been so caught up in their cat-and-mouse exchange that neither had heard or noticed his arrival which had coincided with the departure of other guests.

Jonathan's lips came together in a tight line. "We have not yet established that it is the property of Lady Norwood."

"If she says that it is," David said with cool, but unmistakable menace, "then you may trust that it is so. A gentleman does not question the word of a lady."

Jonathan flushed slightly at this deliberate insult. There was a tense silence as the men took each other's measure. Jonathan's gaze shifted to Evelyn and rested on her for a moment, and then his smile was back in place. "But of course you are right," he said, and held out the locket, letting it swing a little on its chain. "I am sunk beneath reproach to have questioned you, my dear Lady Norwood. You must excuse it to my penchant for exactitude."

Evelyn took the locket with trembling fingers, turned, and descended the stairs, not daring to meet

David's eyes. Dancer followed, saying, "This is an unlooked for pleasure, Norwood. I was not aware that my mother had invited you to our simple entertainment tonight."

David checked his progress down the stairs and turned to Dancer. "I came to fetch my wife. She is yet inexperienced in the ways of the *ton* and has not fully developed her sense of social discernment." Their eyes met and held; one pair held contempt and the other frustrated rage. "I am sure you will say everything that is proper to Mrs. Dancer on Lady Norwood's behalf," he added, casting the words over his shoulder as he crossed the hall.

He addressed not a single word to his wife, not even to ask her if she needed to fetch anything from the saloon. His carriage awaited them in front of the house, and even as they pulled away he still said nothing. The silence in the dark carriage was uncomfortable and finally Evelyn could stand it no longer. "How did you know to find me at Mrs. Dancer's rout party?" she asked, managing to keep a tremor out of her voice, though she certainly felt tremulous inside.

"Danbury" was his succinct reply. His tone was cold and she could not doubt that he was very angry with her, but it was a far cry from the rage she had feared.

"Danbury?" she repeated, puzzled. "Martin Danbury? How could he know where I would be?"

"Martin saw you going to the house with Lady Henrietta," David said in a voice of ice. "He was visiting a barque of frailty he has in his keeping a few doors down and wondered what brought you to this section of town. Then he recalled which of your acquaintances lived there amongst the cits and the lightskirts."

It was an unfair assessment of the neighborhood, but Evelyn wisely let it pass. "I knew you would not like it, but I could not sit about forever waiting for Mr. Stevens to make some sort of progress."

"I told you yesterday that he had progressed."

"Yes," she acknowledged, "but he, and even Mr. Ventry, have only verified what we already knew to be fact." She opened her hand and the locket rested in her palm. "It was nothing so positive as this," she said, some of her excitement at her success returning in her relief that there would be no full-scale battle over her defiance.

"The locket proves nothing in itself," he responded, looking at her and not the locket she held out to him. "Stevens himself told you that."

Since it was clear he did not mean to take the locket from her, Evelyn opened it herself. "There is something inside of it," she said, and this time he did take it to examine it.

"It is hair," he said flatly.

She nodded. "Belonging to my mother and father. My hair is exactly the color of my father's," she added eagerly.

"It could be your own," he replied, and after a moment she realized he was not agreeing with her, but saying that she might have put one of her own curls in the locket.

"How could it be? It is entwined quite intricately with the lock of my mother's hair."

"I am only saying what others will say," he replied levelly and closed the locket. "Is there also a convenient portrait of your father at Limirend?"

She ignored the sarcasm in his tone. "Not as an adult, but there is one of him as a boy with his pony and dogs which was used to hang in the dining room. That, along with the portrait of my mother which shows her wearing this very locket, must be considered telling for my assertion that I am a Fearne."

"It tells that you now have in your possession something which once belonged to Mrs. Fearne. It says nothing about how you came by it."

"And the locks of hair?"

"Your hair is a lovely shade, Eve, not common perhaps, but neither is it unique."

She knew she should be glad that he was not raving at her for going to Jonathan's house against his express wish and that it was unwise to court the anger that was clearly just below the surface in his cold manner toward her, but his skepticism piqued her, and she had no doubt his words were meant to be deliberately crushing. "It is very easy for you and Mr. Stevens to be so cautious," she said, knowing she sounded pettish, but not caring. "It is not either of you who must live with uncertainty and falsehood."

She thought she saw a flash of anger in his eyes, but it was dark in the carriage and it was likely only a glimmer from the streetlamp that they passed at that moment. "Nor have either of us anything to lose. It should be you who counsels prudence," he responded, "but instead you have not only jeopardized your name and mine by going to Dancer's house, you have very likely betrayed yourself and warned him of what is to come. I think in the circumstances it would be best if you returned to Blakenhill until Stevens actually needs you here. I can't have you risking disgrace every time you are out of my sight, and I haven't the time or inclination to play nurse-maid to you. I thought I could trust Jane to keep you out of scrapes, but I see that trust was misplaced."

This speech was so cutting and unfair that Evelyn felt angry tears sting her eyes. "I have no intention of returning to Blakenhill," she snapped. "You are not my keeper and neither is Jane." She took breath to calm herself and then went on with cool dignity, "I apologize for disobeying your wish that I not go to Jonathan's house, but I felt it was necessary. I acknowledge that I need your assistance and I am grateful for all that you have done for me, but I prefer to remain here to oversee the progress of this matter myself rather than waiting passively to be informed of what my fate will be. I appreciate that I am a source of bother and annoyance to you, but when this is all settled, we will begin the annulment proceedings and you needn't concern yourself for my welfare or my conduct in the future."

It was an excellent speech and seemed to silence him, for he said nothing for the several minutes that remained until their carriage stopped before Norwood House. But just as the footman was opening the door and lowering the steps, he gave her a long, clear look and said, "There will be no annulment."

There was no time for Evelyn to respond before alighting from the carriage and when they were in the house he curtly brushed aside her attempt to speak with him and proceeded at once up the stairs. She followed him, catching up with him at the door to his bedchamber. "What do you mean? There must be an annulment; I was out of my senses when I married you." She was breathless because she had had to trot to keep up with his long stride.

He turned to her, a faint sardonic smile curling his lips. "Be that as it may, you are my wife and you shall remain so." He saw that she was about to protest and he held up his hand. "It has been a long and wearisome day, Eve, and I am tired. I have no intention of discussing this tonight and certainly not in the hall. Good night." He went into his bedchamber but Evelyn followed him and he would have had to push her out of the room to be rid of her.

He chose instead to ignore her. He shrugged himself out of his black silk evening coat and removed the pin from his cravat, undoing that evening's creation. Evelyn stood, a little irresolute, and watched him. "We have always said that we shall have this marriage annuled as soon as all of my difficulties are settled," she said finally.

"It is you that have said that, not I."

Evelyn did not know what to think. If she could have believed that he loved and wanted her for his wife, she might have been overjoyed, but she could not believe it. "You cannot wish to be married to a stranger any more than I do," she said.

"It is not the *wishes* of either of us that I am consulting," He removed his seal ring and watch fob. "We have been married for nearly two years, and though you may not recall it, you must take my word for it that the marriage has been well and truly consummated. Certainly, it is what the world would believe even were it not so."

"What does that signify?"

"Not a thing if you choose to live out of the world," he replied. "But the world will not accept you if you have no reputation, and if we dissolve this marriage, that will be the case."

"That is absurd," she said, incredulous. "If it were divorce . . . but it is no such thing. Surely no one could hold against me what I did when I was not in my senses. It was perfectly proper and legal at the time in any case."

"You have been returned to your senses for over a month," he said, pulling his shirt free of his silk evening breeches and sitting down to remove his shoes and white silk stockings. "Yet you have lived with me openly as my wife. It is more than a question of your lost maidenhood, my dear, it is your continued virtue that would be in doubt."

He began unbuttoning his shirt, exposing his bare chest to her interested gaze. It was the most she had ever seen—or at least recalled seeing—of a grown man's anatomy. She was fascinated and she forced herself to look away from him. She picked up one of his brushes from his dressing table and examined the enameled design on the back of it to distract her gaze. "We needn't say precisely when I regained my memory," she pointed out.

"Whatever we say, people will think what they wish."

She looked up at him. "But I don't want to be

married to you," she blurted out in dismay. Even as she said it, she knew it wasn't true, at least in the fullest sense; under different circumstances it would be the greatest wish of her heart.

He returned her look for a moment and then dropped his eyes away. "Nevertheless, you are," he said, his tone clipped. "I shall leave it to you, my wife. I would prefer a normal marriage in every sense of the word, but I won't force myself on you if I am not to your taste. Comfort of that sort is not very difficult to come by."

Evelyn forced herself to keep her eyes on his face. She found herself stung by his easy assurance that his physical need could readily be met without her. "If it is legally possible to have the marriage annulled, I intend to do so, whatever you may say," she rejoined. "The world may think what it wishes."

"Without my cooperation, it would be extremely difficult, perhaps impossible," he said quietly. He stood, his shirt open, and started to remove his breeches.

Feeling something akin to panic rising in her, Evelyn dropped her eyes and turned pointedly away from him. "That is ridiculous and odiously stupid," she said angrily. "I won't be married only for the sake of propriety. The man I marry shall *want* me for his wife."

He came up behind her and said softly into her ear, "Oh, but I do want you, my dear Eve."

She quickly moved away from him toward the door without looking around for fear of what she might see. Color tinted her cheeks and she was aware of her beating heart. "I didn't mean in that way." She heard him get into bed and she dared to look back at him. "You are naked," she said, surprised and accusing at once, though it was an assumption since she could only see him from the waist up.

"We were both wont to sleep this way except on the coldest nights," he said provocatively. He slid down between the sheets. "Join me, Evelyn, or leave me in peace to sleep," he said as he turned on his side and plumped his pillows. "If it's the latter, blow out the bed candles before you leave." He then settled himself for sleep and closed his eyes, leaving Evelyn standing there, nonplussed.

She considered his refusal to properly argue the matter odiously unfair, and his ability to put it out of his mind and compose himself for sleep was nothing short of base. But there was not the least thing she could do about it, so she vented her feelings by stomping angrily over to the bed, blowing out the small branch of candles on the bed table with considerable force and slamming the door behind her as she left the room.

When she reached her own room, she was so filled with frustration, she wanted to cry. She had thought she wanted nothing more from him than for him to believe her, but now that she had that it was not enough. She had no more wish for the marriage to be annulled than he did, but for such a very different reason. All the elation she had felt at carrying off the locket under Jonathan's nose had dissipated, and so did that small flicker of hope that David might feel something more for her than mere desire. If it was love, it was creampot love. He wanted a "normal" marriage and he would make love to her because she was his wife. It was nothing to do with loving her; she was a convenient body toward whom he might feel some residual affection from the time they had first been wed. But she could never be his wife for convenience, whatever the consequences.

Her thoughts continued on in this vein and she added it to her list of grievances against him that his rest was apparently not afflicted by doubts such as those that assailed her. On the next morning, she felt dispirited from lack of sleep. She showed the locket to Jane after breakfast, for there was no reason to dissemble now that David knew of her visit to Grove Street.

Jane groaned a little to learn that Evelyn had so handily deceived her, but she was excited over Evelyn's success and disagreed with her brother that Evelyn's possession of the locket and its contents were meaningless. Mr. Ventry, who came into the room as they were discussing it, was also inclined to agree, though Evelyn, who had by now discerned that there was mutual interest between her friend and the secretary, was not sure whether he truly believed what he said, or was just making himself agreeable to Jane. Whatever his true opinion, he promised to take the news of the locket to Mr. Stevens when he went into the City later in the day on business and to faithfully report whatever the solicitor might suggest.

Neither she nor David made any reference to the events of the previous night. She treated him with cool civility to show that he had not cowed her with his bullying, but it gave her no satisfaction. She knew that the intimacy that had been building between them had suffered, and she scarcely knew whether to be sorry or glad.

Evelyn's dread of meeting her cousin again was not immediately realized. Lady Henrietta called before luncheon and informed her that Jonathan had gone to Spedwell on urgent business. The foolish older woman was convinced that some lovers' quarrel had erupted between them at the party and that this accounted for Evelyn's odd departure from the party and Dancer's precipitate journey to Essex.

Evelyn did not know what to think of this, for she could have no doubt that Jonathan's unexpected departure from town was the result of their encounter on the stairs. If that were true, it must mean that their mutual masquerade was finally at an end and his leaving could well have some sinister purpose. Jonathan was clever and resourceful and she could scarcely believe that simply being discovered in his villainy would be sufficient to rout him. She need only to remind herself how well he had coped both with her sudden disappearance from Spedwell and her unexpected reappearance as Lady Norwood to be certain of it.

Evelyn longed to confide her fears to David and lay her burden in his strong, capable hands, but with the estrangement that now existed between them, her pride forbade her to do so. Jonathan's name never surfaced between them, and if David knew that Dancer had left London, he never mentioned this to his wife.

Evelyn's suspense came to an end exactly one week from her aunt's rout party at a ball given by Lady Ponsonby. It was the sort of affair that was destined to be described on the morning after as a "dreadful squeeze." The cream of the *ton* were certain to be present and everyone with any claim to gentility who could scramble for an invitation had pulled out all stops to receive a piece of the coveted pasteboard. Evelyn did not really care for such large entertainments but she went deliberately with the thought that if Jonathan were in town she would be very likely to meet him there.

She was not disappointed, though at first she thought that she would be. It was an uncommonly warm night and as the evening wore on and the ballroom and adjoining anterooms filled with revellers, the warmth became insupportable. It was close to midnight and the last set was forming before the musicians retired to rest and the guests went in to supper. Evelyn was promised to Martin Danbury for the last set, but she took the privilege of a friend and begged him to excuse her, pleading the heat and exhaustion. He readily complied, and after seeing to it that she was comfortably seated in one of the chairs provided for chaperones, he went off to find her a glass of champagne punch.

Evelyn was more hot and tired than she was hungry or thirsty and she decided that as soon as the country dance was ended, she would find Jane, who was standing up with Roger Ventry, and inform her that she was returning to Norwood House. She had no intention of spoiling her sister-in-law's pleasure in the evening, nor did she wish to seek out David, who, after dutifully standing up with one or two ladies of his acquaintance, had retired to one of the card rooms. She would return home alone and send the carriage back for the others.

She began to scan the room for a sight of Jane or Mr. Ventry, which proved a very difficult task in the overcrowded ballroom. "Are you searching for Norwood, dear lady?" said a silky voice at her elbow. "I saw him just this moment as I passed the refreshment room. He was speaking with his friend Danbury."

Evelyn looked up at her cousin, who was standing beside her chair. On his arm was an attractive young woman with pale, titian colored hair and brown eyes. She was about Evelyn's age and of a similar height and form. Jonathan saw Evelyn's lips part in surprise, and his smile, which was quite mirthless, broadened a little. "Please permit me to present my cousin Miss Fearne to you, Lady Norwood. 'Eve,'" he said, addressing his companion, "this is Evelyn, Countess of Norwood. You see Lady Norwood is called by the same given name as you. Perhaps that may be a bond between you that will foster friendship. I hope it may be so, for Lady Norwood is a particular friend of mine."

The young woman curtsied prettily and murmured a shy greeting, but Evelyn scarcely noticed her. Her eyes were on Dancer, whose eyes were on her. Even before he had performed the introduction, a flicker of apprehension had assailed her. She was utterly nonplussed. Even though David had warned her that it was not out of the realm of possibility that Jonathan would try to thwart her by producing his own "Evelyn Fearne" as a counter claimant, she had not really believed that he would carry it to that length.

"I have spoken of you often to my cousin," he said to Evelyn with a purr in his voice that reminded her of a cat in a creampot, "and she has been most anxious to meet you."

"I—I had no notion that you had a cousin," Evelyn said, knowing it was a stupid remark, but feeling that she needed to say something. "That, is, Mr. Dancer has *not* spoken of you, Miss Fearne," she added, and her eyes, which were sitll on Jonathan said clearly what she thought of him.

"I have been unwell," Miss Fearne replied in a voice that was die away enough to give justice to this statement, "and have lived retired for more than a year, but now I am feeling much better, and Jonathan" —she paused to look up at him with something like admiration—"insisted that I come to town and make my curtsy to the *ton*."

Jonathan patted his charge on the hand in an avuncular way. "You shall do quite well, my dear. No doubt Lady Norwood, who is all kindness to her friends, will assist you by introducing you to her particular friends," he added brazenly. Addressing Evelyn, he then said, "I see you do not wear your mother's locket tonight, Lady Norwood."

Evelyn had known there would be fencing between them on their next meeting, but the remark nevertheless caught her off guard. "It did not suit my gown," she replied coolly, though her heart was beating rapidly.

He raised his brows slightly. "I had thought its value to you was beyond the dictates of fashion."

"Its value is great," she concurred. "So great that it is now in the proper hands for safekeeping." Evelyn thought she saw something pass in his eyes at her words, but could not be certain.

He flicked a speck of lint from the sleeve of his coat. "You are very wise," he agreed with no apparent show of concern. "One cannot be too careful." He glanced toward the doorway. "Ah, here is Mama,

Eve," he said, and Evelyn was still startled to realize
it was not her he addressed. "You will forgive us,
Lady Norwood. My mother has a number of friends
she wishes to make acquainted with her niece." His
smile became odiously triumphant.

Mrs. Dancer approached them, but behind her
David entered the ballroom and Evelyn at once caught
his eye and broadcast her appeal. He acknowledged
this by following in the dowager's wake. "David,"
Evelyn said the moment he reached them and before
Jonathan could speak, "this is Mr. Dancer's cousin,
Miss Fearne."

If David were surprised he had the aplomb not to
show it. Instead he greeted "Miss Fearne" with considerably more cordiality than Evelyn had done. Before there could be further conversation, the final
set was finished and the company began a general
exodus toward the supper rooms. To Evelyn's astonishment, David at once begged permission to escort
Miss Fearne in to supper. A friend of Mrs. Dancer
offered his escort to her and Evelyn was left to her
cousin, who immediately offered his arm. Evelyn
accepted it and used the opportunity to pick up the
gauntlet that Jonathan had thrown down. "Your
scheme will fall flat once the truth is known," she
said, speaking softly so that they would not be
overheard.

His mobile brows went up. "Ah, we are to take the
points off our swords, I gather," he said. "It is better
so, perhaps. Do not be too certain, my dear Evelyn.
The advantage is mine, I think. It will be so much
easier for the world to believe me, you see. Then
there is the question of time. You attained your
majority more than a year ago but have made no
claim to your inheritance."

"I had lost my memory," she retorted.

"So I deduced, and now it is regained, but will the
world believe it? It is so farfetched, don't you agree?
My Evelyn Fearne, you see, has been ill and in pri-

vate care—a fact well known to my friends and acquaintances, and so much easier to credit."

Evelyn kept her expression as pleasant as she could
so that no one would guess at their conversation, but
her eyes flashed anger. "It won't work, Jonathan,"
she said through a false smile. "I won't let you cheat
me of my inheritance."

"Your inheritance?" he said with a laugh that was
meant to be offensive. "It is Miss Fearne who is the
rightful claimant. Who are you, my dear?"

"You know perfectly who I am," she said through
her teeth. "And I shall prove it to the world."

"With what?" he asked as they passed through the
doorway of the supper room. "That paltry locket that
you stole from my house. It is the one from the portrait, is it not? I doubt it will count for much, and it has
very definitely occurred to me, you know, that if you
had something more you would not have risked that
particular theft. In fact," he added, as if musing on the
thought, "if you had any positive proof, I fancy
we would not be having this conversation at all."

"You would be in jail," Evelyn said in a hissing
whisper, and then was angry with herself for telling
him what he had doubtless most wished to know.

The Dancers and the alleged Miss Fearne continued as part of their party even after the Norwoods
were joined by Jane and Mr. Ventry, but no further
private conversation was possible. Evelyn was glad of
it, but her relief was short-lived as she watched David conversing with the impostor. It was reasonable
to suppose that David gave her so much of his attention to learn what he could of Dancer's scheming,
but there was something in David's manner toward
Miss Fearne that Evelyn felt was unnecessarily warm
to the point of flirtation and it was obvious that Miss
Fearne was quite willing to receive these attentions.
Jonathan, watchful for her discomfiture, favored her
with an unpleasant little smile that underscored her
suppressed anger and frustration.

After what seemed to Evelyn an interminable supper, their parties at last separated. Jane clearly was anxious to discuss this development with Evelyn, but the latter, pleading the danger of being overheard, put her off. Evelyn was not equally reluctant to speak with David and managed to draw him aside. At the far side of the ballroom were several sets of doors leading out to small balconies that overlooked the garden. They found one of these unoccupied and offering a reasonable degree of privacy.

"Can you believe that Jonathan would dare to do such a thing?" she said the moment they had stepped outside.

"I believe I mentioned it as a possibility," he said without any smugness. "I am not sure I really believed he would do so, though. He must feel quite certain that you have not the means of exposing him and his impostor."

Evelyn wished to avoid this turn in their conversation, for she was acutely aware that it was her venture to Grove Street that both caused Jonathan's introduction of Miss Fearne and convinced him that it was a risk worth taking. "I wonder where he found her?" she said. "Could he really have had her tucked away all this time against the possibility that he would need her? It seems incredible that he would do so, and yet a sennight is a very short time for him to have found someone suitable and rehearsed her in all that she would need to know."

"What would she need to know?" David inquired. "As far as society is concerned, Evelyn Fearne is a cipher. Who is there who has known you since childhood who could give her the lie? Dancer needed only to school her in the particulars of your background so that she would not appear ignorant if questions were asked. Whatever her character and personality, it will be acceptable because no precedent has been set for the behavior of Miss Fearne, and besides us, only the Dancers know that she is an impostor."

Evelyn digested this. "What manner of woman can she be to do such a thing?" she said indignantly.

"An actress offered generous compensation for the part she is to play. A provincial actress, most likely, for Dancer wouldn't be fool enough to use someone known on the London stage."

"And it was just his good fortune to come across such a one when he needed her?" Evelyn asked with obvious disbelief.

David smiled in response. "It is more likely that he has known her for some time and that she was ready to step into the role should it ever prove necessary. He may even have cultivated her acquaintance with that in mind."

"And now what am I to do?" Evelyn asked, trying to keep despair at bay. "It would have been hard enough to convince the world that I am Evelyn Fearne with Aunt Lavinia and Jonathan refusing to acknowledge me; it will be a thousand times more difficult now. It was stupid to risk confrontation before we were ready," she added with bitter self-recrimination.

David resisted the temptation to say that he had warned her. "I'll speak with Mr. Stevens on Monday," he said, but if this was meant to reassure her, the attempt fell flat.

"Stevens is an old woman," Evelyn said, dismissing the legal skills of a man who represented a fair percentage of the richest and most powerful families in the realm. "He will probably want to interview every provincial and touring company in England, Scotland, and Wales before proceeding."

"And Ireland, too, no doubt," David said, smiling.

"He is plodding," Evelyn insisted.

"He is careful. We must accept that we have lost our advantage, but that is no reason to proceed until we have secure cause for doing so. In fact, it is all the more reason to be provident."

Evelyn was in no humor to be reasonable. "And while we are being so careful and clever, what is to prevent Jonathan and his . . . his minion from liquidating all that I possess and absconding with it?"

"Now that would be incautious. Whatever measures he may take to protect his interest in your inheritance, he knows the truth is on your side and there is always the risk that the truth will out."

Evelyn was not encouraged by this. "If we are able to prove the truth, he will be ruined in any case. He has little to lose."

"He would have his neck to lose" was David's quick response, annoying Evelyn that he could so readily counter all her objections. "Embezzlement could take him to Tyburn. I may be wrong, of course . . ." He paused as his wife made a sound that was suspiciously like a snort. "I may be wrong," he went on, "but I think his motive is to prevent public confrontation. If he can convince you beforehand that he has bested you and that laying claim to your father's inheritance would net you nothing but scandal, you may just give it up."

Evelyn's hazel eyes flashed. "I will never give it up."

"No. I know you will not," he said with a dry smile. "But Dancer has clearly underestimated you before and he may do so again. As my wife you enjoy a fortune far greater than your own and want for nothing. Dancer may well doubt that you would take up the cudgel for a cause that will make you the *on dit* of the *ton* and which may well end in failure."

"He is mistaken," she said, but in a less martial manner. "You think that a slow and steady course will answer?" she added, still doubtful.

"When open confrontation finally comes, it must be from a position of strength." He held out his hand to her and she got up. "We had better go inside before they begin to think we are making love in the moonlight."

"Oh, no one would think that," she said in an offhand way. "We are married."

His tone was bland. "No doubt you are right."

Since her own efforts had not met with particular success, Evelyn agreed to do just as David wished this time, but she quickly chafed under the resolution after she had spoken to the cautious Mr. Stevens on Monday. He did indeed propose a course of action similar to what Evelyn had suggested in sarcasm, though not at such exaggerated lengths. Further, to her annoyance, he insisted on searching the records of other parishes where people of the surname of Fearne where known to reside to see if there had been another Miss Fearne with the Christian name of Evelyn, just in case it were freakishly possible that it was legally the impostor's name. Nor was he particularly enthusiastic about the locket, saying merely that comparing it to the portrait at Limirend would doubtless be a help should they need it.

"In the end, no doubt, all his research will serve to convince *me* that I am not Evelyn Fearne," she said acidly to David when the solicitor had gone. But David refused to be drawn into an argument and Evelyn was reduced to animadverting against lawyers, husbands, and wicked cousins to Jane, who listened dutifully but made it no secret that she agreed with her brother and the solictor.

8

The next fornight was an exceptionally difficult time for Evelyn. Whenever she met her cousin, she read his constant smile as smug and her fingers ached to slap the smirk off his face. It did not help her humor that Jonathan's neglect of her was now equal to his previous attention and that it was generally regarded that he had abandoned her in pursuit of his charge. Within only a few days of Miss Fearne's introduction to society, the *on-dit* was that she and Dancer had had a previous understanding and that their betrothal would be announced before the Season came to an end.

The Season was gradually winding to a close, and already several of the first families of the *ton* had retired to their country seats for a little quiet time prior to converging on Brighton or Cheltenham for the summer. As things quieted down, the gossips seized on any little thing that might interest, and to Evelyn's further discomfiture, she learned that it was being said that David, too, found something to interest him in the newcomer, with the most vicious of the harpies suggesting that Evelyn was about to find herself hoist with her own petard for the talk she had raised by her flirtation with Dancer.

In fairness, she could not call David's attendance on Miss Fearne pointed, but he did occasionally single Miss Fearne out for conversation, at times taking her a little aside so that they might be more private. Evelyn assumed that his attention to her rival was purely for the sake of learning what he could to expose her and Jonathan; but however pure David's motive might be, Evelyn discovered that she found his conduct discomfiting. She would not admit to jealousy because she was determined not to be in love with him, yet every time she saw them together, however innocently, her dislike of it grew.

This situation, combined with the plodding progress of Mr. Stevens, was beginning to erode Evelyn's even temper. The search for some person who might readily identify her, and whose motive for doing so would be unquestionably pure, had still met with no success. Neither had interviewing managers of provincial acting companies discovered any actress of Miss Fearne's description who had recently left their companies.

Evelyn knew her complaints on this subject were becoming tiresome, but it was so much in her thoughts that she was in danger of losing all other conversation. David was surprisingly patient with her, but after a fortnight of listening to her constant lament, he finally suggested that since Evelyn found nothing to please her in town, it might be wise for them to retire to Blakenhill for the summer.

"Where we may sit about doing nothing exactly as we do here," she said irritably.

They were in Evelyn's sitting room waiting for Jane to join them before leaving for an al fresco party being given by Lady Hertford—and, unofficially, the Prince of Wales—at Richmond. David sat slouched in a chair near the open window, catching what breeze he could, for the weather had remained warm since Lady Ponsonby's ball. He turned his gaze from the window and looked up at Evelyn. "What do you wish to do, Eve?" he said, his voice tart. "Do you wish Stevens to bring claim to your father's estate at once, pitting your word against Dancer's? If you do, I shall send him word of it before we leave for Richmond."

In spite of her impatience, Evelyn recognized the foolhardiness of this and was annoyed with David for forcing her to admit it. "What I do not wish," she said acerbically, "is to leave town and the field to Jonathan and That Woman."

"Then we shall remain here," he concurred.

But Evelyn would not leave it be. "I am surprised you would wish to leave town."

He shrugged. "It is a matter of indifference to me. I don't think it matters particularly whether we stay here or return to Blakenhill, but if you prefer to keep an eye on Dancer, we shall stay."

Abandoning subtlety, she said, "Then you may also keep an eye on Miss Fearne." She had meant the words to be spoken in a quizzing way, but her tone was sharper than she intended.

His eyes opened a little wider and a faint smile curled his lips. "Yes, so I may," he said as if it had just occurred to him. "Do you object?"

Evelyn looked away from him and walked over to the window with her back to him. "It is not a personal objection," she said with an indifference that did not quite succeed. "But if you are particular in your attentions to her, you will court the very sort of gossip you have warned me against with Jonathan."

"Have my attentions been particular?" he asked after a pause.

"You could best answer that," Evelyn replied a bit snappishly.

Evelyn's assumption that David's interest in Miss Fearne was purely academic was correct. He was playing the same sort of cat-and-mouse game with her that Evelyn herself played with Jonathan, but David was more optimistic about results. The young actress—though he fancied that was a polite term for her true profession—was becoming increasingly discomfited by his veiled hints that the deception she was practicing would end in something more than disgrace. It was not his intention to arouse jealousy in Evelyn, but he was not displeased by her display of it.

Lady Hertford's al fresco party was to be one of the capping entertainments of the Season, followed that same evening by one of the Prince of Wales' famous musical evenings at Carlton House. The day was talked of and planned for weeks by everyone who was fortunate enough to have received the coveted invitations. The number of guests at Lady Hertford's party would be many, but the matrimonial difficulties of the Prince had prevented him from entertaining in a grand way at Carlton House, and the company there would be relatively small and more select.

The Norwoods received invitations for both because David's father had been a particular friend of the Duke of York and his mother one of Queen Charlotte's ladies. Evelyn had not expected to find her cousin at Richmond, but he had somehow managed to wrangle an invitation for himself and his ward. His presence did nothing to improve Evelyn's humor, for she was heartily tired of deflecting Jonathan's caustic comments designed to convince her that she had been bested, and she certainly had had her fill of Miss Fearne, whose demureness she felt was patently false.

For Evelyn there was little pleasure in the day. Her sharp tongue drove her husband to seek more congenial company, but she was less than pleased to be so abandoned, and she made a point of being cheerful and gay with other of her friends to punish him. After the picnic luncheon had been served, the company broke up into small groups, strolling about the grounds to ease the effects of food that was rich and plentiful. Jane and Mr. Ventry invited her to join them in this activity, but Evelyn declined. She had noted that Jonathan was in conversation with Lord Hertford and Sir William Congreve, and Miss Fearne was for once not attached to his side. She then looked about the stretch of park where luncheon had been served and noted the absence of her husband. It did not follow that the two disappearances were related, but Evelyn had a sick feeling near her heart that she did not wish to examine, but which she could not ignore. She recalled that David had not denied his interest in Miss Fearne, though at the time, she had supposed that his reason was to pay her back for her sharp tongue.

Admitting no objective, even to herself, Evelyn strolled about the garden, refusing all escort. Though her wandering gave no appearnce of purpose, her progress was steady and in a definite direction. Finally, she came to a small copse a little apart from the area where most of the company was to be found, and there she discovered her husband, so deep in conversation with Miss Fearne that neither noticed her approach. There was nothing improper in their behavior other than the fact that they had sought privacy for their discussion.

Evelyn had satisfied her perverse desire to prove that David's interest in Miss Fearne was more than academic, but she was far from feeling satisfaction. Sense told her to be content with her knowledge, but she could not retrace her steps as if her discovery had no import. She told herself that she did not intend to spy on them, but she continued to approach the copse with considerasble stealth.

She got as close to the thicket as she dared and then paused as if she were examining a flowering shrub that was near the tree under which they stood. She could hear their voices well enough, but at first she could not understand what was being said because Miss Fearne was speaking and her voice was soft and low-pitched. But when David spoke, she heard quite well, and wished she had not. "You would do much better to trust yourself to my protection," he said quietly, but distinctly. "I can offer you more than Dancer and I keep my promises." He put a finger under her chin and raised her head, a gesture Evelyn knew only too well. "Trust me and I promise you there will be no regrets."

Evelyn felt as if her stomach had dropped to her toes. She no longer had any wish to know what would occur and she moved quickly away from the trees, not wanting to be seen by either of them. But she was not as unobserved as she had hoped. She had not progressed too far from the copse when David caught up with her and fell into pace beside her. Though Evelyn did not mean to show by what she said or did that she had overheard him offering his protection to Miss Fearne, the emotions this had aroused in her were too intense to be denied, and when he asked her with deliberate casualness if she were enjoying the party, angry tears threatened to choke her, and her response was a brief, but fulminating stare.

"What's amiss, Eve?" he asked quietly.

She did not slow her pace and refused to look at him again. "Why should there be anything wrong?" she replied, having gained control of her voice.

He gave a brief laugh. "You look as if you wish to box my ears."

"It is nothing to do with you," she said, determined to maintain her dignity. "I have the headache."

"Do you wish us to leave?"

"I would not wish to spoil *your* pleasure in the day." She could not prevent the waspishness in her tone.

He gave no indication that he had noticed her acidity. "It wouldn't give me pleasure to remain, knowing you were in pain."

"I was not aware that I was in any way necessary to your pleasure."

Her pace had quickened to the point that conversation was becoming difficult. David came to a stop, and because he had linked her hand in his arm, she was forced to do the same. "Why don't you tell me what we are really speaking of, Eve?" he said evenly.

"I don't know what you mean."

"You do," he insisted. "You are implying that I prefer the pleasure of Miss Fearne's company." She did not reply; her features were rigid in the effort to control her emotions. "You saw us together just now, didn't you," he asked quietly.

"I wish you would not call her that," Evelyn said angrily, her voice rising a little, unintentionally. "It is not her name."

"It is the only one I know," he replied. "If we are going to wash our dirty linen in public, perhaps we had better leave." He started walking again, steering her in the direction of the waiting carriages.

"I prefer to stay," she said frostily, and stopped at the edge of the clearing where the carriages stood. "Though no doubt you would much prefer it were I not present," she added meaningfully.

They were within earshot of several servants who were talking in small groups and playing games of chance. A few looked up curiously at their approach and David turned Evelyn around and returned a few steps in the direction they had come. "If you wish to ring a peal over me for real or imagined crimes, you may do so," he said in a voice that was obviously controlled, "but not until we have reached the privacy of our own home. I have dealt with all the scandal caused by you that I intend to."

"It isn't I making scandal now," she snapped. "I suppose I have no claim on your fidelity, but I would not have supposed you would be cruel enough to make the one choice of inamorata that would be most humiliating to me."

His lips parted as if in surprise and then his features softened and he nearly smiled. "You are right," he said, quiet in contrast to her heat. "You have no claim to my fidelity. But you are mistaken in my intentions toward Miss Fearne."

Evelyn gave a little snort of bitter laughter. "You offered her your protection. I heard you say it."

"The great peril of eavesdropping is hearing words out of context. I was trying to convince her that it was in her best interest to leave Dancer and throw her lot with us."

She pulled her arm free of his hand. "David, I saw you as well as heard you," she said, her voice choking a little in spite of her effort to control it. "You were making love to her."

He did not reply at once. A part of Evelyn wanted him to deny her words, but he did not. "Do you think so?" he asked quietly. "If it were not Miss Fearne, would it matter to you?"

"Not at all," she replied, perilously close to tears.

Jane came up the path toward them. "Good heavens," she said when she reached them, sounding mildly exasperated. "What is the matter with both of you? People are staring and starting to whisper. Do you *wish* to stir up gossip?"

"Evelyn has the headache and is feeling out of sorts," David replied. "I was about to take her home."

"Then do so for pity's sake," Jane said, "before we are forced to rusticate for a month to avoid the stares."

"I am not going anywhere with you," Evelyn said defiantly to David, for she had no wish to find herself inside a closed carriage with him for the length of the drive home.

"Then go with Jane," he suggested curtly.

Of the three of them, Jane was the only one who was truly enjoying the party and had no wish to leave, but she decided that prudence was better than pleasure. "That would be best, I think," she said in a soothing manner. "Come, Eve. As soon as we are home, I shall bathe your temples with violet water and you will soon be more the thing."

All argument seemed to have died out of Evelyn and she followed Jane meekly to their carriage. She dared a quick glance behind them, but David was no longer to be seen. Evelyn felt both heartsick and

furious at once. When they were inside the carriage
and started on the journey home, Evelyn's tattered
emotions overwhelmed her and she began to weep
with great heartrending sobs.

Jane did what she could to comfort her. "Whatever is the matter, dearest?" she asked as soon as
Evelyn began to quieten a bit. "I had thought that
you and David had begun to mend your fences."
Her brow knit into a pensive frown. "You are not
increasing are you, Eve?"

Scarlet flooded Evelyn's cheeks. "No, of course
not. That is, I could not be," she added, her confusion evident.

Jane sighed a little, as if that news saddened her.
"I do not wish to pry, but I am truly puzzled, and it
is only because I care so much for both of you that I
wish to understand what is happening. If you cannot
care for David, why has arguing with him made you
cry so?"

"Because he is the most vexing man I have ever
known," Evelyn said, but she could not keep a slight
quiver out of her voice and suddenly she was overset
again. Jane put her arms around her and Evelyn
wept for a few moments more on her sister-in-law's
shoulder. She had no intention of confiding in Jane,
but she could no longer bear the strain of keeping
her pent up emotions to herself. "He is the most
vexing man I know," Evelyn repeated in a voice
choked with tears, "and at times I think I hate him.
B-but I think I am more afraid that I have fallen in
love with him."

Jane let out an exclamation of joy. "But that is
wonderful! Why should you be afraid of loving David? He is your husband."

"He does not love me."

Jane was genuinely surprised. "That is nonsense. I
think David has been in love with you from the day
that you met."

"That was then," Evelyn insisted, speaking between

sniffs while she opened her reticule to find a hand-kerchief. "It is not the same now."

"I would not refine too much on matters as they stand now," Jane advised. "If David seems cold at times, it is just that he has been heart bruised once, and now he is shy of his own vulnerability."

Evelyn shook her head to indicate her disbelief. "He loved the woman he thought I was when he married me." She spoke quietly, once again in control. "Oh, he has some feeling for me, I suppose, but it is more lust than love, and it is not even exclusive to me. He was making love to . . . to that creature calling herself by my name. That was why we were fighting."

Jane's surprise became astonishment. "I cannot imagine David doing such a stupid, cruel thing. Why on earth would you suppose that he would?"

"I saw it with my own eyes, Jane," she said, a little angry to have her word doubted.

"I don't know what you saw, but there must be some explanation for it," Jane assured her. "Even if David did have an interest in Miss Fearne, he would never be so indiscreet."

"If you do not believe me, ask David," Evelyn said a bit pettishly. "I confronted him and he did not even bother to deny it." The carriage pulled up before Norwood House and Evelyn was very glad to have the conversation brought to an end. Jane's pragmatism did little to reassure her, and she still lacked the sympathy she had hoped for. She pleaded the headache to keep Jane from continuing their discussion and used the same excuse to take dinner in her room. She had no notion when David returned to the house, for he did not come to her and she did not again leave her room. Jane stopped in to say good night as they were leaving for Carlton House, but she was alone and made no mention at all of her brother. Evelyn supposed she had given David a disgust of her which she supposed hardly mattered but which made her wretchedly unhappy in spite of her determination that it should not.

Whatever Evelyn might have seen at Richmond, Jane could not credit that her brother would make love to Miss Fearne under Evelyn's nose. She might have supposed that it was a revenge of sorts for Evelyn's behavior with Dancer, but she knew her brother too well to believe him capable of such petty behavior. Yet Evelyn had seen something to upset her, and hoping as she did that David and Evelyn would again find the love they had shared at the beginning of their marriage, Jane wished she might set Evelyn's mind at ease and remove the fear and misunderstanding that prevented Evelyn from opening her heart to David.

Jane hinted to her brother that Evelyn's headache resulted more from their argument than from any physical cause, but further than that she did not dare go without betraying Evelyn's confidence. David acknowledged this information with no outward display of emotion and gave every appearance of taking unimpaired pleasure in the evening.

The following morning found Evelyn as dispirited as the night before and no attempt by Jane to raise her from the doldrums met with success. This troubled Jane sufficiently that she at last voiced her concern to David. "Eve is impatient and feeling a little frustrated and sorry for herself," he said shrewdly, if unfeelingly, in reply. "She knows prudence will best serve her, but it is a hard course to follow while she watches Dancer play out his hand and take the rubber. But the game is far from over, and a bit of rest may be the very thing for her now."

It was hardly the speech of a man concerned for the happiness of the woman he loved and Jane began to wonder for the first time if perhaps she could be mistaken about his feelings for Evelyn. While Evelyn spent the day quietly in her sitting room with a book that remained mostly unread, David was out for much of the morning, and when he returned, he spent the remainder of the day closeted in his study with Mr. Ventry.

The rumors of Lord Addleby's imminent resignation were rampant as was the speculation that David would be offered his post. Jane knew how very much the appointment would mean to David, and she knew equally how perilously close it was to eluding him because of the threat of domestic scandal. David was a sensible man; it was hard to believe he would risk his painstakingly built political career for a transitory passion or a petty revenge.

She wished she might confide her concerns to Roger Ventry, for his clear thinking always served to put her fears in perspective, but he remained with David nearly until dinner time and then was off on an errand for his employer, so that she had not opportunity to speak with him at all.

Again Evelyn preferred to remain at home for the evening, though they were invited to a ball at Devonshire House and Evelyn had had a new gown made especially for the occasion. Allowing that her brother might be right in his judgment that rest would be good for Evelyn, who had, after all, been under tremendous strain both before and since her memory had returned, Jane did not press her to join them.

As discreetly as possible, Jane spent much of the night observing her brother, and what she saw did not reassure her. He did not precisely dance attendance on Miss Fearne, but he stood up with her twice and a third set was sat out while they conversed on a sofa in a corner of the room. There was nothing in their manner to suggest they were lovers, but the gossips would not care for that.

Jane also noted that Jonathan Dancer followed David and Miss Fearne with his eyes when they were together, and by his expression it was obvious that he was not pleased. Therefore, when a casual search of the room after supper failed to discover either

David or Miss Fearne, Jane's concern was twofold. She feared for Evelyn's sake that they had slipped away to find privacy for their lovemaking and for herself and her family she feared the scandal that would be inevitable if Mr. Dancer sought them out and caused a scene.

Unaware of the turmoil he was causing in his sister's breast, David deftly separated Miss Fearne from her party and maneuvered her with skill through the supper room, an adjoining card room, a short corridor used principally by servants, and into a small sitting room that was the furthest anteroom from the main ballroom. Miss Fearne made not the least objection to this, and a small, self-satisfied smile indicated that she was rather enjoying the attentions of Lord Norwood.

He led her to a small sofa, and when he did not at once embrace her, Miss Fearne made a small *moue* of disappointment. "Do you mean to preach at me again, my lord," she said archly, her accent flawlessly refined. She had either breeding and education beyond usual for a member of her calling, or else she was a particularly good actress who never allowed herself to be caught out of character. "I thought you had quite another purpose for spiriting me away from my duenna."

A faint smile that was seductive and meant to be, played on his lips. "Surely a maiden of gentle birth would not willingly court the advances of a married gentleman?" he said, his voice softly quizzing.

She placed a hand on his arm. "A lady is still a woman," she said, and leaned toward him suggestively.

He bowed his head toward her, his lips close to hers but not quite closing the tantalizing distance. "Do you really believe that a man who would cheat his own cousin out of her inheritance will keep his word to you?" he asked, his voice husky as if he were speaking words of love.

Miss Fearne moved back from him abruptly. "You

do mean to harangue me," she said, annoyed. She stood. "I wish to return to my aunt."

David took her arm and pulled her back onto the sofa none too gently. "It is time for us to remove our gloves, Miss Fearne. I had word from my solicitor today that his assistant has finally located a former servant from Spedwell who is certain she can positively identify Evelyn and is willing to do so. I have sent my secretary into Kent where she resides now to interview her. If he is convinced that her motive is disinterested, he will return with her in hand and then, I fear, the game is up."

Miss Fearne gave vent to an exasperated sigh, but ther was a watchfulness about her eyes. "Why do you continue to insist that I am other than I say?"

"Because we both know that you are not Evelyn Fearne."

"Everyone else accepts me without question," she said, raising her chin. "It is only you who claim otherwise. Yet you haven't the courage to challenge me publicly."

"Tomorrow, or perhaps the next day, I shall," he said quite casually.

"Why should I believe you?" she asked, a wary note in her voice.

"Why should you be concerned if you are innocent of deception?" he countered.

"I am not concerned," she replied, but her tone carried no conviction.

David smiled. "I am the only protection you can hope for. Defrauding the estate of an orphan is a capital offense if there is no plea for clemency. Is whatever Dancer has promised you worth the risk of your life?" She regarded him with the intensity of a mouse cornered by a ferret. "In fact," he added almost as an afterthought, "it is not out of the question that Dancer will throw you to the dogs. He may try to convince the world that he, too, was duped."

Though she remained virtually expressionless, David knew that at last he had broken through her armor and her next words proved him right. "He told me that Evelyn Fearne was dead but that it had happened in a private asylum and no one knew. When you told me that Lady Norwood was Evelyn Fearne, Jonathan said it was a hum, that she was only some sort of distant connection trying to secure the inheritance for herself."

"He lied." David regarded her thoughtfully. "I suppose he promised you a share of the fortune."

"Half."

David's laugh at this was not studied. "I would have taken you for a sharp rather than a flat. You can't have believed Dancer would be so generous, Miss Fearne. By the way, I would as soon not call you Miss Fearne any longer," he added. "I presume you have another name."

"Molly Jenkins," she replied without hesitation. "It seemed a bit good to me," she admitted, "but he couldn't claim the inheritance at all without me."

"He would have found the way to cheat you," David assured her. "It is a mistake to underestimate Dancer. He's determined, and that could make him dangerous."

Molly looked skeptical, but she smoothed her skirt with a restless little movement and said, almost as if to herself. "There have been times . . ." She stopped abruptly and said in a very different way, "Do you truly have the proof you claim, or am I being another sort of fool?"

"The foolish thing would be to trust Dancer," he replied without directly answering her. "I certainly won't promise you half of my wife's fortune, but you shall be well paid, I promise you. And," he added, with just a touch of silky intimidation, "*if* you help us, you may have my word that there will be no prosecution for your part in the fraud."

Molly rose abruptly. It was obvious that a belated disquiet had come upon her. "I should never have told you what I have," she said. "If Jonathan were to know . . ." She left the sentence uncompleted, but an involuntary shiver went through her. She saw that David had noticed and she forced a smile. "Someone walking over my grave," she said lightly. "I am letting myself get caught up in the melodrama. You had best forget what I have told you, my lord. I shall deny it if you do not."

David rose slowly. "But you have told me your name," he said gently. "I shouldn't think my solicitor will have an impossible time tracing your true past, Molly." The look that came into her eyes was definitely hunted. "You are afraid of Dancer," he said, and it was not a question.

"Of course not," she said shortly, and turned away from him. "He is a bit short of temper at times but he has never touched me."

"But you fear it," he insisted. David put his hand on her shoulder and his touch was gentle. "It is all the more reason to throw your lot with me, Molly. There are private papers belonging to my wife's father that Dancer has in his possession. They are probably in a lock box that he keeps in his library or study at Grove Street. Find them and bring them to me, and I shall see to it that Dancer's wrath falls on me instead of you."

"How could you?" she asked without turning around.

"Once I have the proof of Evelyn's identity combined with your defection and the financial records of the Fearne estate, Dancer will have far more to concern him than enacting a petty revenge on you for your duplicity."

She said nothing, but David knew she was weighing his words. "My aunt must be missing me by now," she said at last, and casting David only a brief glance over her shoulder, she left the room.

David retraced his steps to the ballroom at a leisurely pace, but Molly was not much before him. In the hall beside the card room, she stood with Jonathan. David heard no words spoken as he approached them, but their posture made the import of their encounter obvious. Dancer had hold of her by the shoulders, and though Molly met his eyes squarely, there was something in her posture that was very near to a cringe.

They heard his approach and Dancer released her abruptly. Without waiting for David to come up to them, Molly turned and fled into the card room. Dancer remained where he was. He waited until David came up to him before speaking. "My compliments, Norwood. You are not slow to seek your advantage."

David gave him a slow smile that was meant to be provoking. "I don't berate myself on that score," he said.

"It won't help you fix your interest there," Dancer said, his tone easy, but the set of his features belying this. "She may be attracted, but she will refuse the bait, I promise you that."

"Do you? Then you have nothing to concern you." David gave him a brief, contemptuous bow and continued on into the card room.

Shortly after he reentered the ballroom, Jane accosted him, reproach clear in her eyes. "Where is Miss Fearne?"

He looked his surprise. "I haven't any idea. Should I?"

"I saw you leave the supper room with her," she said accusingly. "And if I saw it, so did others."

The corners of David's mouth turned up a little, but his expression was more grim than smiling. "It's of no consequence."

"How can you say so?" Jane said, shocked.

He put his hand on her arm and led her to the near corner of the room. "This is not the place to discuss it, but I think that we are very near to the end of this coil. The errand on which I sent Ventry, should it prove successful, may prove Eve's identity without question, and I think that when that happens, Miss Fearne—who is Molly Jenkins by birth— will decide that it is more in her interest to be *with* us than against us."

"She has agreed to help us?" Jane asked, skeptical.

"Not precisely, but she's no fool. She'll do what's in her best interest."

Jane did not press him for greater detail, for she was as aware as he of their lack of privacy. "Perhaps we should leave," she suggested. "It would be a kindness to Evelyn to tell her that her waiting is nearly over."

"I think I prefer to say nothing to Eve until we can be more definite. Indications may be good, but everything is still very tentative, Jane. We have promises, but no results yet. It won't help Eve to have her hopes built and then dashed. Roger should return by late morning tomorrow and it will be on his information that all else will hinge."

"You sound as tiresome as Mr. Stevens," Jane said, rebuking him. "It is Eve's life, after all; she has the right to know what is happening."

"And so she shall, my dear, but not until tomorrow. She'll be none the worse for the wait." His tone held an edge of command, and though Jane felt it was unfair and perhaps even unwise given Evelyn's odd humors of late and her predilection for taking matters into her own hands, she supposed that no great harm could come from the wait of less than a day.

9

After having spent the entire evening alone in her sitting room at Norwood House, Evelyn was heartily tired of her own thoughts and company and would have given a great deal to have known of any plan to resolve her problems, however tentative. At the beginning of the evening she had been dispirited and inclined to self-pity, but as the evening wore on, solitude and the time to order her thoughts again made her realize that she had behaved unreasonably at Richmond. She had created just the sort of scene that might have been expected of Lady Notorious.

She knew she could not go on living in this self-imposed limbo; it was affecting her temperament in ways that were intolerable to her. Neither did it add to the peace of her mind that she was forced to admit that she had been stupid enough to fall in love with David, in spite of the fact that she believed he was not in love with her. Intellectually, Evelyn knew she could not justly blame David for seeking the comfort of another's arms, but she felt sick in her heart to think of him doing so.

Evelyn acknowledged that she could not help what she felt, but, she decided as she finally crawled beneath the sheets far in advance of her usual hour, it was time she did something to bring an end to her uncertainty. Whatever David might say about Mr. Stevens' thoroughness and the importance of caution, she had had enough of it. Her increasing impatience to denounce her cousin and the impostor he had set in her place was intensified by the hope that once she was independent of David, and no longer in need of his protection and charity, he would no longer look upon her as his responsibility and might begin to see her as the woman she was now, uncolored by their shared past. She had no more wish than he for an annulment to their marriage, but for them to remain together, it had to be the wish of his heart as it was of hers.

She lay awake for some time thinking what she could do to help herself and at last hit upon an idea so simple it struck her as absurd that they had none of them thought of it before. Jonathan, by setting an impostor in her place, was calling her bluff, and Evelyn meant to repay him in kind.

Evelyn took an early breakfast in her room the next morning. She knew it was David's custom to leave the house soon after breakfast and Jane was planning a much put-off visit to Mrs. Drummond-Burrel, so she was reasonably certain that she would be able to leave the house by midmorning without any awkward questions. Jane did seek her out, concerned that she had not come down for breakfast and determined to send for the doctor if Evelyn appeared at all unwell, but Evelyn's much improved humor and the excuse that all that ailed her was weariness caused by the pace they had kept since coming to London, did much to dispel these concerns.

Jane yearned to give Evelyn some hint of her discussion with David at Devonshire House, but she honored her promise to David that she would hold her tongue against more definite proof. Jane left Norwood House in a sanguine frame of mind, but it was nothing compared to Evelyn's optimism, which now was as complete as her pessimism had been before. Evelyn could not be certain that her actions would have any definite results, but it was almost enough for her to be simply doing something again instead of waiting.

In spite of her willingness to flaunt the dangers to her reputation that seeking Jonathan out in his house presented, she knew they still existed. There had been some little talk about her attendance at Mrs. Dancer's rout party, which had quickly evaporated in the speculation surrounding the arrival of Miss Fearne, but it would surely begin again if it became known that she had gone there unescorted, even armed with the excuse of paying a morning call on Mrs. Dancer. Accordingly, Evelyn decided against taking her own carriage, which would be known by its crest, and the hat she wore had a veil attached which she could easily use to mask her identity, should it prove necessary.

If the butler saw anything odd about his mistress asking him to fetch her a hack when the Norwood mews boasted no fewer than three carriages suitable for use in town, he did not question his mistress's order. Once inside the carriage, Evelyn became a little chary that she might again encounter Mr. Danbury in the street that housed his *chèe amie* and she arranged the veil to fall over her eyes.

As luck would have it, Dancer's butler informed her that his master had not yet risen, but Evelyn refused to be put off. She insisted on sending her card up to Dancer. Bowing, the butler did as he was told, giving his tacit opinion of young women who came to the house unescorted, veiled, and asking for unmarried gentlemen by rudely leaving her to stand unattended in the front hall. When he returned several minutes later, he informed her that his master was still dressing and would be down as soon as he was presentable, and only then escorted her into a small saloon.

There was no offer of refreshments while she waited, and Evelyn passed the time pacing about the room going over what she intended to say to her cousin. She heard the door open at last, but when she turned, she saw her aunt entering the room rather than Jonathan. Mrs. Dancer held out her hand and smiled at Evelyn as if this were indeed a morning visit, and Evelyn was assailed with the fear that she would repeat her failure at Spedwell. "How good of you to call, Lady Norwood. It is an unexpected pleasure." There was nothing in Lavinia Dancer's voice to indicate that she knew that Evelyn had regained her memory. Since Mrs. Dancer was part of her son's conspiracy to refuse to acknowledge her, Evelyn had made the natural assumption that his mother was in his confidence. Mrs. Dancer certainly had to know that the Miss Fearne that she accepted as her niece was an impostor, but it was possible that she was ignorant of Jonathan's reason for perpetrating the fraud.

"I have come to speak with Jonathan," Evelyn said levelly.

"I fear that Jonathan is not yet down," the older woman said, seating herself, "but perhaps I may offer myself as a substitute for my son."

"No," Evelyn said, deciding on impulse to bring her knowledge out into the open. "Only Jonathan will do, Aunt Lavinia."

Lavinia Dancer stared for a long moment at her niece, but beyond that gave no indication of surprise or dismay at being addressed with the familiarity. "Very well, my dear, but I fear we may have a bit of a wait. You should recall that Jonathan does not care to hurry his toilette." At this point the butler reentered the room bearing a tray containing glasses and a decanter of pale amber liquid. "Do you remove to Blakenhill for the summer or shall you go to Brighton? In my day Brighton was not in the least fashionable, just another fishing village, you know."

Evelyn was thrown off her stride by her aunt's astonishing willingness to accept her equally as mere acquaintance or niece without any apparent difficulty or chagrin. "Our plans are still uncertain," she replied mechanically, and then said, speaking carefully so that she could not be misunderstood, "Aunt Lavinia, you do realize that I know who I am now and who you are as well?"

Mrs. Dancer looked surprised at the question. "But of course you do. Why should you not?"

Evelyn might have thought that her aunt was being facetious or sarcastic, but she knew the older woman had little sense of humor and no talent at all for irony. "I had an accident when I left Spedwell and I lost my memory for more than a year," she said, slowly, as if to a child. "When I came to London as Lady Norwood, I didn't recognize Jonathan as my cousin."

Mrs. Dancer nodded, looking pleased that she could agree with her guest. "Jonathan told me that. I thought it sounded odd at first, but he assured me it was so. He wrote to me in March when he met you in town and told me that you were still alive but out of your senses, and I came up to town for a day or two to see for myself. I thought it would be a good thing for Jonathan to tell the courts that you were out of your senses and unfit, so that there wouldn't be any more fuss about his management of your poor papa's money, but he said that Norwood would likely kick up a fuss and that it was best to say nothing at all, for it might just be that you never would remember who you were." She dropped her voice to a confidential level. "I was quite vexed with you for running off from Spedwell in that inconsiderate way, Eve, but it is something that you have married an earl. There has never been anyone above the rank of viscount in the family before."

Evelyn had always thought her aunt a vague, vain, and somewhat stupid woman, but she thought this odd response was almost simpleminded. Evelyn refused her suggestion of a glass of Madeira, and the older woman poured out a glass for herself. "I told Jonathan that he could not count on his luck holding true indefinitely, and he assured me that neither did he."

"Hence the woman he has introduced to the world as Miss Fearne," Evelyn suggested dryly.

Mrs. Dancer smiled her pleasure at Evelyn's easy comprehension. "Why yes, of course." Her expression suddenly brightened. "Unless you have decided to elope with Jonathan after all?" she said hopefully. "He said it would solve our difficulties almost as if you had never left Spedwell. But I told him he must not place too much reliance on that, for after all, why should you leave Norwood? He *is* an earl."

"Jonathan could not have supposed that if I eloped with him, he would have control of my fortune?"

"He already has that," the dowager said complacently. "But it is only the income from your estate that he may dispose of as he pleases, not the principal, though he has sold off as much of the estate as he could and invested it in the Funds so that it would be at hand. If he were your husband, he would have control of it all."

"But how could he ever hope be my husband, even if I eloped with him? You know that I am already married to Norwood," Evelyn said, puzzled by her reasoning.

"Well, of course I know that, you stupid girl," Mrs. Dancer replied, the petulance that Evelyn remembered so well coming into her voice. "Jonathan said that Norwood would be sure to think the disgrace of your divorce and remarriage less than the humiliation of having Jonathan set you up as his mistress for all the world to see."

Evelyn's lips set in a grim smile. "He is obviously unacquainted with my husband. I doubt Norwood would have fallen in with Jonathan's plans so readily."

"Nonsense," said Dancer as he strolled into the room, impeccably and elegantly attired, proving that his toilette need not take the better part of the morning after all. "Norwood is a nobleman with political inclinations. These are the proudest breed of all and would willingly cut off their noses if they thought it would save face." He smiled at his pun as Evelyn regarded him stonily.

"No consideration would have persuaded me to have you for a husband in or out of my senses," Evelyn said with such obvious distaste that Jonathan's smile became rather fixed.

"Perhaps your memory is still imperfect, dear cousin. I did not find you unresponsive to my, ah, overtures."

"It was your vanity that thought so," she said with certainty. "I would have preferred begging in the streets. Or worse."

"You have no sense at all, Eve," Mrs. Dancer interjected. "Even marriage to Jonathan must be better than that," she added, aware of no irony in her words. "Though I must concede that he is not always a particularly kind man."

Jonathan flicked an annoyed, contemptuous glance toward his mother. "I think, madam, that it would be best if you allowed Evelyn and me to work out our difficulties alone."

"But you wished me to come down to keep an eye on her," she reminded him.

"I am here now. I shall do so myself."

Her aunt's countenance crumbled. "You are not a good son, Jonathan," she said pouting. "You leave me to molder at Spedwell and then you demand that I come to London without a word of explanation and will not even let me go out except when you say, and now you dismiss me like a parlor maid."

"You may remove yourself to the dower house whenever you please if you are not content here or at Spedwell," Jonathan replied indifferently. "But for now I only require you to remove yourself from this room." He then turned his back on her and crossed the room to a lacquered cabinet that opened to reveal several decanters of wine and spirits. The dowager's lip quivered dangerously, but she managed to maintain her composure at least to the extent that she was able to rise from her chair with dignity, only slamming the door behind her to vent her anger.

Dancer returned to Evelyn, carrying one of the decanters. He pushed aside the decanter of Madeira and poured two glasses from the crystal decanter in his hand. He handed her one of the glasses, saying, "I think you will find this is a particularly fine sherry. It is imported—quite illegally, of course—from a fine old vineyard in Spain with a very select clientele." Evelyn did not respond to this bit of self-importance but she took the glass he offered even though she did not wish for the wine. Taking the chair his mother had vacated, he said in a confidential manner, "You see now, of course, why I do not encourage her visits to town."

Evelyn sipped at the wine absently. "I thought my memory of my years at Spedwell was complete, but I do not recall . . ." She allowed her voice to trail off, for she scarcely knew how to describe her aunt's disconcertingly childlike behavior.

But Dancer understood her well enough. He raised his brows. "Surely you never imagined her to be strong of wit," he said sardonically. "I do admit, though, that her infirmity of intellect has grown in the past year or so along with her tastes for laudanum and strong sherry. But I doubt you have come to discuss my dear mama." With the change of subject his manner changed as well. He had been speaking in a clipped way but now the corners of his mouth turned up again, and he said quite affably, "To what do I owe the honor of this visit, my dear Evelyn? I feel it must be a matter of import if you risked Norwood's wrath to come here."

"My husband is not aware that I am here and I have come in a hack to avoid having my carriage recognized. I would prefer this to be between us, Jonathan." He nodded as if to indicate that he understood and she should go on, which she did. "I have come to tell you that your plan to put that woman in my place to lay claim to my inheritance will not succeed," she said, coming to the point at once.

If he were taken aback at this attack, it was undiscernible in his expression. "No?" His smile broadened. "I rather think it shall. But surely we have already had this discussion—at Ponsonby House, I believe? If you come forward claiming to be Evelyn Fearne, I shall deny it, of course, evincing all astonishment and horror, and since I would be expected to know you better than anyone, I think I shall hold the edge of credibility. And then, though I regret to say it, my dear Lady Notorious, there is the fact that all the gossips are whispering that Miss Fearne has quite cut you out in my affections. 'Heaven hath no rage . . .' and so on."

He finished his wine and put the glass back on the tray. "Your father's estate is far from paltry, but it is scarcely a king's ransom," he went on. "Why can't you be pleased with what you have with Norwood—which I am sure is far superior to your inheritance—and leave matters as they are. So much better for us all."

"Better for you," she retorted. "It doesn't matter if you refuse to acknowledge me." She gave a fair imitation of his superior smile. "I don't need to prove that I am Evelyn Fearne. I need prove only one thing: that your Miss Fearne is an impostor. Once that is evident, I think the remainder of the truth will be quite obvious."

For a moment Dancer's smile faded, and when it returned it had deteriorated into a sneer. "You cannot think me fool enough to leave tracks?"

"I think you arrogant enough not to bother with every detail," Evelyn replied. "If this woman is an actress, and I am sure she must be, it should not be so very difficult to find someone who has known her as such. She is not a great beauty, but she is pretty enough to attract some attention on stage."

Dancer's features were still composed genially, but his eyes had narrowed considerably. "I do not say *touché*, coz," he drawled, "but I do admit that you are no slowtop. It is my sad duty to disabuse you of your conceit, nevertheless. Molly has not practiced her profession for some time. Her profession of acting, that is," he amended. "She was in the keeping of a friend of mine for the past several years until his unfortunate demise a few months ago."

"How very convenient," Evelyn remarked, "but I think that inquiries which are already being made amongst the provincial and touring companies will prove more fruitful than you imagine."

Jonathan said nothing in reply to this. He sat looking at her, his expression unreadable, but set and cold enough to chill her a little. "Norwood won't continue to pursue that line of inquiry when he is faced instead with your ruin," he said with soft mendaciousness. "He cannot be interested in your father's estate for himself, and without you there will be no point in going on."

Evelyn was not sure she understood him. "I never had any intention of eloping with you, Jonathan," she said, thinking that that was what he meant.

"Perhaps not," he agreed with perfect amiability. "But your intention is immaterial. You have been kind enough to come to me of your own volition, which I shall make certain is known. Once that is evident," he added, using her own words to mock her, "the remainder will be quite obvious."

Evelyn supposed he was threatening to kidnap her and she might have laughed at the absurdity of such a desperate measure, but she knew Dancer well enough to know that he seldom made idle statements. Still she regarded it as mere bravado and a sure sign that her bluff had succeeded. "You will catch cold at that, Jonathan," she said boldly. "If you try to force yourself on me, I promise you will have your own back and then some."

"How very Amazonian," Jonathan replied. He gave a small affected shudder. "In the general way, I abhor violence, my dear Eve, but in a good cause one might amend one's values for the nonce. But I doubt force will prove necessary."

He spoke with such confidence that Evelyn was beginning to feel uncomfortable, and since her principal purpose of paying back her cousin in his own coin had been achieved, she thought it prudent to leave. She drank the little wine that remained in her glass and then stood. "I shall leave you now, Jonathan, and I don't think you would be wise to stop me. I shall not hesitate to scream and I can't believe that all of your servants are so loyal to you that no one would come to my aid."

"I am sure you are right," he agreed, as affable as ever.

Dancer did not rise with her, but raised his head to look up at her. He gave no appearance at all of a man who intended to use physical force to constrain her and Evelyn felt a sense of anticlimax. She started to walk away from him but her steps felt curiously light, as if she were walking on a thick carpet of feathers. As she neared the door a sudden thought occurred to her and she turned again to address her cousin. The room spun with her. Then she was certain. She had underestimated Jonathan once again.

Dancer rose with careful deliberation. He walked over to Evelyn and returned her unresisting to her chair. "You see, my dear," he said in a painstaking fashion, "I simply cannot allow you to take your fortune out of the family. The truth is—this is just between us, you understand—it is not quite the fortune it was when it was placed in my guardianship. I have not dissipated it, you need have no fear on that head, but there would be awkward questions. Yes, I very much fear there would be questions."

Evelyn wanted to speak but her tongue felt thick

and furry. Her eyelids were heavy but she resisted the desire to close them. Dancer regarded her intently, but dispassionately, as if she were an insect on a pin. Then all at once his smile spread into a confident grin that for once was quite genuine and he began to laugh. His laughter was the last thing that Evelyn heard as unconsciousness overtook her.

David had only just returned to the house for luncheon when he was informed that a Miss Jenkins awaited him in the gold saloon. He went to her at once, evincing no surprise at her visit. Molly Jenkins, dressed rather primly in a high-necked gown and a knit shawl that was unnecessary for the warm spring day, looked exactly the part of proper young maiden on a morning visit. He greeted her amiably and, when they were seated, casually crossed his legs and waited silently for her to begin.

Molly, searching his expression with professional intent, saw nothing there beyond polite indifference. She had hoped for a more enthusiastic response which would have placed her at more of an advantage, but having made up her mind, she took a breath and said, "Your arguments last night were most persuasive, my lord. I have decided, after all, to accept your offer."

David subjected her to his own, less subtle scrutiny before replying. "Did you bring the papers?" he asked directly.

She did not care for his businesslike approach, for she was used to quite another manner when dealing with gentlemen. She creased her milky brow a bit and said with a note of sharpness, "There are other matters to be discussed first, my lord."

"I have never been known to be ungenerous to my friends," he said, understanding her.

Molly tilted her head and studied him for a moment, her smile returning and expanding. "We might be more than that if you're of a mind."

"Thank you, Molly. I am flattered, of course," he said gently, "but I fear my interests are already engaged."

She shrugged, not in the least offended, and said, "If it's to be business, then I need to know what your generosity would entail."

"Or in other words, how much?" David said, the corners of his mouth turning up in a faint sardonic smile. She nodded, completely unabashed. "I think I should prefer to see your offering before committing myself to a definite figure."

Molly hesitated, shrugged, and stood up to pull a metal box, which her gown had been concealing, from beneath her chair. As she did so the shawl slipped off her shoulders, revealing painful-looking bruises in several places on both arms. David got up, and ignoring the box, which lay on the floor between them, he twitched her shawl from her arms. Molly stood quite still, allowing him to inspect her exposed flesh without comment.

"Dancer," David said. It was only partially a question.

Molly nodded. Her mouth twisted into a wry smile. "There are other bruises, but I won't put you to the blush by showing them to you. It was more a knocking about than a real beating, which I've had in my day, but the thing is, I could tell he enjoyed it. He let me know it was just a taste of what I could expect if I talked to you again without either him or that crazy old woman about."

"And so you've switched horses."

"You said you'd see to him for me," she reminded him.

"You may depend upon it," David replied shortly, and then stooped to pick up the metal box, carrying it to a nearby table. It was smaller than the box he and Evelyn had found in the library at Spedwell, but large enough to contain the records of her father's estate that Evelyn had found in the first box.

"Am I to stay here then, my lord?" Molly asked hopefully while David forced the lock with a penknife. The box was quite full and he removed and examined several of the documents. "I daren't go back to Grove Street if there's any chance that he's missed the box," she added when he did not answer her at once.

"You'll spend the night here at any rate," he replied. "I'll send for my solicitor, who I am sure will be quite interested in this, and after he has taken a deposition from you, I'll send you to Blakenhill for a time until Dancer has been rendered harmless, as I intend him to be." He returned the papers to the box and closed it. He named a figure to the actress which nearly surprised an exclamation of delight from her, but she controlled herself sufficiently to simply nod her agreement. David walked over to the mantel and pulled the bell, which was answered with suspicious alacrity by Tomkins. "'Please ask Lady Norwood to join us," he said to the servant.

"Her ladyship is not at home, my lord."

An annoyed frown creased David's brow. It was late for morning calls. "Did my wife mention where she was bound?"

"No, my lord, but I doubt it was one of her usual calls," the servitor replied to be helpful.

"Why is that?"

"Her ladyship refused her town carriage and insisted that I call her a hack."

David stared at him for a moment and then recovered himself. He cursed under his breath. "Has Ventry returned yet?"

"No, my lord."

David sighed with annoyance. "Is my sister at home?"

At last the butler was able to reply in the affirmative. "I believe her ladyship came in just before you, my lord."

"Then ask her to come to me at once," David said briskly.

Tomkins bowed and left, and in a very short time, Jane came into the room with Roger Ventry, who had just returned, hard on her heels.

"Do you know where Eve has gone?" David asked his sister.

"Isn't she in her rooms?" Jane asked, then she noticed Molly, who had effaced herself in a corner of the room, and her eyes opened quite wide. "Evelyn cried off accompanying me on my call to Mrs. Drummond-Burrel," Jane said, speaking to David but staring at Molly. "Her spirits were much improved since last night and I only thought that she did not wish for the visit, for which I cannot truly blame her."

"Eve apparently left the house after you," David informed her. "She refused her carriage and took a hack."

"Took a hack? But why would she do that unless she . . ." Jane broke off abruptly, but her brother finished the sentence for her.

"Unless she didn't want the servants or anyone else to know where she was going. Exactly." He turned to his secretary. "What is your news, Roger?"

Mr. Ventry, who could only conjecture about the meaning of the previous exchange, spoke a little haltingly. "Just what you'd hoped, my lord. Jenny Bickers, an upstairs maid at Spedwell, left to marry a local man who had a position on an estate in Essex and went into service there with him. Haskell is her name now. She's no grudge at all to bear to the Dancers and remembers Lady Norwood quite well. Is there something the matter here, my lord?"

"There may be," David replied tersely. "Did you get a deposition?"

Mr. Ventry pulled a folded bit of paper out of an inner pocket in his coat. "Mrs. Haskell has sworn that she could readily recognize Evelyn Fearne on sight and is willing to come to town to do so whenever it is necessary, if we are willing to cover her expenses and make good with her employer, a Mr. Rudd, who I had a word with and who is willing to be equally cooperative."

David held his hand out for the paper and Ventry gave it to him. "This should effectively rout Jonathan Dancer." He put it in his own pocket, casting a quick glance toward Molly, who acknowledged his promised success with a faint bow of her head. "Roger, have Tomkins send for my carriage and then pen a note to Stevens and tell him that I wish to see him here within the hour, if that is convenient. Whatever his other commitments, I'll make it worth his while. Have Mrs. Kipp ready a room for Miss Jenkins, who will be spending the night. Also, when Stevens arrives inform him that Miss Jenkins has a statement that she wishes to make to him concerning her part in Dancer's scheme to cheat Eve of her inheritance."

"David, where is Eve?" Jane demanded, feeling that this part of their conversation had never been completely resolved.

"Where do you imagine she would go that she would wish no one to know about?" he asked.

"Grove Street," Jane said at once, though she had harbored a hope that it would not be so.

At these words, Molly rose and ventured over to where the others stood. "Why would Lady Norwood go to Grove Street?" she asked David. "Things being what they are, I would've thought she'd avoid Dancer."

David's smile and tone were both dust dry. "My wife is not blessed with any noticeable degree of patience. She would appear to be obsessed with ignoring prudence to solve her difficulties on her own."

"Surely she wouldn't confront Dancer by herself?" Molly asked, just the faintest hint of alarm in her voice.

David's response to her had been almost offhand, but now he looked at her with interest. "She has done so before," he replied. "That concerns you?"

Molly looked uncertain. "I would not wish to be melodramatic," she said tentatively.

"Why not?" David said sardonically. "I am becoming quite used to living in that state."

"You don't suppose Evelyn would be in danger from her cousin?" Jane asked, not really expecting an affirmative answer. But that was what she received.

"Yes. That is, it might be so," Molly answered. "He was in a rare state after the Devonshire ball. I don't know if he meant the half of what he was saying, but he said he should have killed Lady Norwood when he had the chance—when she was still Miss Fearne, that is, and in his care."

Ventry saw the dawning horror in Jane's eyes and he placed a comforting hand on her arm. "It is just bravado," he said to reassure her.

Once again David pulled on an end of Molly's shawl and revealed the angry marks on her white flesh. "Oh, God," Jane ejaculated, and a stronger curse issued from the shocked lips of Roger Ventry.

"I'm coming with you, my lord," he said in a tight voice.

"No. Just do as I ask, Roger, and quickly," David said. When it was clear that the secretary was about to protest, he added, "I need you to deal with Stevens and to be with Miss Jenkins until I return. You will serve me best in this way, Roger." Ventry could not argue further, and he left the room at once to send for David's curricle.

10

Lord Norwood's servants knew him as a master who expected his orders to be carried out with alacrity, and in the mews the grooms moved with all possible haste. But to David, who chafed at every moment wasted, the wait for the carriage seemed endless. When at last it drew up before the door he took the reins from his groom and refused his company for the journey. David had no idea what would go forward when he arrived in Grove Street and he wanted no witnesses for gossip even among the most trusted retainers. He was not a man given to alarm or fancy but the grim reality of Dancer's treatment of his own confederate when he suspected her of trying to cross him made him genuinely fear for Evelyn's safety.

David disposed of his carriage on the street before Grove, where he found a loitering youth to hold his team. He walked the short distance to Dancer's house, and as he mounted the steps to the front door, a post chaise came to a halt before him with a baggage cart in its wake. David was a little surprised and turned to glance at the equipage before applying the knocker, but the door was opened in any case, and the butler looked past him to the post boy who was dismounting. The major domo nodded the post boy into the house to help the grooms with the baggage, and then turned a haughty countenance toward David.

"I believe Lady Norwood is here," David said brusquely. "I wish to see her."

The butler, recognizing Lord Norwood, and not deaf to the gossip that had earlier circulated concerning his master and the earl's wife, looked a bit nonplussed by this request but managed to say, "Her ladyship was here earlier, but I believe she has been gone some time."

"Did you see her leave?"

"No, my lord. But Mr. Dancer began to make preparations for a journey into Kent nearly an hour ago, so it is safe to assume that lady Norwood left at about that time."

"I wish a word with Mr. Dancer," David said in a voice that brooked no argument.

The servitor hesitated, but his orders were certain and it was better to offend a visitor than court his master's wrath. "I am sorry, my lord. The family is about to retire to the country for the summer months and neither Mr. Dancer nor his mother is receiving."

"Nevertheless, I believe Mr. Dancer will see me," David assured him. "You may inform him for me that at least one member of his 'family' is in my care and won't be making the journey with him. I am sure he will find that of interest."

The butler did not understand, but it was not in his nature to flaunt the commands of Quality and he bowed and left David in the hall while he took the message to his master. David was forced to stand to one side as various servants scurried in and out of the hall with odd pieces of luggage for loading in the cart. There was the sound of a crash in a rear hall and then a woman's voice could be heard shrilly berating a serving girl, followed by a gust of tears from the offending maid. Mrs. Dancer came into the entrance hall, addressing one of the grooms in an equally querulous manner. She stopped short when she saw David, her eyes going perfectly round.

Before she could speak, Dancer came down the stairs far more swiftly than his usual languorous pace and brushed past her as if she were invisible.

"What is the meaning of your message?" he asked in a voice that was also markedly different than usual.

"I'll tell you when you tell me where I may find my wife," David said calmly.

A faint sneer turned up Dancer's lips. "If you have misplaced her, I am surprised you would come to me to find her."

David ignored the taunt. "I know that she came here to see you and she has not returned to Norwood House though my butler informed me that it is more than two hours since she left."

"Perhaps she has gone shopping," Mrs. Dancer suggested, casting a timid glance toward her son, whose attitude was uncommonly bellicose.

"Or to visit other friends, or for a drive through the park, or she may have finally had the good sense to leave you," Dancer continued jeeringly. "Whatever, you can see for yourself that my mother and I are in the process of removing to the country and are scarcely entertaining guests."

"Where is she, Dancer?" David said levelly, refusing to be distracted.

"If you are so certain that she is with me, I am surprised that you want her back."

There was no mistaking the import of his words and David, who had had enough of Dancer's evasiveness, acted on instinct instead of intellect. He planted Dancer a facer that left him stretched out at the foot of the stairs unconscious. The butler, two grooms, and the post boy stood in the hall, interested spectators, but not one of them came to their employer's assistance, and it was Mrs. Dancer, who, letting out a little shriek, knelt beside her son and began calling for burnt feathers.

The butler moved to do her bidding, but David caught his arm and held him. "In what room did your master speak with Lady Norwood?"

The butler bit at his lip, self-interest warring with his dislike of his employer. Then he nodded down the hall where the crash had been heard. "The small saloon, my lord, second door on the left."

David nodded his thanks and strode off in the direction of the side hall, leaving Mrs. Dancer to wail over the prostrate form of her son and the others in the room to gawk their fill at their employer's disgrace. The door to the room the butler had indicated was open, which made it unlikely that Evelyn was there, but David went into the room anyway. As he had feared, the room was empty, but an interior door to his right led into another room and he tried this and found it locked. The hall door into the next room proved to be locked as well and David returned to the front hall, which now held several other servants who had come to see what was afoot, including a kitchen maid who used the occasion to indulge in a bout of hysterics. Ignoring the commotion about him, he summoned the butler and between them they managed to force the door. But the room, which proved to be a saloon somewhat larger than the first, was equally unoccupied.

For the first time, David's belief that Evelyn was in the house began to waver. He hesitated on the threshold of the second room, uncertain what his next step should be. The butler, who was willing enough to think poorly of his employer, regarded him without judgment. "Will there be anything else, my lord? I ought to see that the others return to their duties."

David nodded dismissal and the servant returned to the front hall, where pandemonium still reigned. Not yet willing to admit that his judgment and intuition were at fault, David continued down the hall, trying the three doors that remained and finding them all unlocked and unoccupied. The last room at the end of the hall was a study cum bookroom with leather chairs and sofas and several low bookcases that lined the far wall. David supposed that his search should continue upstairs, but if Dancer were holding Evelyn against her will, it was rather unlikely that he would have carried her, resisting, up a flight or more of stairs.

He entered the room and looked about him. The room was absolutely empty and quiet; not so much as a curtain stirred. Two leather sofas graced the room, one faced him, but the other was turned away toward the fireplace. Knowing he was clutching at straws, David walked over to it and looked down; what he saw made him catch his breath. Laid out as perfectly as if indeed in her last sleep, was Evelyn, her complexion appropriately ashen.

"Dear God," David cried aloud, and at once knelt before the sofa, taking one of Evelyn's white hands in his. It was cool to the touch and his alarm rose by leaps and bounds. He cradled her in his arms and put his ear against her breast. He heard the flutter of her heart and sagged with relief. He shook her and called out her name and was rewarded by a faint moan. On a table near a window was a small vase of flowers and David cast these out and poured the water on his handkerchief, heedless of the liquid that poured out on to the carpet.

It took a minute or two of applying the wet cloth to her forehead and temples before Evelyn at last opened her eyes. The first look that came into them was one of alarm, but as soon as she perceived that it was David and not Jonathan who was with her, she cast herself into his arms and gave in to a fit of tears in sheer relief.

"Has he hurt you?" David said in a voice that might have chilled the miscreant had he been present.

Evelyn shook her head. "No. But he gave me sherry with laudanum in it."

David called Jonathan Dancer by an epithet that should have made Evelyn blush, but with which she heartily concurred. "There's nothing to fear from him now, Eve; it's finally over. Roger has found someone who can identify you, and Miss Fearne, who is an actress named Molly Jenkins, admits that she was brought here by Dancer to lay false claim to your inheritance."

Evelyn expressed her delight with a joyous exclamation, and then promptly dissolved into tears again.

David, realizing that the laudanum Dancer had fed Evelyn was contributing to her fragility, said gently. "It would be best if I carry you to the carriage. You're in no condition to walk."

Evelyn shook her head and managed to restrain her sobs. "No-no. If you would just give me your arm . . ."

"But I wish to carry you," he said with mild complaint.

The look of fear she had surprised in David's eyes when she had first regained consciousness and the gentle concern evinced there now made her heart beat with hope, and as he scooped her into his arms, she leaned against his strong shoulder and gave a little involuntary sigh of contentment. The most terrifying thought that had come into her head as Dancer's drug had taken effect was that she would never see David again, and she knew in that moment that she would never have left him, whatever the urgings of her pride.

They had only gone a few steps toward the door when Dancer came into the room, pushing the door shut behind him. His appearance was now the antithesis of elegance. His hair looked uncombed, his coat had a patch of damp near the shoulder and his shirt was soiled and peeking out between his waistcoat and breeches. His eyes blazed with anger, and his mouth worked as if he were trying to say something but could not find the words. He raised his hand from his side and it held a pistol. "Put her down," he commanded, waving the pistol at them in a random and alarming way.

Deciding that for the moment it would be best to obey, David set Evelyn on her feet, but she leaned against him for support since her legs were still wobbly. "Put down the pistol, Dancer," David said in a voice that carefully expressed neither anger nor concern. "You can't possibly use it. There is a house full of people who know we are here."

Dancer did not reply to this. Continuing to regard them, his expression intense, he spoke. "That fortune has been in the Dancer family since Henry V gave Sir Archibald Dancer his first land grant," he said, sounding more petulant than menacing, "and it should have passed to my father and then to me."

"Your father had his portion of the estate," Evelyn replied, "but he gamed it away."

"It isn't right to give portions to girls," Dancer insisted. "It breaks up the estate and enriches those who haven't any claim to it."

"As you have none to Eve's fortune, which you well know," David said, and then repeated, "Drop the pistol, Dancer."

The other man shook his head. "I have plans for you and I shall need it," he said, almost matter of factly. "Actually, I should be grateful to you for coming here and drawing my cork. It makes everything so much easier now that I can actively dislike you both. I was not entirely sure that I would be able to put a period to Eve's existence in cold blood, but now I shall kill you both, and since it will seem like a tragic accident, I needn't fear retribution or trouble my conscience."

"You haven't any," Evelyn said, clinging even more closely to her husband as if that would be enough to save them both from her cousin, who she now suspected had inherited his mother's mental infirmities.

Dancer was unconcerned by her outburst. "Eve and I have been the Crim. Con. story of the Season, and everyone knows what a pretty dance your young, and regrettably fast, wife has led you, Norwood. I shall say that you followed Eve here when you discovered that she had come to me and, as you say, there are witnesses. I tried to protect Eve from your wrath but was bested when you knocked me down in my own hall. You found her, you fought, and in a moment of passion you shot her. You then came after me and in the ensuing struggle you met your own untimely, but not undeserved, end. Then Miss Fearne shall be free to take up her inheritance quite uncontested. Neat, don't you agree."

"Too neat," David said with a faint, mirthless smile. "Where is Miss Fearne, Dancer?" Dancer regarded him without comprehension, and David went on, "You must know she is not in the house."

"She has gone to the lending library with Lady Henrietta to exchange a book," he said mechanically, obviously annoyed by this inconsequential interruption.

"Miss Fearne is at Norwood House," David said succinctly, for there was really no need to say more.

The raw fury that blazed forth from Dancer's eyes frightened Evelyn so that she was certain he would shoot them at once. David still gave no evidence of concern. "There is nothing you can do to prevent the truth coming out now, Dancer," he said levelly, "and I doubt even your own servants will back up a story which they must know is patently false."

"Do you think so?" Dancer asked, some of his old, urbane manner returning. "Yet I think it worth the risk." He raised the pistol. "On the whole, my dear," he said, addressing Evelyn, "I think you would have done better to have had me for a husband."

Dancer stood in front of the closed door; suddenly it flew open, slamming into him and causing him to pitch forward. David, fearing that the pistol would go off, pushed Evelyn to the floor, out of the line of fire. But the pistol merely slipped from Dancer's fingers and dropped harmlessly to the floor. Dancer, regaining his balance, reached for it, but David was quicker. A punishing left caught him squarely on the jaw and once again sent him sprawling.

Into the melee sprang Roger Ventry, fists raised

and ready to be put to use. But this proved utterly unnecessary, for Dancer, his jaw obviously of the glass variety, lay quite still as David picked up the pistol. "Thank you for your timely entrance, Roger," he said with a heartfelt smile. He handed the pistol to Ventry. "Dispose of this, if you will." Then he turned toward Evelyn, who had picked herself up and was sitting, looking a bit stunned, on the one of the leather sofas.

At these new sounds of upset the same troop of curious servants with Mrs. Dancer in the vanguard came hurrying into the room. When the dowager perceived her beloved son once again prone on the floor, she flew to him, but this time instead of cursing David, she said with absolute lucidity, "This must stop. I shall tell the truth even if Jonathan refuses to do so. I have always known Lady Norwood was my niece, but Jonathan forbade me to say so because he did not wish to have to return Evelyn's money to her." Sudden tears filled her eyes. "But look what has become of it. My poor boy, he is always so foolish about money, just like his poor papa." She brushed her son's disheveled locks back from his forehead and her weeping became more audible. Everyone in the room felt an awkward, embarrassed pity for her, and the servants, who were getting more of an eyeful and an earful than they could have hoped for, began to disperse without being told to do so.

Whether due to his mother's ministrations or a natural cause, Dancer again became conscious. He pushed his mother aside and forced himself into a sitting position. He glared at David with pure venom. Ignoring his mother's offers of assistance, he stood up, swaying slightly. "Damn you, Norwood, this isn't over," he said, but his tone lacked its previous menace.

"I'm afraid it is, Dancer," the earl responded quietly. "You never did have any hope of success, you know, and I think it would be in your best interest to accept that now. I could make matters very uncom-

fortable for you by laying a complaint in Bow Street
or even simply by letting the complete truth get
about in a more insidious manner. However, much I
may dislike it, you are kin to my wife and I would
prefer to cast as little scandal as possible on her
name. But I shall, you know, if you force my hand.

"I think you would be wise to rusticate for a
time," he continued when Dancer's only response
was an impotent glare. "Whatever story we put about,
I cannot prevent the whispers that are sure to circu-
late when the world learns that Miss Fearne was an
impostor. I doubt they will be generous to you."

"So like his dear papa," Mrs. Dancer murmured
again, as if to herself. "Always risking all on the turn
of a card."

"Get out of my house," Dancer said, his anger
sounding more and more like the frustration of a
thwarted child.

"We shall and with pleasure," David assured him.

Dancer turned on his heel and almost collided
with his major domo, who was the last of the servants remaining in the room. "What the devil are
you standing about for?" he said furiously. "Send
Peters to my room at once with sticking plaster and
violet water." Before the butler could reply, he
stomped from the room, leaving the servant to follow in his wake.

Lavinia Dancer still stood by the door, her expression anxious. "Will you go to Bow Street, Norwood?"

"Not unless your son creates difficulty for Eve."

The dowager looked thoughtful. "If you will wait
a few more minutes, I shall write out a statement
acknowledging Evelyn as my niece, and when I have
done so, I shall tell him what I have done. Archie
was always sensible about matters once they were a
fait accompli," she added cryptically, and scurried out
of the room to find paper and pen.

"I shall be forever grateful, Mr. Ventry," Evelyn
said as she rose to stand beside her husband.

"As shall I," said David. "Even if you did ignore my order to leave the matter in my hands," he added with a dry smile.

The secretary looked a bit uncomfortable but said judiciously, "I thought you might wish for someone to help you after you had matters in hand."

"Rather like mopping up," David suggested blandly.

Mr. Ventry seized on this explanation. "Exactly, my lord."

"Cut line, Roger," his employer advised him. "You came *ventre à terre* to our rescue and I am in your debt for it."

The secretary looked a little embarrassed. "Thank you, my lord, but you owe me nothing."

"As you wish," the earl replied with apparent disinterest. "But there is something I wish you to do for me, Roger. Return to Norwood House immediately, find Jane, and tell her all that has happened, for I am sure she is on pins and needles waiting for the outcome."

"Of course, my lord," Ventry replied, eager to accomplish a command exactly in line with his own desires.

"Then, when you have done that," the earl continued, "I want you to take my sister out to the rose garden—I can personally attest to the efficacy of the setting for romantic purposes—and ask her to be your wife."

"M-my lord, I scarcely know what to say," said the young man, speechless with happiness.

"You shall know exactly what to say," Evelyn assured him. She glanced up at her husband, and the proprietary smile he gave her nearly made her shiver with anticipation.

"But say it to Jane, not to us, Roger," David advised. "Neither I nor my wife has any intention of providing you with any more problems in which you can prove your mettle, so you had better take my word for it that I wish you well of my sister. There is one final thing," he added.

"Yes, my lord?"

"Stop calling me my lord."

"Yes, my l—," Ventry began, and then broke into a broad grin. David assured him that he need not remain with them until Mrs. Dancer returned, and the secretary took himself off happily to do his employer's bidding.

David glanced at Evelyn and noted that her expression had become melancholy. "You are feeling the effects of all this," he said. "I'll take you home and then return for Mrs. Dancer's statement."

"No," Evelyn said firmly. "If we do not wait now, she may change her mind and we shall never have her statement."

"We don't really need it now," he assured her.

"I would be more comfortable having it," she insisted.

Mrs. Dancer came back into the room. "He will be furious with me, I suppose," she said as she handed a folded piece of foolscap to David. "But I shall make him see that it was for the best. It was not good for him to have the means for racketing about town and I am glad it will be at an end. Town life never did agree with Archie," she added, once again confusing her son and her dead husband.

David unfolded and scanned the paper to be certain that it was what Mrs. Dancer had promised; when he saw that it was, he and Evelyn left Grove Street with a haste that was less than polite, but which was not objected to by the house's occupants.

As they left the house they saw that it had begun to rain and that Roger Ventry had thoughtfully taken the earl's open sporting equipage and left for them the closed town carriage. It hardly mattered anymore that the Norwood crest was emblazoned on the doors for the world to see.

As they started off, Evelyn recalled that the last

time they had ridden in this particular carriage alone
together the circumstances had been quite different.
When he had told her that night that there would be
no annulment, she had been certain that he had said
so from duty; now she was ready to believe that he
had had quite another motive.

"Now we may get on with our lives," she said
leadingly, looking out the window at the passing
street.

"Do you still wish to do so alone?" he asked
quietly.

His response was encouraging, but Evelyn treated
his question lightly. "I hope you and Jane do not
mean to abandon me now!" she exclaimed. "I shall
need friends now as much as before."

"Is that how you view me?"

Evelyn glanced up at him and then away again.
"Yes, of course. I hope you feel that you are my
friend, too."

"I am your husband as well," he reminded her in
the same quiet tone, and then without warning bent
his head and kissed her gently. "Do you still wish for
the annulment?"

Evelyn's heart was a hammer in her breast. "You
said I would have no hope of it if you fought me,"
she replied evasively.

"I want your happiness, Eve. If you can't be happy
with me, I shall let you go and find some way to
silence the gossips."

Evelyn found his generosity anything but comforting. "Would you still wish to be married to me after
all the trouble I have brought you?" she asked, meeting his eyes, her own dark and liquid.

"With all my heart," he responded without hesitation. Evelyn's lips parted, but she did not speak and
he took advantage of this by kissing her in a way that
this time was not at all gentle. Her response was all
that he could have wished for, and when he released
her, he looked down at her with a heart-melting

smile. "In fact, I am especially looking forward to our wedding night."

A little rosy color came to Evelyn's cheeks and she dropped her gaze from his. "Our wedding night took place nearly two years ago," she informed him primly.

"But you told me that it was unmemorable," he chided.

"I had no memory at all then," she amended.

"And have you the memory of it now?" Her deepening color told its own tale, and he laughed aloud. "How long have you remembered?"

"Not long. A few days," she admitted.

"What do you remember, Eve?" he asked softly.

"That you are given to asking impertinent questions," she countered to avoid answering.

He laughed again, and before she could protest, she found herself enfolded in his embrace. For several minutes she happily lost herself to the delights of requited love. But as passion grew between them, she finally pushed him aside. "It is not yet our wedding *night*, my lord," she said with mock seriousness.

"A figure of speech," he assured her. "We shall have a wedding afternoon, I think."

"David, we cannot," she said, scandalized.

"Why not? Lady Notorious would not be such a wet goose."

"I am not Lady Notorious," she said a little coolly.

"Yet I rather thought that you did not entirely dislike playing the role of a dashing matron."

In spite of a wish to look stern, a dimple appeared in her cheek. "It was rather amusing to flirt with so many handsome gentlemen. It might not do, you know," she added, giving him a sidelong glance, "for me to abandon the role all at once. People might wonder at it if I became a sedate matron overnight."

"They won't when your figure begins to thicken," he said baldly.

"David!"

Once again he swept her into his embrace. "I mean for you to be cast in one role for the rest of your career," he said, his voice deepening. "My loving wife." And then he took her again with his lips, and when they reached the house, he received no further objections to continuing with their wedding afternoon.

About the Author

Originally from Pennsylvania, Elizabeth Hewitt lives in New Jersey with her dog, Maxim, named after a famous romantic hero. She enjoys reading history and is a fervent Anglophile. Music is also an important part of her life; she studies voice and sings with her church choir and with the New Jersey Choral Society. All of her novels for Signet's Regency line were written to a background of baroque and classical music.